Unexpected Monet

By K.A. Stead

JaCol Publishing Inc.

Copyright 2018 © by JaCol Publishing Inc.

Illustrations Copyright © 2018 by JaCol
Publishing Inc.
FIRST PRINTING

Nov 2018
All rights reserved

JaCol Publishing Inc.
195 Murica Aisle
Irvine, CA 92614
818-510-2898

Editor-in-Chief: Randall Andrews
Managing Editor: Jessica Collins
www.jacolpublishing.com

ISBN: 978-1-946675-30-9

Acknowledgement

Dedicated to Patricia Stead, my mother, who always encourages me to be the best I can be and to live the life I want. My sister, Julie Davis, for her never ending love and support. My father, Lloyd Barrie Stead (5.10.30 – 1.11.94) who I know is looking down on me and saying "Go on you can do it." Joseph Stiell, my son, for the endless cups of tea and IT support. Not forgetting the incredible people in Writers World who critique honestly and brutally with their hearts and souls. To Karen Brosinsky for her awesome cover design, and last but not least randall 'Jay' andrews for creating this amazing group of writers from all over the world and believing in me and pushing me to write.

Table of Contents

Chapter One 1

Chapter Two 9

Chapter Three 14

Chapter Four 18

Chapter Five 25

Chapter Six 30

Chapter Seven 32

Chapter Eight 39

Chapter Nine 43

Chapter Ten 48

Chapter Eleven 53

Chapter Twelve 56

Chapter Thirteen 63

Chapter Fourteen 66

Chapter Fifteen 71

Chapter Sixteen 78

Chapter Seventeen 81

Chapter Eighteen 89

Chapter Nineteen 96

Chapter Twenty 99

Chapter Twenty-one 104

Chapter Twenty-two 108

Chapter Twenty-three 116

Chapter Twenty-four 127

Chapter Twenty-five 138

Chapter Twenty-six 149

Chapter Twenty-seven 157

Chapter Twenty-eight 163

Chapter Twenty-nine 171

Chapter Thirty 176

Chapter Thirty-one 193

Chapter Thirty-two 201

Chapter Thirty-three 210

Chapter Thirty-four 218

Chapter Thirty-five 226

Chapter Thirty-six 233

Chapter Thirty-seven 240

Chapter Thirty-eight 246

Chapter Thirty-nine 251

Chapter Forty 259

Chapter Forty-one 269

Chapter Forty-two 277

Chapter Forty-three 285

Chapter Forty-four 293

Chapter Forty-five 302

Chapter Forty-six 306

Chapter Forty-seven 313

Chapter One

Over breakfast, Andrew abandoned the iPod as the morning news misted over with steam from his coffee. He mentioned their long-planned weekend away and sparked hope when he insisted they'd go the weekend after next. She made a mental note to cancel her book club scheduled for the same weekend. He hated it and considered it a poor excuse for her to gossip with her cronies.

Her tongue stung with the sharpness of the freshly squeezed orange juice as she contemplated her busy day ahead. A perfunctory kiss brushed her cheek before he left. Auto-pilot kicked in as she organised herself to leave before the commuter rush hour started. She didn't want to be late for her appointment at The Salon. She wanted a new look for the summer months, and she hoped for once Andrew would notice her.

"Good morning, you're here bright and early, Emma. What do you have in mind? I see you booked in for a restyle." Tracey showed Emma to the swizzle salon chair in front of the long mirror.

"Yes. I want something different. I feel so dull at the moment. I'm not really sure why. What suggestions do you have?" Emma sat and swirled the chair around to face the mirror.

"Well, I could add some layers and trim the ends to shoulder length and a translucent colour wash would look amazing. It isn't permanent so it won't damage your hair but it will bring out the chestnut highlights. In fact we can lighten a few strands at the front for that sun kissed look. It's quite classy and I think it will look fabulous on you" Tracey ran her comb through Emma's hair. "What do you think?"

"You don't think the highlights are too young for me. I'm in my late forties you know. I don't want to look like mutton dressed up as lamb." Emma grinned.

"What, in your forties? No way. You look great. No signs of grey yet and your skin has a lovely glow. Tell me your secret. The new look will look amazing on you."

"Thanks. I use a simple cocoa butter moisturizer, not much make up and I guess I have good genes. But you're the expert with my hair. I trust your judgment." Emma gave a thumbs-up to Tracey.

"Great. Come over to the wash basin and we'll get started."

Emma's mind drifted as Tracey massaged her scalp and washed her hair. She wondered what had happened in her life, when did a trip to the hairdresser mean so much to her.

Didn't they say life began at 40, since 40 my life seems to have slowly disintegrated. I feel so distant from Andrew and don't know what to do to get closer to him. He constantly works and some days I can do nothing right for him. I look forward to seeing him every day but when I do we have nothing to say to each other apart from the pleasantries and not even that some days. I hate his constant anger towards me, and demands on my time as if I'm his handmaiden. This is not what my marriage should be about.

As Tracey worked on her hair; pasting the chemicals and wrapping the ends in foil, Emma caught sight of a black Mercedes slowly driving down the High Street.

AM1. That's Andrew's car, but what is he doing here at this time. He said he had a meeting in the city today with some new investors in one of his overseas projects.

The car picked up speed and disappeared from view. Emma turned her mind back to Tracey's handiwork, but her mind puzzled over the black Mercedes and why her husband would be driving down High Street at this time in the morning.

I'll call him and find out.

She reached for her handbag to find her phone, but as she did an image of it on the hall table sprung to mind.

Damn. I left it at home.

"Tracey, how long will I be? I left my phone at home and I need to make a call."

"Well, the colour takes about 40 minutes and then we need to rinse and cut then finish so maybe around an hour and 15. Do you want to use my phone?" Tracey offered her phone to Emma.

"Thanks but it's okay. No problem. I thought I saw someone I knew but never mind." Emma knew Andrew wouldn't answer a call from an unknown number and would be furious she had used someone else's phone to call him. She pushed the thoughts to the back of her mind and picked up a magazine. She flicked through the pages but the puzzling thoughts of Andrew's movements returned with a niggling doubt.

"How do you like your new look?" Tracey flashed the mirror around the back of Emma's head.

"Wow. It is great. I love the chestnut tones mixed with the golden highlights and the length is perfect. Thanks so much." Emma hugged Tracey. "You always know exactly what to do. Thanks again." She left a generous tip and dashed to her car. High Street had cleared of traffic and she sped home. She wanted to pick up her phone and call Andrew. She didn't usually check up on him, but puzzles and doubts in her mind had stolen the pleasure of being pampered at The Salon.

A superb light blue Jaguar XK convertible sat on the lane approaching the house. A new car with 15' plates. It was her dream car, and her heart fluttered thinking Andrew might have bought it to surprise her at dinner. She sighed and pushed the thought out of her mind. She needed to find her phone and put her mind at rest.

When she put her key in the door, the bolt slid and locked instead of unlocking. She stopped, nerves on edge.

Why was the door unlocked? I'm sure I locked the door and set the alarm.

She caught the keys as they slipped out of her hand. She inched the door open, and waited for the alarm to go off. She held her breath. Nothing. She hesitated, not knowing what to do. Go in and find what? Call the police? What if she had forgotten to set the alarm and lock the door, then it would be a wild goose chase and a waste of everyone's time. Her hands shook, her heart pounded.

Pull yourself together, Emma. Come on now. You're a big girl. You can deal with it.

She gave herself a pep talk, removed her shoes and entered the house like a cat burglar, creeping around not making the slightest noise.

She scanned the lounge and kitchen, open plan with few hiding places. Nothing. She avoided the creaky treader as she crept upstairs to look in the bedrooms. Nothing. She doubted herself again, when she heard a faint noise, like someone had stifled a moan or a giggle. It came from the guest bedroom in the annex. The only place she hadn't checked. Panic set in. Someone was there.

What should I do?

Andrew would know. She found her phone on the console table and dialed his number. She heard a faint ringing.

Don't tell me he forgot his phone as well.

Her heart sank, but he answered.

"Hello, sweetheart. You don't usually call me at work. What's wrong?"

She frowned. Her mind liked to play tricks. She had been positive she heard the phone ring in the house. She continued toward the guest bedroom.

"Oh I just wanted to say hello. You left so quickly this morning. We hardly had time to discuss the weekend." Her voice remained composed but she continued to puzzle over why she heard the phone ring in the house.

"Well sweetheart, can we discuss that later as I'm in an important meeting now. You know how busy things are at work for me at the moment."

The door to the guest bedroom swung open, and the reflection in the hall mirror stopped her, mid step. She hung up, but continued to speak.

"Andrew?" The calm in her voice surprised her.

Realisation dawned, and he froze. The expression on his face at being discovered 'in flagrante delicto' etched into her memory. Shock combined with the look in his cold calculating steely blue eyes. His phone slipped to the floor as he scrambled to grab the sheet from the bed. Palpitations ran through Emma's heart as he turned and the red scratch marks running down his muscular back spoke volumes. The naked woman screamed and ran in to the ensuite.

"It's not what it seems."

"Isn't it? Then tell me, Andrew, what is it? Because from where I am standing there is no ambiguity."

"She fainted at work, and I was making sure she had a comfortable place to recover."

"Bullshit, Andrew. Please do the decent thing and be honest with me. You owe me that much."

"For Christ's sake, Emma. Why are you even here at this time in the day? Shouldn't you be collecting my dry-cleaning? You know I have an important business trip tomorrow. I need those suits. What about my shoes? Have you taken them to be mended? And the desk diary? Where is that? What about the weekend away? You should be gossiping with Harriet, and booking it shouldn't you? Instead, you are snooping about in the house. Have you been following me? How dare you?"

Her voice quavered as his power consumed her, as it always did. He could play 'wrong but strong' very well. She knew that.

"How dare you, Andrew? How dare you bring that, that—whoever that is, here? Into our home. You couldn't even go to a hotel? You make me sick." Her voice crumbled and tears streamed down her face. Hot angry tears gave way to a heavy sadness that overwhelmed her heart. Fear fogged her brain. Any semblance of calm drowned in the waves of nausea that overwhelmed her. Her gut wrenched and twisted in embarrassed hurt. She needed to be strong. She clenched her fist, and her nails dug into her palm. The pain fuelled her repugnant anger, and quelled her fear. "Get out of my house."

He laughed, and the woman reappeared from the guest bathroom, clothed. A secret revealed.

"You whore. Get out of my house."

The woman slid her arm around Andrew and smirked. "You gonna make me, sweetheart."

Andrew responded before Emma had chance. "Leave. Now. Quickly." The woman raised her eyebrows, surprise written on her face, and left.

"Who is she?"

"She's—"

Emma raised her hand. "Stop. I don't need to know. Get out of my sight. Leave me alone." Emma sobbed, unable to control her emotions, raging like a fire burning out of control.
Andrew's shoulders slumped as he left. "I'll be at the Marriott if you need me."

"Leave." Emma closed the door to the guest bedroom and sank into her favourite chair in the conservatory. She sobbed into a towel until her tears ran dry. She didn't understand. One word ran around her mind: Why?

Chapter Two

The cool air in the conservatory disappeared under the stifling heat as the day progressed. Emma woke with sweat dripping down her neck. She wondered why she sat in the conservatory at that time of day. She had so much to do. A wave of nausea passed over her as realization of the day's events dawned. Her head pounded. A sharp pain thudded behind her right eye. The beginning of a migraine. No wonder. She hauled herself out of the chair and staggered into the nearest bathroom. Her nose crinkled at the overpowering scent of *Poison* by Dior. She barely made it to the toilet before her breakfast reappeared.

A splash of cool water on her face refreshed her senses, a couple of Paracetamols dulled the headache, and an opened window released the oppressive scent. She needed no lingering reminders. She would get her housekeeper to clean up the rest. If only the housekeeper could clean up the turmoil in her mind.

She found her phone full of messages and ignored them. She called the one person who could help her make sense of it all. Beth had the uncanny ability to tell it like it was. She called "a spade a spade" when she felt people were too pretentious.

"Hiya. How are things?"

Beth's happy voice made her feel better.

"Not great. Can you come over on your lunch hour?"

"Oh gosh. What has he done now? That bastard. I hate him already, and I don't even know what crime he's committed, but I know it's bad."

"Just come." Emma sobbed.

"I'm on my way. It's a slow day in the office today so they won't miss me. I'll just tell them I have a family emergency."

Beth arrived in record time. Emma opened the door and fell into her arms. Beth didn't say anything but held her tight until her sobbing subsided. Emma led her into the conservatory. The voiles billowed in the fresh breeze and chased away the stagnant, dirty air. They sat together on the sofa.

Beth whispered, "Tell me what happened, Emma. You need to let it out." She wiped Emma's tears.

"I caught him."

"Caught him?"

"He was with another woman. Here in this house. How dare he?" The fire in Emma's voice dried up the last of her tears. She told Beth the entire sordid details.

"Oh wow. That's unbelievable. He has a real cheek. He must have planned that, and I bet it's not the first time they've been here. Did you recognise her? Does she work for him? Girl. Come here. What a bastard."

Beth enveloped Emma into her arms and held her tight. Emma's body relaxed into the hold and she sighed. Beth brought comfort to her like a mother brings to a child. They were old school friends. Best friends, forever.

"I didn't recognise her, but you know recently he's kept me away from the company unless absolutely necessary. I only see Sarah, his secretary, these days. Beth, he makes me so angry. I do so much for him. I feel like I live my life for him. Even now I'm worrying about picking up his dry cleaning, taking his shoes to be mended, and he wanted a new desk diary."

"Girl, forget that. He has his secretary to do all that kind of stuff. Not you. You deserve better than that. But you know what I think about him. He uses you. He always has. Emotional abuse followed by a nice dinner or roses. Emma, you need to snap out of this. This is reality. This has been going on for quite some time, I am sure of that, and just look how fabulous you are with your new style. It takes years off you. You look thirty-five not forty-five. Who did that for you, Tracey?"

"Yes, she did, and I'm forty-eight not forty-five. Thanks that's sweet of you. I love it, but Andrew—I don't know. I love him. I'm sure he loves me, but why would he do such a thing."

"Because you let him, and it has to stop. You give him his power, but you need to reclaim it. If it was me I would divorce him and take half of everything. That's what you deserve."

"Divorce! Oh my! I'm not sure I'm up to that. Where would I live? What would I do? I don't know if I can live on my own again after so long."

"Of course you can. Don't be stupid. It's the only option. Otherwise you will never move on. Look if I did it you can do it. You know I'll be there for you. You can count on me. Yes, he would probably fight it tooth and nail, but he is in the wrong and now you have grounds for divorce—adultery. If you stay with him he will win and continue using you and having sex with other women. Believe me I know this isn't the first and won't be the last.

Wake up! Emma!" Beth slammed her fist and the coffee table magazines jumped.

"Hang on a mo. That's him calling me now. Let me get this." Emma picked up her phone. "Hello, Andrew. What is it?"

"I hope you haven't forgotten the charity."

"No, I haven't forgotten but didn't think you would want me there after what happened."

"This is important, and I need you there, will you be there?"

"Yes, of course I'll be there. Okay, you can pick me up at eight for it."

"Will you wear the black gown?"

"Yes, I'll wear the black halter neck gown. Goodbye."

The door slammed as Beth walked into the garden. Emma followed her.

Beth spun around. "Are you deaf and stupid? Did you not hear what I told you? Forget him and there you are agreeing to go somewhere with him. He controls you. He makes me sick. I don't know what to do with you." Beth breathed in the cool fresh air. "I need to clear my head."

"He needs me. You know this is a long standing invitation and we, McKenzie Associates, are the guests of honour. I can't let down the Children of Hope. It's my favourite charity, you know that. Why don't you come along as well? Moral support." Emma wrung her hands and pleaded with Beth. "Please. I need you."

Beth raised her eyes to the sky and sighed. "I'm a good friend, Emma, but no. If I come along and see him I'll give him a piece of my mind, which would embarrass you as well as him. I'm not going to do that. If you go, you go alone, but remember what he did each time you look at him. Come on let's go inside and have a drink. I've got some Pinot Grigio in the fridge. I think we both need that. You can tell me about your new hairstyle. Are those highlights and did you get one of those new translucent colour washes. It really does look good, girl."

"Yes. Tracey knows her stuff. You should get one."

Beth laughed. "Come on. You know that would never work on this Afro hair. I like my natural wild style. Wash and go I call it."

The best friends hooked arms, like they used to when they walked home from school together, and returned into the house. The cool wine refreshed both women, and Emma began to relax. Giggles chased away trouble with Andrew, as the girls relived their teenage escapades.

Chapter Three

"Tell Luisa to come in to my office." Andrew snapped the blinds of his Managing Director's office at McKenzie Associates closed, poured a whiskey, and grimaced as the strong fiery liquid hit the back of his throat. He did not intend to lose control of the unfortunate situation he found himself in. His groin stirred as the woman entered the room and took her place on the couch. She beckoned him over, leaning forward, one too many buttons on her shirt undone, revealing just enough. Andrew turned away to compose himself. He ran his hands through his hair. He needed his wits about him. His head needed to rule this conversation. Passion would come later.

"This morning was unfortunate but expected. You need to be careful now. Very careful; Emma is not someone to be taken lightly. She can be very determined when she wants to be, even though she doesn't always seem like that. You, my dear, need to do something about your appearance. A wig. Change your hair. Go to the salon and get it dyed or cut or something. You know exactly what to do. I need you at the event on Saturday, but you cannot risk being recognised."

"Sexy. God you are so sexy when you're angry. Come here. You don't know how much I want you right now. The last time as the old Luisa. I will be brand new for the weekend." Her long sweeping lashes raised up and her voice lowered. "You know how good it feels to be inside me. You know how much you want me."

Andrew swallowed hard. His control eroded by the incredible woman in his office. He knew he should not let this happen. He had to control himself but for once in his life he didn't know how. An unknown force pulled him over to her, and she closed in. Their bodies entwined. He quickened his pace and relinquished control.

How can that feel so good. Such a relief after the stress of the morning.

As abruptly as it started, it ended. Her face flushed and replete. Her eyes half closed. She appeared to be in a dreamlike state.

"Get dressed. Sort yourself out. Take the rest of the day off, and do whatever you need to do to look different. Expense it. Entertaining clients. You know the drill."

She straightened herself out and left.

Andrew opened the blinds and motioned to his secretary to come in. "I need to see Francesca from Marketing and PR."

His secretary scurried off.

Whilst waiting for Francesca to make an appearance, he straightened the crumpled cushions, and tidied away his whiskey glass. He was back in control. He sat behind his desk and checked through his emails. His secretary screened everything, so he didn't need to deal with the daily nonsense from everyone wanting to be his friend, or those who thought they were his friend. He had few friends.

Francesca appeared. She shuffled in to his office, her plaid skirt skimming her knees, her blouse with the scarf tied in a neat bow, not a hint of sexiness. Perfect for what he needed her to do. "You wanted to see me, Mr. McKenzie."

Andrew smiled to himself.

Polite, courteous, maybe a little afraid. He could use that.

"Yes. Sit down, please. I have an important job for you in public relations. You will need to be discreet and careful. The person concerned is usually on the ball but maybe a little thrown off balance at the moment. We will only have one chance to get this right. Do you understand me?"

"I think so, Mr. McKenzie. Can you explain a little more, what it is you want me to do for you?"

"All you need to know now is that your presence is required at the Children of Hope Ball on Saturday night. My secretary will arrange for an invitation, and my driver will pick you up at 7.30 p.m. He will explain everything else you need to know. Okay."

"Well, I don't think I'll be able to attend the ball as my sister is visiting from Italy, and we have a large family dinner planned for Saturday. I really cannot miss it as I am the host."

"Re-organise it. This is more important. Please understand me, Francesca, when I say I can make life very, very unpleasant for you and your family, if you do not do what I want. If I understand correctly, you are in the UK on a European Union working permit that can easily be reversed with a simple call to the Foreign Office. I am sure whoever it is you are running away from in Italy would be more than happy to meet you at the airport on your return." Andrew refilled his glass. He did not want any more problems, family dinners could wait. This was far more important. Nothing would get in his way.

Francesca's face paled as she whispered, "Mr. McKenzie. Please. It's okay. I'll be ready to leave at 7:30 p.m. on Saturday. Thank you for the opportunity. I appreciate it. Can I leave now?" Francesca escaped to the door. Andrew smiled as she teetered on the threshold, waiting for his okay.

"Go. Don't let me down. Speak to my secretary on the way out for the invitation." Andrew threw the amber liquid down his throat, the strong alcohol warming his stomach. He needed some lunch, preferably a liquid one. He had accomplished what he needed for the morning. He called Ken, his old golfing buddy, always good for a long lunch and arranged to meet at the club. Time to forget women and their complications, he needed some guy time.

Chapter Four

The crunch of wheels on gravel. Emma peeped out of the window, nervous since her discovery a few days before. An unexpected encounter with the other woman would not be welcome. A sigh of relief. Her ride to the Children of Hope Ball had arrived. She motioned to let the driver know she would be ready in a few moments. She put the finishing touches to her lipstick, found her handbag and left the house. On the way, the driver chatted about the 'boss,' his generosity and kindness towards such a worthy cause, how he had employed him as a driver when he was down and out, and desperate. The boss had saved him. Polite words of agreement stuck in her throat. Kind and generous. If only he and others like him knew the truth. She couldn't listen. She knew a very different side of the 'boss.' She excused herself and closed the privacy partition.

She contemplated the evening ahead.

How would I react to Andrew, when I see him?

That would be the first time since the discovery. The sight of them together still haunted her every night before she went to sleep.

Maybe this was a mistake. Maybe I should have listened to Beth and not agreed to attend this event.

A silent tear rolled down her face. She scrambled in her handbag for a tissue and realised she had brought the wrong clutch. She had grabbed old faithful on the way out the door, which didn't do the elegant gown any justice.

Andrew would have reminded me. He would have told me to change my handbag before I left the house. Maybe I do need him after all. Life alone, after so long was hard.

She wondered if they could go back for the handbag, but the flashing headlights of other cars on the motorway told her otherwise. Not enough time.

Nerves almost got the better of her, and she steadied herself against the driver who held the door open. A few deep breaths and she stood tall. Andrew greeted her like nothing ever happened. Bile rose in her throat at the touch of his kiss on her cheek and his arm around her waist. Another deep breath. She needed every ounce of inner strength to get through this test. She regretted ever agreeing to attend this function, and excuses began to run through her mind.

I could faint. No too obvious. Food poisoning. No that would put too much blame on the caterers. Twist my ankle on the dance floor. Trip on the steps.

Clarity of thought evaded her.

"Sweetheart, you seem far away. This is Mr. and Mrs. Kaneko. The Japanese investors I told you about."

The reality of her position with Andrew hit home. She bowed to the Japanese. "I am honoured to meet you. Mr. McKenzie informed me of your presence here tonight and we are truly privileged to have you attend this important event tonight. Please come this way. I will show you to your table." Glad to escape Andrew's hold, she led the Japanese to their table and made sure the waiter understood his role—to look after their every need.

"Sweetheart, I lost you. I thought maybe you decided to abandon me after all. Now you know that wouldn't do would it?"

She swallowed hard at the hand placed around her waist. She needed a drink to neutralise the metallic taste in her mouth. "Of course not. Can I get a G 'n T please? I need a drink to take the edge off. I'm sure you understand." She smiled at Andrew as she felt eyes from all corners of the room on them. Keeping up appearances could be tiring.

Andrew signalled a waiter. "Gin and Tonic for the lady and keep them coming. I do not want to see her glass empty. Understand." The waiter disappeared before she had time to protest.

"I only want one, Andrew. You know that I don't drink much."

"Relax. Enjoy yourself for once. You know what you need to do." He turned and greeted other guests clamouring to shake his hand, to receive his business card, to get the okay to call him. Strangers running after the so called big prize.

The ice cold drink slipped down with ease. It refreshed and lifted her mood. The waiter kept them coming as instructed. The room wobbled, and the lights flashed in time to the music. She thought the electrician very clever. She would have to ask his name and get him to do the same next time she and Andrew had a dinner party.

Andrew leaned into her neck and whispered into her ear, "Would you like to dance with me for old time's sake?" Her guard collapsed. The drinks, the music, the soft touch on her neck. His familiar smell—safe and secure. She stumbled as he took her hand

and led her to the centre of the dance floor. A space cleared for them. He twirled her around in time to the music. Her head did double time on the twirls. The lights spun. The music thumped louder and louder. She put her hand out to him. "Stop. Andrew. I need to go to the bathroom. Sorry."

"That's okay, Sweetheart. Whatever you want? I'll be waiting for you at the bar." He steered her in the direction of the bathroom.

She leaned on the vanity, glad to escape the heady music and lights, and glad of the respite offered by the ladies room. She studied her reflection.

What am I doing dancing with him, who a few days ago brought another woman into my house? Am I crazy?

A light tap on her shoulder interrupted her thoughts.

"Mrs. McKenzie? Emma, isn't it?"

"Yes. Who are you? Do I know you?" The woman smoothing her pixie cut had a familiarity about her but she couldn't place it. She racked her brain as to where she had met her before.

"I'm Luisa. I think we met a few days ago with Andrew. Maybe you don't remember?" Still no recollection.

Damn that gin, and those double measures.

"Oh I'm sorry I really don't recall. It is lovely to meet you. Are you enjoying the evening? It's such a wonderful charity isn't it?" Emma gave a standard polite response and waited for the woman to leave. She really had no idea if she had met her before and had no intention of making a new friend.

"Yes it is, and there are some very interesting people with very interesting behaviour here tonight."

What a strange thing to say.

Her head spun from the gin. She needed to compose herself before she faced Andrew again.

"Yes. Well if you can excuse me. I see there is a cubicle available now. Lovely to meet you." Emma disappeared into the free cubicle. Privacy at last. She waited a few moments. The woman, Luisa, had left the bathroom. Emma fixed her makeup before leaving the bathroom to rejoin Andrew.

As she left the bathroom, she collided with another woman rushing in. Her handbag dropped to the floor. She sighed as the contents scattered.

"Oh gosh, I apologise to you, Madam. Let me give you an assistance." The woman sounded Italian, and helped scoop up the remaining contents. Emma held out her open bag. "Drop them in. It's okay. It was in a mess in any case. A bit of a handbag black hole to be honest. Once something is in there it is lost forever." They both laughed. The woman apologised again and disappeared into the bathroom.

Emma found Andrew at the bar laughing and joking with Ken, one of his golfing buddies. "Here she is. The love of my life. The wonderful Emma McKenzie. I gave her that name to last a lifetime you know."

"Aye. She's a grand lass. She's as loyal as my Highland Terriers." Ken sniggered at the reference to his dogs. Emma turned away in disgust. She had never liked Ken. She only tolerated him. He had no class, but Andrew seemed to enjoy his company and any friends were precious, she knew that. Another G 'n T waited on the bar for her. The sharpness of the gin combined with the bitterness of the tonic and the lemon, refreshed her palette. She knew she had had enough but one more would be okay.

Wouldn't it?

She could count on Andrew to make sure she got home okay.

"Emma, it's time to go. Come on. I'll drive. Make sure you get home in one piece. I can't leave you to the mercy of anyone else." Andrew held her close to his tight body, his musk sparked passion deep within her and his eyes twinkled. Emma breathed in familiarity, as her head spun around and around from that last gin.

Maybe it was twinkling with the stars in the sky. The stars are twinkling in Andrew's eyes. I must tell him that.

She barely made it to the vehicle. Andrew fastened her seat belt and set off on the drive home. She chattered on the way, telling him about the stars twinkling in his eyes. He laughed and told her about the lights spinning in time to the music on the dance floor. Comfortable banter on the drive home. In no time at all, they slipped back into old ways.

In the house, she floated up the stairs in Andrew's arms, drifting in and out of a gin induced sleep. She relaxed into his arms, strong and safe. She loved him. She offered no resistance when he kissed her and when he caressed her neck, her passion rose. A warm glow travelled over her body as she hungrily devoured him, and he devoured her. Their bodies lie entwined, spent after the heady night of drinking, dancing, passion, and emotion. Sleep came easily for once, for both.

The heat of the morning sun, streaming in through her window, woke her. Her head thumped with the remnants of gin from the night before. She rolled and grabbed a Paracetamol from her bedside cabinet.

He sat up. "Morning, sweetheart. It's good to be back."

She rubbed her eyes to wake as the memories of the night came flooding back.

Oh god what happened. No. I can't believe that. He is my husband and that was unbelievable sex last night but this cannot be happening. I cannot forgive him so easily.

"Andrew. You do know that last night was a mistake. I was drunk. Completely. I believe you plied me with drinks and planned the whole evening to get back here. I know you, Andrew. And what happened last night does not forgive what happened on Monday." He reached to pull her against him, but she pulled away and stood by the window.

"No. Andrew. It has to stop. Right now. Leave please. If you have any respect for me you will leave."

"Sweetheart—"

"I cannot forgive you, Andrew. You understand that don't you." She gathered his clothes scattered around the room and threw them at him. "Get dressed and leave."

Chapter Five

The house shook as the door slammed. The gravel crunched as his car pulled away. Relief surged over her, and her headache subsided as a strong dark coffee hit its mark. He left. She relaxed. She knew she had made a mistake, a very big mistake. She relished her time alone in the house, with only herself to look after, no one to pick up after, no one to demand anything from her. She liked her newfound freedom; she did not want to give it up. She needed to talk and work out her feelings.

"Beth, I hardly dare tell you what happened last night. Come over and let's finish that bottle of Pinot Grigio." She deserved a roasting from Beth, and hardly dare hold the phone to hear it.

"I heard already. Don't expect any sympathy from me. You made your bed, you lie in it. You know that. But yes, I'm on my way, honey. You wait 'til I get my hands on you. And make sure you have more than one bottle of that wine."

Heard already? Who from? More people must watch me than I realise.

Another bottle in the freezer, and she took out two steaks. She knew she had a long day ahead and needed to sweeten Beth from the sounds of it. Steak topped with garlic butter accompanied by a green salad with lots of crunch would hit the spot.

"I can't believe it. How could you dance with him like that? Look at this picture in the society column." Beth rushed in like a whirlwind, and slammed the local newspaper onto the kitchen counter. "Look. Seriously. That photo there looks like you were holding on to him for dear life, and look at that woman in the background. Who is she? Look at the expression on her face. If looks could kill, you, my dear, would be six-feet under."

"Hello. Beth. How are you too? I had no idea there were any hacks there. Wow. You are right. I look terrible and who is that woman. I have no idea but look at her face. Caught on camera. What does the caption say? Those hacks are usually very good at naming people in these photos." Emma studied the photo and the caption. "It says, Luisa. Oh, that rings a bell. I vaguely remember meeting a Luisa there, but I can't remember who she was at all. I had so many G 'n T's I lost count, and I think they were all doubles. He plied me with drinks you know. He knew exactly what he intended to do."

"Well, I would say that this Luisa character, whoever she is, does not look very happy with you and Andrew dancing. Do you think she could be his woman? The one you found him with?"

"I don't think so. The woman who I found here had much longer, lighter hair, but apart from that I don't really remember too much about her. But Beth, the photo is the least of my worries."

Beth's eyes met hers. "Oh. Don't tell me. You didn't. Oh Emma. You did. He brought you home and you had sex. Oh, my god, Emma! No. Why? Were you seriously so drunk? I know he can be very persuasive. I bet he kissed your neck. He knows that gets you every time."

"You know me so well. From what I can remember it was great. Amazing actually. I don't know where it came from. It reminded me of our first few years together, twenty years ago. When we lived off our love. We were invincible back then, when love conquered all, as they say. I don't know anymore. He used to be so kind and generous. Nothing was too much trouble for him and he always made me feel like a princess, like I was the only woman in the world for him, not a handmaiden which I feel I've become. Maybe he is trying to go back in time but too much has happened over the years we've been together. I don't know. Could he, we, go back in time to what we used to have if I gave him another chance? But, Beth, you know, a few days without him being here, and I have begun to realise how I can enjoy my own time. Even when he went away on business trips, he always left a long list of things for me to do. This time it feels different. I feel free from him, and it is a terrible thing to say about my own husband, but I like that freedom."

"You know what I think. He used you and continues to use you. Look at last night. He played you like a pawn, and you didn't see it. I think he's been having affairs for years, but you haven't realised until now. He must. He has too many business trips. Too many excuses for a man who is so controlling over his business. Remember that time you told me he had gone to Paris in July, on that business trip but you know the 14th July is a public holiday in France. The French don't do business on their precious Bastille Day. I didn't tell you at the time but I called Pierre. You remember Pierre. The delicious French exchange student I met at the gym."

"Ooh, yes. The lovely Pierre. Anyway, what did he say?"

"Well he said that the whole of France, and especially Paris is closed on Bastille Day. No business happens at all. It would be a sacrilege. Andrew must have taken a woman with him that weekend or met a woman over there. Otherwise why would he go? It doesn't make sense. Do you have his credit card bill from last month? I bet you'll find the hotel they stayed at. We could get Pierre to call the hotel, pretend he's Andrew and he left something. What do you think?"

Emma took a big gulp of wine and neutralised the bitter metallic taste rising at the back of her throat. Her thoughts jumbled.

Do I really want to find out? Is it better to let sleeping dogs lie? I know the truth but have been unable face it, until now it stares me in the face. Nowhere to hide anymore.

"Hang on a minute. I think he left it here in his bedside cabinet. I'll go and get it. You can make a start on the salad for lunch, there's steak too. I'm starving." Each step took her nearer the truth, which she needed but dreaded. The truth she had been hiding from all these years. Beth knew, which is why Emma needed her so much.

Beth munched on salad as she filled the bowl. The seasoned steaks sat in the dish waiting for the skillet to reach searing point. Emma returned and slumped into the seat at the breakfast bar, her voice broke. "How did you know?"

"It's not hard, hun. It doesn't take an idiot to put two and two together. Let me look." Beth scanned the credit card bill. "No need to call Pierre. All the evidence you need is here. Hotel George V. One room with two guests. It couldn't be more obvious. I'm sorry. I hoped not but knew the truth. Maybe he wanted you to find it, if he left it lying around. Maybe he wanted you to discover him with the woman, if he brought her to the house. It doesn't make sense to me. But at least you know for certain now. Oh, sweetheart. Come here."

Emma sobbed in Beth's arms. She couldn't help it. The blatant evidence before her cut to the core. She had secretly hoped that the woman she found Andrew with had been a one off, but this proved otherwise. It had been going on for quite some time. She didn't want to know how long. That had no importance. Trust had been broken. She knew it could not be repaired. He had gone too far. He had betrayed her love and loyalty. But no more. Her tears dried up. She reached for her glass and emptied it.

"Steady on, girl. You don't want to get raging drunk again, or do you? Tell me, what's next?" Beth held her hand.

"I'm going to book into the spa for a few days to detox and rejuvenate. He can pay for that. He owes me, and I'm going to make sure he pays. Then who knows what will happen, but one thing is for sure I am not going to cry over him anymore."

Beth refilled both glasses and raised hers towards the ray of sun streaming in through the crack in the blinds. Emma followed suit. "To new beginnings."

Chapter Six

Luisa jumped as he slammed the daily on the table.

"Look at that photo. If you call that discreet, I do not! One look at your face in the photo and anyone can tell what you are looking at and thinking. Woman! You are going to get both of us in serious trouble." Andrew stabbed at the society pages, and the only photo of the night before charity event. "How on earth did that hack get your name? You could at least have given a false name. She is not stupid you know, and she will put two and two together. Thank god she had so much to drink last night. You didn't speak to her did you?"

"No I didn't speak to her. I'm not so stupid you know. And that hack, as you call him, happens to be a good friend, so he didn't need to ask my name. I guess it was a lucky shot." Luisa's eyes met Andrew's as she told her blatant lie. She had years of practice, learnt from the master of deceit himself. She loved him but hated him. Two sides of the same coin as the old saying goes. Love and hate. Her addiction to their passion, and the hold she had over one of the most powerful men in the city would be hard to break. She didn't know if she could go cold turkey and do what she had planned with her so called hack, but as events moved along, it became all the more evident to her what she needed to do.

"Come here. You need some relief, my darling Andrew. Forget that. She has no idea who I am. You know those gins were all doubles so she was very much under the influence when you danced with her. She was on such a high and so emotional over

you, my lover. If only she knew. Come here." She closed the blinds
and locked the door as she spoke. The couch groaned and shifted as
they fell onto it, clothes scattered over the office floor. Oblivious to
everything around her, consumed by passion. The phones rang
unanswered. No acknowledgement of a knock on the door. She
knew his secretary understood the nature of their meetings, and
her job depended on her discretion. There would be no more
interruptions. She held his head in her lap and saw tenderness and
love in his eyes.

"I—"

"I know you do." She stroked his hair. His breathing slowed
and his body relaxed. Elation and power surged through her, and
she smiled. She had him where she wanted him.

Chapter Seven

"I'll park your car in the usual place, Ma'am, and send your bags to your room. Please check in with reception. They are expecting you."

Emma smiled at the valet. "Thank you."

The receptionist welcomed her like an old friend in safe, comforting surroundings. A lump formed in Emma's throat and tears welled.

How silly. It's Angela.

"Hi, Angela. How have you been keeping?"

Angela held Emma's outstretched hand. "I'm great and pleased to see you here, my dear. You look so tired and drawn. I hope to see you leave looking rejuvenated and back to your old bouncy self, Emma."

"Thanks. I am tired. I've a lot going on at the moment and really need these few days. Have you booked me in for my usual treatments?" Emma didn't want to release Angela's hand and give up the warmth and comfort emanating from it—like a child clinging to his mother on the first day of school. "I'll go to my room, get changed and go down to the Hibiscus Room for the first massage. Can you let them know I'm on my way please?"

"Yes of course. Enjoy and relax. Let us take away all your worries."

Emma loved The Spa. Everything had been so well thought out and aimed towards the emotional and physical wellbeing of guests. She relished her time there and intended to make the most of everything on offer. Marcus greeted her in the Hibiscus Room. "Welcome, my darling Emma. I have missed you. Oh my, you look so tired. I have the perfect remedy. Lay down, close your eyes and relax. I will rejuvenate you."

The hour massage passed too quickly, and before Emma knew it she had a magazine in her hand, waiting for her pedicure.

A soft foreign accent interrupted. "Scusi. The magazine? You finish him?" Emma raised her eyebrow and offered the magazine in relief. It bored her. She reached for her kindle instead and had just begun her favourite Hemmingway novel, 'The Old Man and The Sea,' when the foreign woman touched her arm. "Scusi. Can I ask how was your massage? This is my first time, and I hope it is excellent."

"Oh, Marcus does amazing things with his hands. He understands exactly what you need and more importantly where you need it. Is this your first time here?" Emma closed her kindle, leaving the boy and the old man. This woman wanted to chat and seemed harmless enough so Emma indulged her.

"Yes, this is my first time. I have a cancer you know so the doctor advised to get a treatment to assist. It is expensive here."

"Gosh, I am sorry to hear that, and yes it is very expensive here, but it is absolutely worth it. I know nowhere else which is as good."

The woman looked Emma in the eyes. "My boss paid for me to come here. He is such a wonderful man. He looks after me and everyone else in his company so well. He told me if his people are happy then he is happy. He gave me as much time off as I need."

A cold shiver ran down Emma's back but wasn't sure why. As if someone had walked over her grave. She shrugged.

Maybe a breeze. Nothing.

"That is lovely. You must be very lucky to have such a kind and generous boss. Where do you work?"

"McKenzie Consulting. In the nearby town. Do you know it?"

Emma inhaled a deep breath to regain her composure. She grasped at the nearby glass of water and cleared her throat. "Yes I am familiar with it. "

"Mr. McKenzie is such a wonderful man. He is kind to his staff. It is not like a boss, he is a like a father to everyone there. You know he paid for Jonathan in accounts to finish his university course. He helped Amanda in customer service to repair her car when it broke down. He does all kinds of things for us. All he asks is that we work hard for him. And we all do. You look pale. Are you okay? Do you need some more water?"

"Yes. Thanks. I'm okay. I think I need to relax a little more after the massage." No escape. Emma's head thumped and cold sweat trickled down her forehead. Black spots appeared before her eyes as the walls of the room closed in. She breathed deeply. "I need a little fresh air. Please excuse me."

Outside, the breeze refreshed her as she sat on a bench in the Lavender Garden. She crushed a purple flower head to release its calming scent. She inhaled, and her calm and composure returned.

Surely a coincidence. Did Andrew know I was here and had he sent the woman to spy on me? Telling me those lies.

A movement across the garden caught her eye. It was the woman from earlier—on her phone. Her body language gave away her agitated conversation. Hands waving all over the place, a European trait. Maybe Italian. A few words floated on the breeze.

"Told her that—no idea—deal—kept my promise—keep yours."

The topic of conversation intrigued Emma and an idea sparked. As she reentered the Hibiscus Room, Marcus swept her into his arms. "Emma, my darling. They told me you had a funny turn. Are you okay? Here let me give you another relaxing massage but this time Reiki with hot stones to reset your chakra."

"Thank you, Marcus. I appreciate it." Emma relaxed into her massage and let her stress drift away.

Emma floated out of Hibiscus to her room. Her eyes closed, and her dreams raced from the charity ball, to a huge bottle of Poison balancing on a light blue Jaguar XK.

As it tipped over someone whispered, "Keep your friends close but your enemies closer."

Her eyes opened. She knew what she had to do. Shafts of sunlight peeped into her room, and she knew it was past dawn. She jumped out of bed. The garden appeared inviting and peaceful—perfect to chase away the night demons.

Keep your friends close but your enemies closer.

She intended to do exactly that. On the return from her walk, she left a message with reception.

The conservatory was perfect for lunch, and she chose a table looking out on to the lavender garden with a light breeze to keep her cool. The waiter signaled to her, and the woman from the previous day walked in. She elegantly picked her way through the tables and met Emma's gaze when she greeted her. She had class. "Hello again and thank you for inviting me to lunch." She extended her hand.

"It's my pleasure. I wanted to get to know you a little better. You sounded so interesting, as did your boss." Emma motioned for her guest to take a seat. Emma ordered water and the house aperitif. "You said you had cancer. That is a terrible thing to be living with. What is the prognosis? Oh, but please excuse my manners. I haven't even introduced myself. My name is Emma, and you are?"

"Francesca. And yes, the cancer is terrible but the doctors say it should go soon with the medication, good diet, and good exercise."

Francesca's eyes pierced Emma, bringing a strong image of déjà vu; she knew this woman, but where from. "Wait! Do I know you? Have we met before?"

"No I don't think so." Francesca bowed her head aligning her napkin with the edge of the table.

"Yes, we have. I think I met you at the charity ball. Didn't you bump into me as I left the bathroom towards the end of the night? You helped me collect all my things. Look I even have the same handbag here." The words tumbled out of Emma's mouth as the memories came flooding back, and she realised it was true. A pink flush and guilt riddled the woman's face.

Caught on camera. Like a deer frozen in the headlights and not knowing what way to run, Francesca shuffled in her chair, played with the menu, and almost knocked her drink over. "No, that wasn't me. I wasn't there. I need to get this call. It's important."

She grabbed her phone from her bag and walked away from the table. She shot a pitiful look at Emma and left.

Emma remained at the lunch table, her head resting in her hands.

What happened? I can't quite believe it.

She knew Andrew had something to do with this but how on earth did he know she was here. She had only told Beth, who would not tell Andrew. This was a mystery she did not understand. Why would Francesca be here at the same time? This was too much of a coincidence. Her brain hurt. She had come here to relax and clear her head, but instead had found more confusion. Their lunch aperitifs arrived, and she gulped both down. The bubbles of the champagne making her swallow hard and hiccup. She giggled to herself. That hit the spot, and she knew what she had to do.

Sadness tinged the drive home. She enjoyed her stay at The Spa and hated to leave early, but she needed to be at home with all her comforts. The emotional goodbye from everyone at The Spa hadn't helped her state of mind. As she turned down the lane, two cars left the drive from the house, and drove the opposite way. She knew one as Andrew's black Mercedes, but the other was the light blue Jaguar XK, which she had coveted over days before. She caught sight of the number plate as it sped away. LU15 ZA. She stopped her car, as realisation hit her. LU15ZA, Luisa. The woman from the newspaper photo who seemed so angry. She had appeared so different that night, but then it was nothing a visit to a good salon couldn't fix. The overpowering scent of Poison filled the house. She grasped at the console table to prevent falling.

Unbelievable.

They had been here together again. At her house. Her sanctuary.

Her shirt caught on the door handle as she slid to the floor, her legs unable to support her. Her shoulders shook and emotions raged through her body: anger, sadness, frustration. Tears soaked her handkerchief. When she thought she had made progress, she found herself in tears. It was an emotional roller coaster she needed to lose at the next stop. She knew the next stop had to be divorce, and through her tears and all her emotions, she made a promise to call her solicitor in the morning to begin proceedings against the only man she had truly loved.

Chapter Eight

"How was the spa? It always sounds amazing, and I wish I could afford it." Beth nibbled on her Panini at Luigi's. The girls had managed to grab their favourite table at their favourite haunt.

"Beth, he follows me everywhere. Even to my sanctuary." Emma took a long swig of Prosecco. Cool, refreshing with a hint of bubbles. Perfect for serious girls talk.

"What did he do now? Tell me what happened?" The Panini forgotten, Beth reached out, and held Emma's hand.

"I loved The Spa as always, but I met a woman who is obviously being employed, or cajoled, or I don't know what by Andrew to follow me. She bumped into me at the charity ball and sent the contents of my handbag flying. I recognised her, but she denied it, and when I confronted her about it again, she practically ran off. I'm sure somehow he found out that I had checked in, and he sent her to spy on me. She started by singing his praises; that he paid for her cancer treatments blah, blah, blah." Emma unwound her hand from Beth's and swirled her drink around. She finished it and signaled the waiter for another.

"Steady on. It's lunchtime you know." Beth laughed, but didn't cancel the order.

"I know. There is an edge. It needs taking off. You know that. But Francesca, that's her name. The one that works for him. She is the least of it. They were at it in my house again." Emma's voice hardened, as she spoke. No tears this time.

"What, who? Andrew and Francesca?" Beth coughed and spluttered, as the Prosecco disappeared the wrong way down her throat. Emma patted her on her back.

"Are you okay?"

"Oh hell yes. Was that Andrew and Francesca you saw at the house?"

"No. Andrew and Luisa. You know the woman from the photo in the newspaper. She is the one that drives the blue Jag. Personalised number plates as well. LU15ZA. That must have cost a pretty penny. I bet he paid. Well, I am going to make him pay. He is going to pay for everything. For all my heartache and tears. There will be no more tears over him." The salt and pepper shakers jumped as Emma's fist slammed the table. "He thinks I'm a walk over but no more. He will see."

"You go, girl. But how disrespectful. I wonder how long it's being going on for? How long has he been doing that behind your back and for her to have a car like that? He must have paid for it. Wow. What is your next move?" Beth squeezed Emma's hand. "Whatever you do, you know I'm here for you. Don't you?"

"Yes I know. I'm going to speak to Kathy and apply for a divorce. She has always given me good advice. I'm worried about Anthony and how he will feel about it though, but it's not as if he is a kid anymore. He's at university living his own life now, and I need to start reliving mine. I feel relieved to be honest. I need to get out from under Andrew's clutches. He is controlling. He lies. He is deceitful. I've been thinking, and I know a huge amount about his business. He thought he hid things well, but I watched quietly from the wings, and there are some things I turned a blind eye to. Even you don't know, Beth. I think I could be in a good position to be honest. Thanks for being here for me through this. I haven't even asked how you and Richie are doing these days."

"Oh gosh, Richie is great. Let's get you through this, girl, then I'll update you with what Richie's been up to." A slow smile crept onto Beth's face at the mention of her lover.

####################

Kathy hugged Emma when she arrived at her office. "It's been a long time my friend. What can I do for you? It sounded very intriguing on the phone."

"No beating about the bush. Kathy, I want a divorce. He has been cheating on me for, well, I don't know how long but I'm sure it's long enough. I just found out. I walked in on them two weeks ago. It was awful. I thought I could maybe get past it, but I can't. There is no trust anymore. I can't be with him anymore and I need to be free." Emma had meant to set the scene but relief took over and brought a smile as her words tumbled out.

Kathy reached for her legal pad and began taking notes. "Okay, I thought it may be something like that. Please take a seat, and I'll go through the necessaries. It should be pretty straightforward—adultery. I doubt he will contest, but I'm sure he will have terms for you."

No shock. No surprise. I wonder if he has already spoken to her. He gets everywhere. How does he know my every next move?

"Kathy, you don't seem shocked or surprised. Has Andrew already spoken to you about this?" Emma knew the answer.

"Yes, he came to visit me yesterday. He explained that you may make an appointment, and said that he will not contest, but he does have some terms that you will need to comply with. His lawyer, Jones and Jones, will send them over once the proceedings have begun. Sorry." Kathy couldn't look her in the eye. "I should have told you immediately, Emma. You deserve that much. It isn't a conflict of interest, but if you wish to go elsewhere I understand. You know I will do my absolutely best for you. Did you tell him you were going to visit me?"

"I didn't tell him at all. I have no idea how he found out. I only discussed it with Beth, yesterday, but there is no way she would betray me like that. How did he find out? I don't want to go elsewhere. We have known each other for years, and there is no one else I would trust to do this for me. Don't worry about Andrew coming to see you. I'm sure we will find out what happened sooner or later." Emma touched Kathy's arm. "I know you'll do your best for me."

Would Beth betray me like that? Why would she? Beth hated Andrew and had always been totally loyal.

Emma shook her head in disbelief.

No it must be something more. Whatever he had planned, I intend to find out and put a stop to it.

Chapter Nine

Emma downloaded her emails, and there it was. An email from Kathy Clark Legal Services. She knew exactly what it contained. The last mouthful of coffee helped calm her nerves and 8am seemed too early for anything stronger. She walked away from the laptop and sat in the conservatory. The sun shone through the cracks in the half-closed blinds, painting stripes across the room. She opened the blinds fully. She needed the bright light of a new day. The light breeze passed through and refreshed her mind.

This is what I wanted isn't it? It's too late to change my mind. Why do I feel so wretched? I don't want to read that email as I know it's so final. Come on. Pull yourself together, Emma.

She jumped out of her chair and marched back to the kitchen where the laptop with email sat waiting. As she read it, sadness enveloped her and tears poured down her face.

Twenty years gone in a simple email. What about the promises they made to each other? In sickness and in health, to love and cherish until death do us part. Or more like, until Luisa came along.

Just the thought of that name brought a bitter taste. Emma reached for the whisky. The harsh alcohol burnt her throat and numbed her mouth. For the millionth time, she wondered if she had acted in haste requesting a divorce. Both Beth and Kathy advised her to go ahead. That she had done the right thing, but now what. She was alone and lonely. No one to discuss the day with. No one to cuddle up to. No one to cook dinner for. No one to laugh with. No one to wipe her tears.

Not that Andrew had done those things recently, but he used to when we were first married and he could have. Couldn't he? No. He had changed so much he would never do any of those things again. And neither would I by the sounds of the terms of the divorce.

She reread the email and the attachments. Seeing the terms they had discussed, in black and white, with the stamp of the court, seemed final and harsh. It became real. No dating anyone connected with the business. Keeping up appearances as his wife attending various social functions and business dinners. She had a home as long as she did not remarry. Terms which once seemed trivial grew in stature with harsh reality.

Maybe I should have argued against his requests but I still loved him. Despite everything I find it hard to hate him. It was the least I could do as he had granted the divorce so easily and given me everything I wanted.

She craved fresh air and left the cloying stagnation in the kitchen for the garden. The roses were in desperate need of pruning, and she had purchased some lovely bedding plants earlier in the week. Gardening lent itself perfectly to thinking or forgetting. She soon engrossed herself in her flower beds and the day slipped by.

"Mum, Mum. Where are you? Mum, I was expecting a pot of food on the stove but here you are still in the garden. I don't know why you don't get Albert to do all that for you." She jumped as Anthony picked her up and swung her around. "It's so good to see you, Mum. You're getting small."

"You too. Silly you're getting big. Each time I see you, you seem to get bigger. Have you been working out? Have you been looking after yourself? I remember what Uni days were like you know. Living in digs with your mates. Lots of parties. Not much housework or cooking." She held her son's face, and her eyes met his. "You know, the decree absolute came through today, don't you."

"Yes that's why I'm here, Mum. I tried to get here earlier but the trains were a nightmare. Nick gave me a lift to the house on his way to see Jennie. He'll pick me up later and we're going out for dinner. I want you to come along with us. We all do. They are all concerned about you," Anthony squeezed her hands, "and yes I am looking after myself. Remember how you taught me to cook. It came in very handy and really impresses the girls you know."

Tears again, but this time of joy at being in the company of her son. She loved him more than anything. Perfect timing. He knew her so well. If anyone could lift her spirits he could. "I'd love to come for dinner with you guys. If your friends don't mind your old Mum coming along."

"They suggested it. They all love you, and are all devastated at what Dad did. How could he?" Anthony dropped her hands, and kicked the nearest plant pot. "I couldn't believe it when you told me. He won't speak to me about it. Just says that it's adult business. Doesn't he realise I'm 22. An adult myself. "

"Sweetheart. Of course he realises, but you know how he is. He is very private about these things you know. I can understand why he doesn't want to discuss it with you. I doubt if he has discussed it with anyone. Maybe that dreadful Ken who he plays Golf with but this made me realise I am the one with all the friends, and he only has business acquaintances. I almost feel sorry for him." Emma held her son's hand. "Don't hate him. He is your father, and whatever he has done to me, he will always love you, and has always been and always will be a good father to you. You do know that, right."

Anthony played footsie with the stones under the bench where they sat. "Yes I do, but you know that he gets me to do stuff for him, don't you, Mum. He asks me to deliver documents and collect packages, in return for my allowance. I feel indebted to him, as if he likes to control me. You know I couldn't live at Uni without the allowance, but I hate having to run around after him. I wish I didn't have to rely on him for that, and our relationship was easier and simpler."

"I had no idea, sweetheart. I thought he just paid it into your account every month. What kinds of things exactly? Nothing illegal. No, it wouldn't be. Maybe he is just making sure that you understand that you need to work for everything you get in life. There is no such thing as a free lunch. You know how he is. Try not to worry about it." Emma shivered and shrugged her shoulders chasing away the same chill she felt at The Spa. An uncomfortable feeling she couldn't put her finger on. "Look at the time. We need to get ourselves organised if Nick is picking us up for dinner. What time did you say he was coming?" She had no desire to discuss anything further with her son, and wanted to shake her growing suspicions. "I'm sure you've brought laundry for me to do whilst you're here?" They both laughed and walked into the house hand in hand. A mother reunited with her son.

Chapter Ten

Emma and Anthony entered the restaurant, hand in hand, to a chorus of 'It's so lovely to see you again, Mrs. McKenzie' from the girls, and the boys teased, "look at Tony holding his Mum's hand."

"I love my Mum and I'm proud to hold her hand." Anthony high-fived the boys and kissed the girls on their cheeks. "You all remember my Mum. She said you should call her Emma, as Mrs. McKenzie makes her feel old. Everyone this is Emma. Emma this is everyone." The warmth and friendship around the table overwhelmed Emma. A comforting glow spread over her realising what wonderful friends her son had made. They all seemed very supportive to her, and more importantly, to him. At least one of her worries lifted. Laughter rang around the table with the unabashed stories from university. Anthony featured highly in most of the stories, but Emma suspected that was for her benefit rather than anything else. A little like getting the baby photos out for a new partner. Pride and interest tinged with embarrassment.

Everyone enjoyed themselves with the light banter, and Emma didn't want to end it, but her head spun a little with the never ending flowing wine and the heat in the restaurant made her feel uncomfortable. "Anthony, thank you so much. I need to go so I'm going to call a taxi. You stay and have fun with your friends. I had an absolutely wonderful time here tonight. It was just what the doctor ordered. Your friends are lovely." She squeezed her son's hand. "Thank you."

"Are you sure you're going to be okay? I can get Nick to drop you home." Andrew signaled Nick to come over, but Nick only had eyes for Jennie. "Well maybe not. Sorry Mum. You know how it goes."

"Oh don't worry. I'll be fine. Look I've got Z-Cars on speed dial. They know me, are always on time and very pleasant." Emma rang the number. "Please pick me up at Luigi's. Okay, 5 minutes is perfect." She hugged Anthony. "They are on their way. Please say goodbye to all your friends. I can't remember all their names, but they are great, and thanks again." She stood and waved a general good bye to the group. The taxi already waited for her.

"Where to Ma'am?"

"The Marriott please."

"Okay."

The fresh air outside the restaurant cleared Emma's head. She knew exactly where she wanted to go, and what she wanted to do. She hoped no one else had the same thoughts. At the Marriott, she made a quick call at reception before entering the lift to the Penthouse Suite. He smiled as he opened the door. "You are the last person I expected to see tonight. Come in."

She pushed past him, and stood by the window. She caught her breath as she gazed out on the lights of the city below, beautiful, but she hadn't come to look at breathtaking views. "What have you been asking our son to do? For his allowance. We both agreed we would assist him at university so he could concentrate on his studies and not worry about work. It seems to me you are giving him more stress than is necessary." The wine gave her courage. She confronted him again. "He feels you control him. Do not do that to your own son. You will lose him. Like you lost me. Is that what you want, Andrew."

"I think it's good for him to learn that there is no such thing as a free lunch. Hard work pays off. He just handles a few deliveries and collections for me, each month end. For that I make sure his allowance is paid." Andrew turned towards her. "It is all above board you know that. Don't you? I would never involve him in anything else. Did you have a nice dinner with him and his friends tonight? I guess they are all very sympathetic towards you aren't they?"

Emma gasped. *How did he know? I hadn't told him. Anthony hadn't told him. And how did he know I had been with Anthony's friends who were sympathetic.* "What? How do you know we went to dinner?"

Andrew gave a sly smile. "I have my ways and means. Emma you should know that by now. We were married for over twenty years. Did you get the decree absolute today? Shall we have a drink to the end of an era?" He handed her a whisky and soda. "Cheers" His smile widened as she sipped the strong drink.

"Thanks. Yes I did. Here's to freedom. You can do exactly what you want now with no guilt." She felt the alcohol burn her throat and combined with the wine from earlier, and the heavy meal, she reached for the nearest seat. The sofa facing the seductive view. "What are you going to do, Andrew? Tell me how you felt when you saw the email this morning."

"Emma." He knelt on the floor at her feet and took her hands in his. "Emma. You know me. You know what I felt. Do you really think I've changed so much over the years? I cried, Emma. I was sad. You know you are the only woman I've truly loved. I've been here all day. Alone. Remembering what our love used to be; what our life together used to be. We were invincible together, remember. We ruled the world, well, we ruled our little corner of it. I love you so much Emma. I would do anything for you. Looking at that view that I know you love so much. I regret my actions, you do know that. But I also know that you cannot forgive me." His head faced down on her knees. His tears rolled down her leg.

She couldn't help herself and reached out to stroke his head. *Had she made a mistake? Look at him. She loved him with all her heart. Why did she divorce him?*

"I know. Andrew. I know. I cried as well. It made me very sad. Come here." She raised his head to hers and kissed him. He tasted salty from the tears, but sweet from the whisky. She finished her drink in one.

He smiled at her. "Are you sure?"

"Yes."

He picked her up and carried her to the bed. They lay together, side by side, looking at each other for the longest while, until the combination of whisky, wine, and passion took over, and she kissed him again. He nuzzled into her neck, and they lost themselves in their memories of better days, full of love, hope, and trust. Days where they woke up each morning, ready to conquer the world together.

52

Chapter Eleven

"...You are my sunshine, my only sunshine...." She woke with a start as she recognised her son's ringtone. She grabbed the phone before realising where she was.

Oh no. What happened? Andrew. That's what happened. What am I going to tell Anthony after last night?

"Hello, sweetheart. Yes. I'm okay. I ended up staying at the Marriott. I had some business to attend to with your father, and as it was so late I took a room here. Sorry I didn't call you. It was all very last minute. No, don't worry. You don't need to come and get me. Just help yourself to breakfast, and I'll be back soon." She dropped the phone and sunk back on to the bed.

No Andrew. Thank God. Damn that wine, whisky and that amazing view.

She smiled to herself as she remembered the night. Despite the situation she found herself in, she had had a wonderful time with Anthony's friends and had to admit they had been good for her soul. Lightness had come over her, like her worries had been lifted. They had given her an insight into how life could be lived. They laughed and joked and ate and drank and enjoyed life. The young teaching the old or the middle aged. Nothing wrong with that.

"How are you this morning? I went for a swim and found some breakfast for us on my way back," Andrew interrupted her thoughts, "I know you will probably hate me and want to leave immediately, but please consider staying for the day. We can spend the whole day here like we used to."

"No. I need to go. I can't go back. I need to move on. I can't believe I let you take advantage of me again. You knew that whisky would be too strong for me and you played me. Crocodile tears and kissing my neck. Andrew, I don't know how you knew I'd been out for dinner with Anthony, but please keep out of my business in future. I will comply with the conditions of the divorce but I want no contact from you for the near future until I get myself over this. Please grant me that much." She pushed past his offer of coffee into the bathroom. The cool water refreshed her and washed away the remnants of the night's passion. She grabbed the coffee and a croissant as she left Andrew sitting on the sofa, presumably contemplating his next move. She no longer cared. He had used her once too often.

In the hotel lobby, she stopped to find her purse with the number for the taxi when she felt a tap on her shoulder. She swung around expecting Andrew but instead saw Harriet. "Emma, Emma is that you? What are you doing here? This is the last place I expected to see you."

"Harriet, likewise, what are you doing here? Shouldn't you be at work?" Emma brushed down her skirt and glanced at the mirrored column to make sure she looked presentable. She had dashed out of the Penthouse and wore the night-before clothes. "But Harriet, it is lovely to see you. Can you have a coffee or are you busy?" She regained her composure.

"I'm working. We have a big promotion on Norwegian Cruise Lines at the moment. Some great deals if you and Andrew are interested in going on a cruise. I know you always said you would but never find the time." Harriet pointed to her marketing stand and colleagues, setting up their cruise promotion in the lobby.

"Actually that sounds like a perfect plan, but for just myself. Andrew will be too busy at work to attend." Everyone would hear the news soon enough. No need for her to play town crier just yet. She needed to get used to the idea herself. "Tell me all about it."

When Emma walked out of the hotel, she had booked herself on a week's cruise in a premium sea view cabin. She had signed up for various shore excursions, an art class, and a yoga class on board. A happy glow spread through her. This was freedom. No one to ask if she could do this. No schedules to work around. No vacations booked then cancelled. She could just go when and where she pleased.

Chapter Twelve

"Welcome aboard Norwegian Cruise Lines. The purser will take your bags and show you to your cabin."

Emma grinned with excitement like a schoolgirl leaving the school gates at the beginning of the summer. She felt free for the first time in a long time. When she walked into her cabin she sent a silent thank you to Harriet for the 'friends and family' upgrade. The scent of summer days lifted her spirits as she appreciated the fresh cut flowers. The veranda gave her the perfect people watching spot, overlooking the Lido Deck. She hugged herself as a wide grin spread across her face. Just what Emma McKenzie needed to restart; the first thing she planned to do was nothing at all. As she leaned back in the old fashioned deck chair on the veranda, memories came flooding back of summer days of her childhood spent at the East Yorkshire Coast, with its traditional seaside towns of Filey, Whitby, and Scarborough. Each one had an abundance of striped deck chairs for rent on the beach. Of course a quick paddle in the sea turned lips blue and brought goosebumps, especially in the late summer, but everyone had had so much fun. And the memories. Priceless. She remembered the summer of '76, with hose pipe bans and scorched lawns. She had been ten years old, with no cares but to play on the beach, and swim in the sea to cool off instead of freeze. The memories brought with them a feeling of gratitude from deep within her soul. Those childhood days had been free, and she needed to recognise that freedom again.

Dusk fell and sparkling lights ignited around the ship. The beautiful sight filled her with peace. Just like the photographs and postcards. She pulled her wrap around her, and settled into her chair, overlooking other passengers like tiny ants scuttling around the deck below. She felt at peace with herself. Her journey to freedom had begun. Her stomach grumbled, reminding her she hadn't eaten since the plane left London, quite some hours ago.

Do I need to get dressed for dinner. Some cruises can be very formal.

She reviewed the welcome pack. Norwegian had introduced 'Freestyle,' a new way to cruise and dine. Informal dressing, eating when and where you wanted.

Perfect. Who would I sit with? Myself? Sally No Mates.

Nervous anticipation replaced the earlier excitement, as she contemplated the logistics of dining alone.

Maybe I should take my Kindle. A good book is always good company.

She chose the Asian Fusion Restaurant because it appeared to be relaxed and informal from the information she had read earlier. Memories of visits to Singapore and Hong Kong assailed her as she entered. The sounds and smells of freshly cooked food. Saki and soy sauce. She sat at the Sushi Bar and marveled at the speed the chefs chopped and rolled to make the masterpieces presented to guests. It all looked too good to eat. She ordered her favourite; California Roll with Tuna Sashimi and tried the exotic sounding Asian Pear Mojito.

Heaven. Delicious food. Relaxing atmosphere. No need for the Kindle here with those chefs to keep me entertained.

"Can I buy you a drink?" A tap on her shoulder turned her head. Her neighbour at the Sushi Bar, obviously alone, and clearly looking for company by the look on his face.

"Thank you but no. One is enough tonight." She politely declined, turned her back and inched her stool away from him.

"Are you alone as well?" He moved his stool closer.

"Yes I am, and I don't need company, thank you." She inched away again and signaled for the waiter to approach. "I'd like my bill, please. In fact, can you put in on my cruise tab?"

"Of course, madam." The waiter scurried away to his station, and she climbed off the stool.

Her neighbour had disappeared.

Funny. He went so quickly after being so persistent.

Back in her room, she breathed deeply. The scent of the fresh flowers lingered. She had found a true haven. Her eyes closed as the mojito hit the spot, and long needed restful sleep carried her away. Sushi floating away on a sea of sparkling lights, washing up next to the whale bones of Whitby, with children jumping waves and collecting seashells for school projects, filled her dreams.

####################

The high sun streaming in the window, along with the next port horn, woke her. She snuggled deep into the cool linen pillows, to catch the last few moments of sleep before rising. She breathed the clean fresh air drifting in from her veranda and smiled at the sea of colourful houses, squashed up against each other on the hillside, all vying for the best vista of the Almalfi Coast. The bustling town of Naples, waking up to the morning's business serenaded her ears; *Ciao bella, pronto, pesce fresco.* She loved Italy, and the Italians always friendly and generous with their hospitality. She could hardly wait for her excursion that day, "Sorrento and Amalfi by Land and Sea." She grabbed a quick breakfast, there would be plenty of wonderful Italian food to eat along the way, and made her way to the Muster Point for the passengers taking excursions. She met pure chaos, passengers milling around, no one knew what to do. A high level of excitement added to the chaos and noise. She found her group, 'SALS,' and followed the tour guide to the coach. She usually let others go first, but she pushed her way to the front. She wanted a window seat for the best view along the way, and she did not intend to give that up easily. Once everyone settled into place, the tour began.

Daniella, the tour guide had grown up in the area and entertained the group with her stories about local Italian life, transporting the passengers back in time. As the coach travelled through the countryside, Emma's mouth watered at the spicy sweet aroma of fresh oranges, and she imagined herself as child running through the streets after the fruit and veg cart, hoping to catch a fallen apple or orange.

As she reached for a traveller's mint, someone tapped her shoulder. "Do you mind? Could I have one of your mints, my mouth is watering with the smell of the oranges, and I need something to suck."

"Of course not. Please help yourself." Emma turned and offered her mints to her fellow passenger, who pushed his dark brown hair out of his eyes.

"Thank you so much. My name is Julian. Are you enjoying the excursion?" His cobalt blue eyes seemed to pierce into her as he attempted to engage her in conversation.

"Yes it is wonderful. Just what the doctor ordered so as to speak. And you?" She turned away to escape his uncomfortable gaze, and to return to the wonderful sights along the way, besides she would probably never see him again.

"It is much more interesting than I expected, to tell the truth. I had been told that it would be a little tiresome but I am not finding that at all."

Emma raised her eyebrows and turned back to her neighbour. "I can't imagine who told you that. Italy is anything but tiresome. I do hope you enjoy the rest of the day. Please excuse me as I didn't come to make small talk, I came to experience Italy."

Julian half smiled and winked. "Of course, Emma. That is understandable. No offense taken. Enjoy your day."

She returned the smile but not the wink and turned back to the spectacular hills surrounding Sorrento.

What a strange thing to say? Tiresome. How could Italy be tiresome and what was that wink about? Some people are very strange and intense.

They stopped for a farmhouse lunch, where the local fresh buffalo mozzarella melted in her mouth and contrasted with the sweet plum tomatoes topped with aromatic basil. The Caprese Salad accompanied freshly caught sardines, grilled to perfection. Her taste buds thanked her as they travelled to foodie heaven. She understood all the fuss about fresh, simple ingredients. After a crisp Pinot Grigio washed down the delicious food, everyone boarded the motor launch for the second half of the tour. She searched for the stranger, Julian; she had no wish for any more small talk or strange undecipherable winks. He had disappeared.

That's a relief.

She lost herself in the rest of the tour, imagining life on the Amalfi Coast. How it would be to live somewhere so beautiful.

Back on board, she settled down into her favourite spot, illuminated by the twinkling lights on the lido deck, and contemplated the day. The buffalo mozzarella tasted spectacular. She wondered if she could purchase any to take home but then how would she keep it fresh for the journey. Best forget that. And the guy on the coach who disappeared so mysteriously. He did seem familiar somehow, but she didn't know where from. A bolt out of the blue hit her. How did he know her name? He had called her Emma; she had not told him her name. Her brow knotted. Maybe he had heard the tour guide mention it. But had she? She couldn't remember. There had been so much chaos at the beginning of the tour. A niggling thought crept into the back of her mind, but she dismissed it.

Had he been sent to spy on me by Andrew. No. He wouldn't do anything like that would he? He didn't even know I was on the cruise. I used my own account to pay and told him I was visiting my sister for a week.

She decided to ignore it. The guy probably heard the tour guide call her name out before they boarded, or a lucky guess. She opened her Kindle and resumed reading, 'The Old Man and The Sea' by Hemingway, but as the lions crept into the old man's dreams in the book, the niggling thought returned like a lion stalking prey, she had nowhere to hide and the thought refused to leave.

Chapter Thirteen

"I have made some contact but she is keeping to herself. She wasn't very friendly to be honest. She is attending art and yoga classes. The yoga is for women only so I can't join in or follow her there. The art class, well, art really isn't my forte, and again it would look very strange if I joined an advanced class as a complete novice. I think it's best if I keep a low profile for now. I don't want to draw too much attention to myself."

The ship to shore connection crackled, and Andrew's words came staccato down the line to Julian, "Sorry you need to repeat that. This is quite a bad connection but is the best way as it is untraceable." More crackles as the connection reset itself. "Yes I understand. I will make sure you get a full report of her activities. I've managed to take quite a few photographs but as we are at sea for the next few days, there is no WiFi so I can't email them to you. As soon as we reach the next port which is Florence, I'll find an internet cafe and send them. That should be anonymous. But to be honest, Mr. McKenzie, there is nothing to be worried about. She just appears to be relaxing. There are no friends around her and definitely no male admirers." Heat flushed Julian's face as he finished his conversation with his employer. He found lying uncomfortable in the best situations, and the situation in which he found himself did not bode well.

He had never met such an amazing woman. Beautiful. Stylish. Elegant. He had been led to believe otherwise by her ex-husband, who had convinced him she had revenge motives. He had been briefed to report back on her clandestine meetings with other so called enemies plotting against McKenzie, but he had found nothing but an innocent woman who appeared to be enjoying her own company. It had taken all his will power not to strike up conversations with her. He forced himself to disappear into the shadows, whenever her eyes wandered in his direction, when in reality he desperately wanted to meet her, touch her and kiss her, with the passion that rose within him each time she appeared in his vision. A powerful force engulfed his body whenever he sensed her presence and it took all his willpower to battle against it. He wondered, not for the first time, if fate had anything to do with this, and how he would complete his assignment. In all the years he had been a private investigator, he had always produced results. Not always what the client wanted to see, but results nevertheless. This assignment challenged him the most. He thought about resigning so he would be free to meet her, but he knew there would be consequences from McKenzie. He knew how powerful his employer could be and did not want to jeopardise the business he had worked so hard to build with integrity and honesty.

A heavy pensiveness descended upon him as he left the communications room in search of his target. A good way of keeping fit on an all-inclusive cruise. He walked the lower passenger deck, then the upper deck. Walking helped him think. He knew where she would be but wanted to prolong the anticipation of seeing her. His nerves sung like starlings in the cherry blossom trees at night. A deep breath as he rounded the corner and his procrastination paid off, almost too much. He walked into her as she rushed out of the yoga studio. "Oh I'm so sorry. Are you okay?"

"Yes I'm fine. Don't worry about it. Sorry I rushed out without looking where I was going. I am late for my art class. Sorry again." She retrieved her yoga mat as a moment of recognition crossed her face. "Oh, don't I know you? You're the guy who sat next to me on the coach trip the day before yesterday aren't you?"

"No. I hate coach trips. That's not me. If you are okay. I'll be on my way. Next time, look where you are going will you." Irritation and anger rose in Julian's voice. He needed to put distance between them otherwise his game would be up. He hated himself for it; when the passion inside him clambered for release.

Colour flushed her face, and she hurried away, muttering to herself, "Okay. It was an accident you know, and I did apologise. Some people are so touchy."

He leaned against the wall with his head in his hands. He inhaled to quell his anger, but the tingling in his groin remained as did the acrobatic butterflies in his stomach. He had never felt like this before over a woman he hardly knew and had not quite met. This warranted another walk around the ship, this time tuned into a podcast. He needed a distraction from himself. He needed to reset his reality.

Chapter Fourteen

Excitement, like that of a child on Christmas morning, woke Emma. Florence. She had always dreamt about visiting Florence and that day was the day. She carefully chose her dress—a stylish and elegant sundress. The sun already blazed into her room. She needed to be comfortable but knew that Florence had expectations of its visitors. She did not want to disappoint. She smiled at herself for visiting Florence like visiting an aged relative, where you put on airs and graces and conduct yourself with respect.

The usual on shore excursion chaos followed, but she had learnt the ropes by now and bided her time. She found her spot on the coach, at the front next to the window, and placed her handbag on the seat next to her, to ensure she would only get a neighbour if the excursion coach was fully booked. She sat back to enjoy the sights and sounds of the birthplace of the Renaissance and one of the original fashion capitals of the world. Daniella, the cruise shore excursion guide, gave an informative commentary on the way into the city, and Emma immersed herself in the history and culture of this unique city. The passengers had the choice of a guided city tour or free time to explore. She chose free-time to explore and knew exactly what she wanted to do. Time to replace the old handbag. She headed towards Via Vacchereccia, and found the tiny door with the unassuming sign. The pungent aroma of freshly tanned leather goods bombarded her nostrils as she entered. She breathed in the rich atmosphere of The Bridge, one of Italy's oldest artisan leather goods stores. Surrounded by everything leather;

handbags, luggage, wallets, a primitive almost sensual feeling excited her. A true mecca for a woman who loved her handbag. She walked around, running her hand over the different leathers, the seductive touch of the smoothed leathers, the roughness of the natural leathers, the textures of the reptilian leathers. She knew she had a hard decision ahead.

"'Scusi, Signora, Desidera?" The shop assistant tapped her lightly on her shoulder, "Inglese? Engleesh?"

"Oh yes. I am English and I am sorry I don't speak Italian."

"Ees okay. I speak a little. What do you look for? I can help you find?"

"Yes I need a new handbag. I'm afraid mine is very old and worn out. Look." Emma proffered her handbag to the shop assistant and smiled as the girl wrinkled her eyebrows.

"I see. Let me show to you the new ones for the season. They arrive yesterday from our factory, here in Florence. They are made with natural leather from Italy. They are beautiful." The assistant guided her towards the display of new season goods.

Emma stood for a moment to appreciate the sight. She loved leather goods, and especially to see all these handbags, fresh from the factory. She picked out a few and tried them on for size. Eventually she decided on one called Messenger; modern yet elegant, in smooth black leather to match any outfit she chose to wear. She resisted the up selling of cleaning and conditioning products for the handbag, and thanked the assistant. She squinted as she left the store and reached for her shades. A clock in the distance, struck 3pm, and she had spent far longer in the store than she had intended. No time to peruse the fashion district now, but maybe that was a blessing in disguise as her new purchase had been more than she had anticipated, but Euro for Euro she knew it would be worth it. She clutched her package close, and hurried through the maze of Via's and Piaza's back to the coach waiting to return to the ship.

Back on the coach she couldn't help but smile to herself as she held her package. She gently pried open the tissue, beautifully wrapped around her new handbag, and breathed the distinct smell. Like a child waiting to play with a new toy, excitement and anticipation enveloped her. She had been very kind to herself. She noticed Julian watched her intently from the seat across the aisle. A wry smile crossed his face, but settled into gazing at the passing vista on the return journey to the ship.

Back on board, Emma restrained herself from sprinting to her room. Her excitement at her new purchase overwhelmed her. She threw down her old handbag, scattering the contents over the bed, and unwrapped the new handbag with care and attention. The aroma snaked its way into her nostrils, and she breathed deeply. She loved that smell. She ran her hand over the smooth leather and smiled with admiration at the exquisite stitching and handiwork of the Italian artisans. A beautiful purchase she knew she would treasure. It already held memories of her wonderful day in Florence and the cruise that brought her here.

She began sorting out the life accumulated in her old handbag over the years, now strewn across the bed. Some things needed to be binned. A female condom brought a chuckle.

Where did that come from? Oh yes it was the hen night that Beth organised a few months ago.

The memories of the hilarious night with sex toys, a stripper and a fancy photo booth came flooding back.

Should I keep it for posterity? No. Bin it.

She continued with the task. Numerous corners of paper with chewed gum. She liked gum but only until the flavour disappeared. After that it made her nauseous, so she used the corners of receipts to dispose of it discreetly. She hated to throw it on the ground, ready to stick up a passing shoe.

Definitely bin.

Lipsticks found their way back to her makeup case, as did the mascara and the eyebrow tweezers.

How did I even get on the plane with eyebrow tweezers in my handbag? Aren't they on the list of dangerous items these days?

Headache tablets and other random medicines found a home in one of the numerous inside pockets of the new handbag, as did her phone. Finally a place where she could always find it, without scrabbling for it at the bottom of the handbag and missing calls.

What on earth was this thing?

She came across something that could be a silver flash drive but had a flashing green light emanating from the usb connector.

Where did this come from? Did it belong to Anthony? I would have to call him when I return. It looked so strange though. I have never come across a USB flash drive with a flashing green light. Weird.

Whilst technology sometimes bypassed her, she did try and keep up to date and had not seen anything like this before. She decided she would keep it and do a google search in the hope of finding out more information. That cold shiver crept down her spine and the niggling thought, that she was being watched or monitored, chased away by the shopping trip and new purchase, returned anew.

Chapter Fifteen

Walking hand in hand along the Lido Deck, looking up at the stars and deep into each other's eyes, Julian turned to Emma, unable to control his passion any longer. When he kissed her, the stars above shone brighter than ever before. A gunshot rang out, and he reached out for Emma as she fell from him into the arms of Andrew. Her eyes open but empty and as vast as the sea beyond. He fell backwards over the rail into the dark abyss below.

Julian shivered and woke in a cold sweat. He untangled the sheet from around his leg and pulled it under his chin. Thoughts of Emma ran circles in his mind. Over and over. Hard workout sessions in the gym hadn't distracted his mind, only made him tired but sleep evaded him. When exhaustion took over, vivid dreams invaded his mind. She seemed omnipresent. Wherever he went on the ship, he felt her presence. He tried to escape but it followed him, enveloping him into a dreamlike state. He needed to concentrate on his assignment to find intel on his subject. It didn't help that his subject had now become the object of his attraction.

How could he remain objective when he felt like this?

He had never had such strong feelings for anyone in his life. Not even his ex-wife in the heyday of their passion.

He wrapped the sheet around him as he climbed from his bunk. The ocean seemed vast beyond through the tiny porthole window.

One more day at sea then back home.

He hated to admit it but he had never looked forward to the end of an assignment as much as this. He knew he would refuse if Andrew asked him to continue.

How could he continue with these feelings and this passion he felt for a woman he had watched but never met.

He hoped he had collected enough information. The kettle sung as it reached boiling point. The tea soothed his mind and his body relaxed into the pillows. He drifted off again, into a more restful sleep.

####################

The call of the seagulls welcoming the ship into port woke Emma from her deep sleep. The last day on the cruise. She intended to make the most of it. They were in Palma, Majorca, one of Spain's Balearic Islands. She planned to wander around the old town, and maybe take in a local lunch of Paella. Her guidebook had lots of recommendations for women traveling alone. Majorca seemed to be quite safe.

She wandered out of the cruise ship terminal into the old town with rambling streets and picture book houses. She immersed herself in the sounds of the locals shouting to each other, hands waving and gesticulating in that passionate Southern European way. She found the restaurant recommended in the guidebook, took a seat outside and ordered the shrimp paella. The sun, high in the sky, reflected off the mirrored building opposite made it difficult to see. As she stood to move tables, her handbag had disappeared. Her heart sank and brought a foreboding feeling in the pit of her stomach. Her purse, her credit cards, her money, her keys. Everything.

What had happened?

The guidebook warned about pickpockets but also that this restaurant was safe because the proprietors were related to the local police. The paella arrived and the wonderful aroma of fresh herbs and seafood wafted over her. Her stomach grumbled but what could she do? She had no money to pay so she couldn't eat it, could she? She wondered if she could communicate her predicament to the waiter whose English left much to be desired for a restaurant in such a tourist area.

She called him over, "El chef, por favor." She indicated towards the kitchen and hoped he understood she wanted to speak to the manager or boss. The chef appeared, talking in fast and furious Spanish. She could only presume he thought she didn't like her food. She gave him the thumbs up pointing to her food and a big smile. He seemed happy and retreated back into his kitchen.

What now?

Around her were locals, chatting away in Spanish, with no one who looked like they could assist. Her hunger gave way to nerves again as she held her head in her hands.

"Excuse me, Miss."

Emma looked up at an old couple stood at her table.

"We noticed what happened. Have you lost your purse? I think there were some kids who passed by and they took it. It can happen but it is rare here in this quarter."

"Yes. Thanks. I don't know what happened. The sun blinded me for a moment and when I turned, my handbag had disappeared. I just don't know what I'm going to do." Relief flooded over her. Someone recognised her plight. "Where is the nearest police station as I will need to make a report to claim for my credit card and other possessions?"

"It is bad, pero ahora, how do you say, today is public holiday and the police are closed today for reports of thieves." The woman spoke in broken English. "I see you worry about your paella. It is good. The chef, he is our son and he will understand." She called the waiter over, and then chef returned, this time full of smiles and apologies. "You see. It is good. Paella is on the house, I think you say. Don't worry. You can make a report tomorrow." She held Emma's hand and kissed her on her cheek. "You have luck with you my dear. You will see. Luck will find you." The couple smiled, held hands and walked away.

Emma called after them, "Thank you so much." She didn't know if they heard as they chatted amongst themselves.

That was amazing. But how am I going to do the police report.

She had intended to explore the rest of the old town of Palma but with the day marred by the theft of her lovely new handbag, she yearned the safety and solace of the ship. Her shoulders slumped as she trudged back to the cruise terminal.

Maybe I could report it to the purser and he could assist.

On board, she found the purser's office empty with a note on the door. 'Purser taken ill. Please return tomorrow.'

Typical.

She returned to her room and fell on the bed. She grabbed the pillow to cover her face. She wanted to hide from the world.

How could this happen on the last day? After such a perfect vacation. I have had a wonderful time. I feel I've made progress coming to terms with my divorce and my confidence is returning. This is a setback. Maybe these things were sent to test me but do I really need any more tests. I want to get on with my life. It seems to be a constant uphill struggle. My beautiful handbag. My new prized possession. I wasn't even accustomed to it yet. I still savoured the smell and loved to feel the smooth new leather.

A tear trickled down and left a salty taste in the corner of her mouth. She sighed, not sure what to do. Her phone and kindle had been in the handbag. Maybe she should make a list of what was in the handbag ready for her report to the purser. She found a paper and pen in the console table and started to write. She heard a knock at her door. She wondered who would be visiting at this hour. Too late for housekeeping, and she hadn't ordered room service. "Hello. Who is it?" She called out.

"Housekeeping. I have something for you. Please open the door."

She didn't recognise the voice as that of Maria, her usual housekeeper, and her nerves tingled.

What now? Should I open the door or press the panic button?

"What do you have?"

"I have something which belongs to you. A man gave it to me to deliver to you. Please open the door."

Emma moved with caution towards the door and inched it open. "Hello" She saw a woman dressed in a housekeeping uniform with a cruise staff badge of, 'Lisa, Housekeeping Manager.' She pushed the door wider and Lisa offered a plain black plastic bag to her. She accepted it and peeped inside. Her handbag. Joy chased away her earlier sorrow.

The lady at the restaurant was right. I am lucky.

"Where did you say you got this from?"

"A man, I am not sure who, gave it to me to give to Ms Emma McKenzie in Suite 501. That's you right. I asked his name but he just said to say it's from a friend who saw what happened earlier. He wishes you well. Are you okay? You look pale. Is there anything I can get for you?"

"No, no. I am fine. Thank you very much. If you see the man again, please give him my thanks. Good night." Emma closed the door and staggered to the sofa. She held her handbag like a child who had been lost and now returned to a mother's arms. She made a quick inventory of the contents, everything in place, even the strange USB drive, still flashing away.

Was it a tracking device and someone following me had managed to track my handbag and return it? But why are they following me and why would they return my handbag?

It made no sense. Happiness surged through her along with gratitude for the luck. She appreciated the moment, the last night on the cruise and tried to forget the niggling doubt rising to the surface of her mind.

"Did you deliver the package?"

"Yes I did. She seemed to be very happy, but shocked I guess."

"Thanks very much. Here's a little something for your trouble." Julian handed Lisa an envelope. She stuffed it into her pocket and disappeared. He smiled.

It feels good to do something nice for Emma. Even though she doesn't know who and maybe never would know. Thank goodness I followed her and saw those kids steal her handbag. That tracking device planted by Francesca on the night of the charity ball earned its keep for once.

A wry smile crossed his face as he remembered how the kids had scattered in all directions when he burst in. A flutter of emotion flew over him as he recalled holding Emma's handbag close to his heart trying to feeling close to her. He knew how precious a woman's handbag could be and more importantly how precious this particular handbag was for Emma. He had waited for hours outside the store in Florence where she purchased it. He just couldn't imagine ever taking so long to purchase anything.

Women, such strange creatures.

He smiled at the thought of Emma's face when she received the handbag.

If I never see her again after this cruise, I would always know that I had been responsible in a small way for making her happy.

Chapter Sixteen

"How was it? I'm dying to know. I didn't realise a week could be so long without you to chat to." Beth called Emma as soon as she walked in the door.

Emma laughed. "It was amazing actually. I feel so refreshed and invigorated now. I have a gift for you. Come around after work and we can catch up."

"Oh wow, you shouldn't have, but I'm glad you did. I'm on my way. Put that Prosecco on ice."

Emma unpacked and sorted out her laundry. She put her old handbag away in one of her storage bins. She couldn't bear to throw it away just yet. Maybe one day. It felt like an old friend, they had been through so much together.

Silly really. It's just a handbag.

Beth rushed in. "Tell me, tell me, and what did you get for me? Oooh, it's so exciting. You need to go away more often." Emma hugged her friend and gave her a small bag marked, The Bridge. Beth took it, a huge smile spread across her face. She opened the bag, savouring each moment, carefully peeling the tape holding the tissue. She took the purse out of its wrapping. "Oh it's beautiful. Just look at the finish and the workmanship. And smell the leather. Delicious. I love it. Thanks so much."

"It's an absolute pleasure. I'm so glad you like it. How have you been?"

"I'm great and did I tell you I met a new guy at the gym. He is yummy. Biceps like, well you know, biceps. And guess what he has a—"

"Oh Beth. I don't know how you do it. What happened to the last guy? I thought he was the one with the biceps and the rest?" Emma held her friend's hand.

"Well, yeah he was okay but you know, still lived at home with his mum and he was 40 years old. Seriously. It turned out he was looking for a replacement mother and we both know that is not going to happen with me." Beth grinned. "The new guy, Tony, told me he has a great friend, John who is looking for a date on Saturday night. You interested?"

The Prosecco fizzed around Emma's mouth. "Oh I'm not sure. I mean. You don't think it's too early to start dating after my divorce. What would Andrew think?"

"Who cares what Andrew thinks? He isn't your problem anymore. You are free from him now." Beth looked Emma in the eye, "You are your own woman, Emma. You need to start living life a little more. The cruise kick-started that process, but moving forward, what are you planning to do? Live here on your own from now on? You are still young. You are beautiful. You have a great personality and sense of humour. Why shouldn't you date again? There are plenty of men out there who would kill for a woman like you to be at their side. Andrew was a fool to play around, and you know and he knows, he will never find anyone as wonderful as you." Beth finished her Prosecco. "Pour me another."

Emma poured and watched the bubbles fizz to the top of the glass and then subside. How her emotions felt at the moment. They ebbed and flowed. She wondered if she could date, if she was ready and emotionally stable.

Why not? Beth is right I need to start living again.

"Ok Beth, why not? Set me up with this guy but make sure he knows I'm not interested in any one-night stand. I read in Cosmopolitan what dating is these days. It's a long time since I dated."

Beth squealed with delight. "Fantastic. I'll set it up for Saturday night."

Emma gave a wan smile to her friend, nerves started their attack on her stomach already and Saturday was five days away.

I need to pull myself together. Beth is right, I know that.

Chapter Seventeen

Emma applied the last of her makeup and checked in the mirror. Viva Glam lip gloss by MAC - it could make anyone feel like a million dollars. She needed that for her first date in over 20 years, and a blind date at that. She smiled at her reflection in the long dress mirror by the doorway

Nerves tingled as she walked into the restaurant alone. Anticipation mixed with fear produced an adrenaline rush. The urge to run began to overpower her. She inhaled and fought against it. She needed to do this as part of her healing. Doubts and second thoughts swamped her mind. She had no idea what he looked like. She was unsure what to do.

If he wasn't there how long should I wait for him? What was acceptable? What constituted too long so everyone knew I'd been stood up? That would be shameful.

The Maître'd approached and asked if she had a reservation. Several different men sat at tables, alone. She wondered which one waited for her, but no one seemed interested as she stood next to the podium. She confirmed the reservation with the Maître'd, who led her to a table at the rear of the restaurant, where a handsome man with angular features sat scanning the room. As Emma walked towards him, his face lit up with a warm welcoming smile. He stood to introduce himself. "I'm John, lovely to meet you."

"Emma, nice to meet you." Relief calmed her nerves.

Maybe not so bad after all. I can do this.

He gazed down at her five foot five inch frame. Her head came to his shoulder.

He looks like he works out. Biceps bulged under his short sleeved shirt. He appeared younger than she expected but she couldn't tell. She had always been bad at working out a person's age.

It was so hard to tell these days.

He held her chair, and waited until she sat.

Good manners.

He handed her a menu and made some suggestions, "I had a little time to look at the menu and I've already decided but please take your time. I think the duck sounds good or the fish of the day. Those are the recommendations from the Maitre'd."

Whilst she reviewed the menu, he studied the wine list. He asked what she planned to eat so he could choose a complementary wine. The gesture made her smile. Andrew had always chosen whatever wine he preferred with no consideration for her taste. She drank what he liked over the years. Emma found John refreshing.

"So, at the risk of sounding like a cliché, do you come here often?"

She gave a wry smile. "I came here once when it first opened but I haven't been back since, you?"

"Same here. I thought it was going to be a one hit wonder to be honest but it seems to have done quite well. Although I'm not sure what the mirrors on the ceiling are for. Do you think the Maitre'd turns tricks when all the guests have left? It makes me wonder. He is so dour but helpful at the same time."

Her laughter burst at the image it conjured up. His eyes twinkled as a sly smile crossed his face. "Oh stop. You are too much." She begged as he developed the scenario with the Maitre'd and the mirrors.

"Ok, well I could ask you your life story but I thought I'd save some questions for our second date. What do you think?"

Smooth, very, very smooth, "Let's not rush into things. We haven't even chosen our dessert yet."

"You could be my dessert." He murmured, his eyes smoldering with intensity. She could hear her blood pumping through her veins, and her groin tightened slightly. Worry grumbled in the pit of her stomach. "I'd prefer a chocolate espresso cup with homemade vanilla ice cream. If you don't mind"

"Not at all. I couldn't resist. Sorry. I don't mean to scare you. You look a little apprehensive now. You shouldn't be. You have no need. You can trust me. If you want to walk away now you can. I would prefer if it you stayed, but the choice is yours, and I wouldn't think any less of you if you went. I know how difficult it must be for you doing this. Beth told me a little about you and your divorce. I do understand as much as I can."

His kind words put her at ease and a sense of calm returned. She smiled at him. "I'll stay. I am enjoying myself and thank you so much for everything."

He smiled. "I worried as well you know. I don't usually do this kind of thing. I like to find my own women, but Tony begged me to do this. I gave in to him. Do you know just how beautiful you are?"

His words surprised her. Beautiful. She had not been called beautiful in a long time. She glowed and couldn't help but give him a knock-out smile.

"You really are. Your gorgeous hair with just a tinge of grey that shows character. Your laughter lines. Don't you dare call them wrinkles. You appear to have lived life well. I feel you have a spirit that you shouldn't hide. Can I ask you a personal question?"

"You may." The flow of compliments made her giddy like a schoolgirl on a first date. She reveled in the attention.

"How old are you if you don't mind me asking?"

"I'm, I'm, well, I'm 48." Nerves on edge, maybe her age would put him off. "How old are you?"

"Younger than you," is all he said.

The meal was over, time to leave. They realised the restaurant had emptied of guests and the Maitre'd who had been so helpful and considerate earlier showed signs of frustration. Their table had been cleared quite some time ago, and their bill had been presented. He clearly wanted to go home. John paid the bill and waved her away when she offered to pay her share.

Again, a sign of a gentleman.

Her husband always left her to pay the bills and despite it being joint money, he left her feeling used, like a secretary, always ensuring everything happened as it should, for the boss.

Outside, the slight chill of the clear summer evening refreshed Emma, after the stifling heat in the restaurant.

"Do you fancy a walk by the river?"

Emma didn't want to go home just yet, "I'd like that."

As they walked together, he hooked his arm in hers; it felt natural so she left it. They reached the river and found a bench to sit on. The ripples of the running water reflected the moonlight. Peace and contentment calmed her soul. The perfect end to a perfect evening.

He whispered, "Come home with me." She barely heard him above the low murmuring of the river. She gasped. The spell was broken. All the thoughts of this being the perfect evening, ground to a screeching halt. As she felt him waiting for an answer, a question entered her consciousness.

Could I be so brave and daring? What would happen if I did?

She heard his words, "You are so beautiful, so perfect. I don't want this evening to end. Come home with me. It will be okay. Trust me."

She took a decisive breath. "Okay. Why not? You only live once."

His smile ear to ear, and everything lit up around them. He rushed, "I don't live far. Just the next block across. Let's go now."

"Okay."

They walked in silence. No idle chit chat, Emma contemplating the rest of the evening ahead. Their pace quickened. The moon cast light around them, so wondrous earlier, lit their way. They reached his house, a new duplex building at the side of the river. They entered the communal entrance, and walked up the stairs to his private door. He waved her in like a courtier opening a door.

"Would you like a nightcap?" He moved to the fridge and waited her answer.

"Yes please, anything."

"Whisky Ginger with crushed ice?"

"Perfect." He turned to prepare her drink. She decided against sitting on the sofa, with all the cushions arranged so neatly, and walked around the glass coffee table and Kilim rug, through the floor to ceiling windows onto the balcony. The flat reminded her of a show house, deliberately minimalist to attract buyers who could imagine their own paraphernalia in place, throwing stylish parties with soft music drifting from the high-tech entertainment centre below the flat screen TV suspended on the wall.

"Are you okay?" he handed her the plain stubby glass.

"I am now. This is an amazing view. Thanks." She lowered her eyes from his piercing look, took her drink and turned away. He stood too close. She swallowed her nerves with her drink and coughed slightly. The whisky had a strong bite, and combined with the wine from dinner, spun her head slightly. She set the glass on a small table, leaned on the railing and breathed deep in the cool night air. His free hand slid around her waist and she noticed his scent. Lemon musk. Irresistible. The stirring in her groin returned with intensity. Nervous anticipation joined the party in her stomach. He ran his fingers through her hair. "You really are." He murmured into her ear.

She shivered. "What?"

"Beautiful, so unbelievably so and more so because you have no idea." His fingers stopped at her neck, and she trembled with his touch. A heat rose inside and began to melt her core. He eased her head to him and kissed her. He tasted of strong alcohol mixed with honey. She offered no resistance. They explored each other. He nestled into her hair and neck and his deep breaths seemed to carry her in to his very soul. "Come," he held her hand and walked her towards the bedroom. "It's okay to say no, you know." He reassured her.

"It's okay. I want this. I want you." Her words tumbled out, and she surprised herself.

His eyes pierced her soul, leaving no uncertainty as to what he desired. He undressed and her nerves disappeared with her rising passion. She wanted him. Her dress dropped to the floor, and she saw pure desire in his eyes. Under other circumstances she would have felt vulnerable and naked, but with him it felt so natural. He kissed her again and ran his hands down her back around into her core. Her throbbing gave way to a flood of wetness as his light strokes intensified. He bent down and explored her with his tongue. Savouring her until he found the spot. Pure ecstasy and desire burned inside her, and she cried out with pleasure. He caressed her until heat rose from deep inside bringing a gush of warm fluid combined with a low moan as her climax exploded. He gave her a few moments to catch her breath then entered her. She held her breath as he did. Euphoria filled her soul. Their bodies entwined. Their passion for each other wanton. They made love and didn't want it to end. They separated and rolled over, spent.

Lying on his bed, his beauty brought joy to her eyes and his youthfulness revealed itself to her.

Just how young was he and should it matter?

He had asked her age but not completely answered when she had asked his. He had just said younger.

Should I ask him again and spoil the moment or just leave it?

Age is just a number; Beth says when she dates men who are much younger. She averted her eyes from his torso.

He seemed to read her thoughts. "You know I'm 35. I could tell that you were wondering by the look in your eye. Age is just a number you know."

She laughed with relief of finally knowing. "I've heard that before from Beth and her younger men"

"Really it makes no difference. If I hadn't told you, you wouldn't have known would you."

"I would have guessed eventually."

"Mmmm, maybe." He went quiet. "Let's just enjoy the moment and each other."

She didn't reply. She let her eyes feast on his youthful body. A poignant reminder of days gone by. This delicious and unexpected adventure had given birth to her new beginning.

She dressed as John sat, comfortably naked, in a chair. "Thank you. You don't know what you have done or how you have helped me. Maybe you never will. But I'm so very grateful to you." She adjusted her belt and he stood. He smiled and kissed her cheek.

"You are good. Let me know if you want to do this again."

She patted his jaw with no promise and walked to the door.

Chapter Eighteen

Emma tightened her wrap around her as she left the comfort of the warm and cozy duplex on the park. The damp, cold air swirled around and enveloped her. Her earlier euphoria changed to apprehension as she considered how to get home. Deserted streets with neighbouring houses, restaurants, bars and cafés all locked up in darkness, did not bode well. As she fumbled around in her purse to find her phone, heavy footsteps broke the night silence. Fear stopped her in her tracks.

What or who was that?

She swallowed her fear and turned towards the sound, her mouth dry; her eyes darted and strained to see in the darkness. A large figure emerged from the shadows and came towards her. A gasp escaped her as she froze to the spot.

"I thought you may need rescuing, my pretty damsel in distress. There are no cabs around at this time of night and you left your phone on the kitchen counter." Relief flooded over Emma as she heard John's friendly voice.

"Oh my. I'm so pleased it's you. Anything else doesn't bear thinking about. I think I need another drink to calm my nerves before you take me home. "

"No problem. Come on. This time you can tell me more about yourself. "

Warm, and inviting, a safe haven from the dark foreboding street, Emma appreciated John's flat again. She wondered how he could afford such a nice place.

"Tell me what you do?"

"Go on dates with beautiful women of course."

"No, I mean for work. This place is lovely but it isn't cheap to live around here. The house prices are crazy at the moment. Everyone knows that."

"Oh. Well, I guess I'm pretty lucky. This was the original show house or flat rather, and the development belongs to my father so I got this as a birthday gift a few months ago. Pretty nice, eh?" John slouched back on the sofa, and patted the seat beside him.

"Okay. Now it makes sense. I heard Mr Smithfield had sold all the apartments and I think someone said he gave one to his son. So I guess you are the son, then." Emma took up his offer and sank into the cushions.

"Yes. Do you know my father?"

"Yes, well no. Well kind of. I attended various functions that he hosted. That was when I was still married. Andrew had all the connections and the invites. Well they dried up a little once we divorced, although, well, you know how it is. Oh, no you probably don't at all."

"You'd be surprised. My parents are separated you know. They just live together for show. It's all about appearances with them. In reality my mother would love to just pack her bags and leave but she is tied to him in so many ways. I think the Facebook status is something like 'It's complicated.'" John laughed. But Emma noticed something different about him as he did so. Different from his easy laugh at dinner. This seemed wistful as if he wished it was different between his parents. She recognised that from her son's recent reactions to her since her divorce announcement. But she didn't know John's reality nor did she want to ask too much or pry. She finished her whisky and ginger and felt warm inside. Maybe from the cosiness of the flat, maybe from John's easy demeanour or just the alcohol. Maybe a combination. She retrieved her phone from the kitchen counter, and called a cab. "What is the address for the cab company?"

"No 1, The Gables, Riverside Walk. Tell them to come down Rivers Drive. It is easier to find that way."

"Thanks." Emma relayed the information to the cab controller, and turned to John. "It will be just a few minutes. They have someone in the area. Thanks again for your kindness and your impromptu rescue mission. "

John grinned. "Well it's not every day I get to rescue such a beautiful damsel in distress."

Emma smiled, glowing inside. Although she had only known him a few hours, she had to admit she felt safe and secure, but most of all appreciated, with him. She relaxed back into the cushions on the sofa, John's conversation drifted into a dull murmur in the background as her eyelids drooped closed, tired from the eventful evening. A shrill sound woke her with a start from her blissful reverie.

What was that? An alarm clock and where am I?

She came back to reality to find John tapping her arm, "Hey sleeping beauty. That's a first. Women don't usually fall asleep on me, but that's okay. The cab is here now and that was the doorbell.

Let's do a quick inventory check. Do you have your phone, handbag, purse, house keys?"

She checked her handbag. "Yes I have everything. Thanks so much."

"I'll walk you down and make sure you don't get lost."

"Thanks."

They walked down the steps into the street where the cab waited. John turned to Emma, "So, pretty lady, can I call you?"

"Yeah sure, why not." Emma smiled, still feeling grateful and thinking she should somehow repay his kindness.

"Great," John's eyes twinkled with a look she couldn't quite interpret.

On the way home, Emma lost herself in her thoughts about the evening. A strange feeling crept into the pit of her stomach as she entered her home, everything felt so familiar and comforting, yet strange. A cup of her favourite green tea or a shower and then straight to bed. She decided on the tea, hoping the calming properties would work on her feelings that had been awakened.

She tried to rationalise. He was young, in fact much younger than her.

Was that such a bad thing? Was this a moment of complete madness? Have I turned into one of those dreaded cougars? Women like me don't behave like this.

She had read about the so called cougars who run after their toy boys. What was the phrase her father used to use? 'Mutton dressed as lamb.' She cringed. She watched them on TV and read about them in those trashy magazines, like *Hello* or *Now*, she encountered in various waiting rooms and surgeries.

Is this what it had come down to?

PING: A text. Surprised and wondering who would be sending messages so late in the night, she searched in her handbag for it. At the bottom as usual. A number she didn't recognise. <Just checking you got home okay.>

PING: <Sorry. I couldn't resist. I looked in your phone for your number. You really need to put a lock on it.>

She stared at the phone, surprised but with the same warmth from earlier creeping over her. She couldn't decide what to do. Message him back or ignore him. If she messaged back then it would probably encourage him further, and she didn't know if she wanted to take things further, or if she ignored him then he would think her rude after his kindness that evening. Rescuing his damsel in distress as he put it.

PING:<I guess you are sleeping. Sweet dreams beautiful.>

He had presented her with a perfect excuse so why did she feel forlorn now she didn't have to reply. She reached for her phone.

<Thanks. Yes I got home okay. Just having a cup of tea before sleeping.> SEND.

She reread the text. Polite enough. Not encouraging. She felt unsure about what she wanted.

PING:<I worried when I didn't hear from you. I had such a great evening. One of the best I've had for a long time. I'd love to do it again sometime?>

No ambiguity in that message. Warm comfort turned into excitement and anticipation followed by ridicule.

Seriously. What am I thinking?

Exhaustion rained down on her, with the nights events replaying over and over in her mind. She made her way up to her bedroom. She breathed in his musky fragrance that lingered on her clothes as she hung them to air and her groin stirred. She twisted her hair around and the same smell wafted into her nostrils. She savoured it, knowing it would be soon gone and maybe forever. With a slight regret of losing the precious scent, she showered with the hope of washing the pervading thoughts of him out of her mind. When she finally lay in her bed sleep came quickly.

The trill sound of her phone woke her with a start. The time on the bedside alarm clock showed 10am. Unheard of. She usually woke with the dawn chorus. She swallowed hard as she reached over and answered the unknown number showing on her phone. Her nerves on edge. She did not want to speak to John so soon after last night. "Hello"

"Hiya. It's me. I'm calling you from my friend's phone; mine ran out of battery power. How are you? How did it go last night? What was he like? Do you know he's been on the phone already this morning to Tony wanting to find out more about you? You must have made quite an impression on him."

She sighed with relief at the excited gush of questions from Beth. "Oh. Gosh. I, err, well I had a great time but we need to meet and debrief. Oh Beth, he was lovely but he is only 35. Did you know that before Tony set me up?"

Beth shrieked. "Wow. No way. Oh, he didn't tell me that. He just said he was one of his gym buddies but one of the nice ones. You know what some of them are like. Pure Adonis and full of themselves. All abs and no personality. I hope this guy was different."

"Yes he certainly was different. He was lovely but 35. Beth. You do know I'm 48? That's 13 years."

"You go girl. So tell me everything."

"Not on the phone. Let's go for a coffee at Luigis. Although you may need some vodka once you hear what happened."

Another shriek from Beth. "I can't wait. What time?"

"About 11.30, let's make it an early lunch. I don't feel like cooking today."

"Okay, great. See you there."

Chapter Nineteen

The glass-panelled building reflected the passing clouds and, under other circumstances, would have given an air of calm, but from the bench where Julian sat, contemplating what to do, the image irritated him. His mind flooded

"Good morning, Mr McKenzie. I hope you are well." Julian swallowed his bile and replaced his hatred with politeness as he offered his hand.

"Yes. Thank you. I hope you have the report you promised." Andrew reached out to shake his hand. "I told you she would be tiresome, so I hope you didn't get too bored, but it is your job after all. I bet you've had much more exciting assignments in your years as a Private Investigator, haven't you?"

"On the contrary, I didn't find it tiresome at all. She is a very passionate woman intent on enjoying her life. She joined the cruise alone and left the cruise alone. I found no evidence of any men accompanying her. She attended art and yoga classes as I mentioned during our telephone call. She seemed to spend a lot of time reading or just looking out at sea contemplating life, I guess. I tried to strike up a conversation with her but she didn't appear to be interested in making friends. She really did keep to herself. Here is my report in full, documenting her daily movements. And as you know, she still has the MemQ device in her handbag. I noticed she changed handbags but after the incident when her handbag was stolen and we managed to retrieve it, I checked the contents. The device was still there and active. She either didn't notice it or she doesn't know what it is and has maybe forgotten about it." Blood pumped hard through Julian's veins as he kept his composure and his emotions under check. He delivered the report in a cold and deliberate tone. He had no wish to give his game away to his employer. "If that is all, Mr McKenzie. I have a few other cases I need to work on, and it seems in this case there is nothing out of the ordinary to report. I presume you received my invoice." Julian made direct eye contact with Andrew. He needed to end this assignment and be firm about it.

"Thank you. I will read the report. You did a good job. I appreciated the update from the cruise, and that I could assist in retrieving the handbag. I know how precious a woman's handbag is to her. I don't want to hurt her anymore. I think I've done enough. I received your invoice, and have made a payment as you requested into your account. However, the case is not closed. It is not as simple as that. I am going to pay you for the next two months with a very generous tax-free bonus which I think should more than cover any income you may make from other jobs. I need to monitor the situation until a critical business deal has been signed. There is a lot of information that she was privy to, which could jeopardise the deal if it falls in the wrong hands. I need to know all her movements now she is back. Who she talks to. Who she sees. What she does. She may not actually realise she holds this information or was privy to it, but I know she knows much more than she realises. I hope you see fit to extend the contract." Andrew pushed the brown envelope on the desk towards Julian. "It would be a shame for you to start having financial difficulties and especially as your wife, oh sorry, ex-wife is now requesting additional maintenance from you."

Julian tightened his fists as his eyebrows raised and his forehead wrinkled in surprise.

How did he know? Am I being investigated myself?

He inhaled and held his breath as he reached for the envelope and popped it open. He exhaled as he estimated how much money the envelope contained. He didn't know the exact amount but the wads of crisp red and purple notes bursting out looked like more than he had seen in a long time. It would certainly ease the way with his ex-wife, and even be enough for him to move out of his dingy flat into the new duplex he had his eye on.

It wouldn't be such a bad thing. I could get an opportunity to become closer to her. This is amazing, so much money.

"Thank you, Mr. McKenzie. Yes I can extend. I will continue immediately. I presume in the same fashion as before." The envelope burned in Julian's hand as he accepted further betrayal of the woman he loved.

Chapter Twenty

"I'll have the Panini with mozzarella and tomatoes with a glass of Prosecco, please." The waiter scribbled down the order and turned to Beth.

"Me too. That sounds delicious. In fact, we'd like a bottle of Prosecco. Thanks." She reached out and took Emma's hand in hers. "Don't worry. Everything will be okay you know. It always works out for the best. Now tell me about John. He sounds delicious."

"He is delicious, and would be perfect if I were ten years younger, but I'm not. I can't believe I did what I did. I have never done anything like that before. Not even when we were at Uni. You know I met Andrew in the second term and that was it. We've been together so long. I couldn't ever imagine intimacy with anyone else, but John was so—" Emma sipped her Prosecco, the bubbles fizzed and refreshed her mouth.

"Cheers to so, then." Beth clinked glasses with Emma and winked. "Don't worry. Just enjoy it. He's keen. Like I said he called Tony several times already this morning to find out more about you, not that Tony knows that much. You've only met him twice I think. Every time he called, Tony asked me what to say. I couldn't stop laughing. The important thing is that you had a great time. Life is for living you know, Emma. I sometimes think you forgot that when you were with Andrew."

Emma laughed. "Yes, cheers to so—actually he made me feel very special. He knew how to be considerate; he gave me space to talk and made me laugh. He's got a great sense of humour. You know we went to that Greek restaurant on The Square. Have you ever been? It's hilarious. There are mirrors on the ceiling but neither of us could work out why, anyway he made up this whole story about the Maitre'd turning tricks when the restaurant was closed." Tears rolled down her face as she recounted the story through her giggles.

Beth leaned over the table and hugged her friend. "I haven't seen you laugh like that in a long time. This man is good for your soul, Emma. Don't give up on him just because he is younger than you. Thirteen years is nothing. I am absolutely positive you can get over that quite easily. You're glowing and it can only be a good thing."

"But, Beth he is only 35. Yes he is great fun, and he rescued me when I left his place and forgot my phone. He came to find me, to check I was okay. It felt good to be looked after again. Do you really think we could have a relationship and make it work? Isn't it too soon after Andrew? I mean the divorce only came through a few weeks ago."

"I told you already, forget Andrew. You know exactly what I think of him. A waste of your time and energy. Always has been. I never knew what you saw in him. He is controlling and single-minded about his precious business. I know he has made a huge amount of money, but life isn't about money you know. It's about love and happiness. It's about being at peace with yourself. If you don't have that you don't have anything in my opinion." Beth finished her Prosecco and signalled for the waiter to bring another bottle. Emma rolled the base of her glass around the edge of the beer-mat as she contemplated her choice of words.

"I do know what you think of him. Oh I meant to ask you something before I left for the cruise but didn't get chance. Don't take this the wrong way, but did you tell Kathy about our conversation about the divorce. When I went to meet with her, she already knew and he had already spoken to her. I found that very strange. You were the only person I'd discussed it with. I hadn't mentioned it to Andrew but he seemed to know exactly what I wanted." Emma flushed as she caught Beth's eye. She knew she may be skirting an issue if Beth had spoken to Andrew, but she trusted her friend implicitly and needed to know if that trust had been broken.

"What? No way. You know me. I can't stand him. I would never betray you. How did he find out? Do you think it may be a coincidence that he spoke to Kathy at the same time as you?" Beth refilled their glasses with the fresh bottle of Processco, and met her friend's eyes as she spoke.

Emma squeezed her hand in a sign of reassurance. "I didn't think you had, but I had to ask. You understand that don't you. I just don't know what's going on. I think he may be following me or having me followed. On the cruise there was this man who kept appearing then disappearing when I tried to talk to him. He bumped into me outside a yoga class, and I recognised him as being on one of the land excursions with me but he denied it then disappeared. It was very strange. Oh and when I switched handbags I found a weird thing. No idea what it is, but I'm now wondering if it is a transmitter or something. Look." Emma pulled the flashing USB device out of her handbag and placed it on the beer-mat.

Beth prodded it with her fork. "What on earth? I've never seen anything like that. Are you sure it's not a USB from Anthony; you mentioned he was back from Uni a few weeks ago. Maybe he gave it to you to hold and forgot about it. I can't imagine anything so small would be able to transmit anything significant, but you never know with technology these days. You should take it into that new spy shop that's opened on The Esplanade. Tony told me about it. It's full of boy's toys; you know watches that turn into boats and the rest. All very James Bond, 007 and Q. "

Emma's eyebrows raised and her eyes widened as she smiled. "Really. Wow. I had no idea. I'll pay them a visit next week. I hope they can get to the bottom of it as it's been preying on my mind ever since. I didn't want to throw it out just in case it did belong to Anthony and had some important work from Uni on it." She picked up the device, wiped it clean and dropped it back into her handbag. She raised her glass. "To new beginnings and old friendships. I love you Beth." Beth followed suit. "To old friends and making new friends. Be gentle on yourself. Be kind to yourself. You deserve it." They drank and ate and became engrossed in themselves.

####################

A man sat at the table opposite, buried his head into his newspaper, and blended into the background of the busy restaurant—a single man eating brunch on Sunday morning with his newspaper and cappuccino, a man who listened to every word they said with an occasional knowing smile crossing his face.

Chapter Twenty-one

"We may need to retrieve the MemQ from Mrs McKenzie. She is beginning to suspect something. She found it when she changed over her handbags and although she thinks it is a USB that belongs to her son, I think she may take it into 'Spy High' on The Esplanade to get them to take a look at it. What do you want me to do?"

Julian shivered as he held the old phone to his ear. Pay phones had the advantage of being virtually untraceable and anonymous. Their location, however, did not lend itself to long conversations especially in the waning summer months. "Okay, that's not a problem. I'll visit them tomorrow and make sure they understand the importance of discretion and reassurance." He fed more coins into the slot.

He sat on the bench next to the phone to decide what to do next. Guilt trampled over him as he replayed the conversation with McKenzie. Betrayal left a bitter taste and he forced himself to think about the sweet gains coming his way at the end of this assignment. The emotional morning had taken its toll. He yearned to reach out to Emma, to comfort her and pull her into his safe secure world, yet he had hidden behind his newspaper to hide from her. He couldn't risk being seen as she would recognise him from the cruise. She had confirmed that in her conversation with Beth. He realised he had underestimated her. She knew about the MemQ, although she still had no idea what it did, but that was only a matter of time. She had been on a date and went back to the guy's place, just for coffee, he hoped, as a twinge of jealousy poked him in the ribs. She had noticed him on the cruise even though he thought he had been discrete. She had begun to live her life again, and maybe she would be more of a challenge than he had originally anticipated.

####################

Emma smiled at the song playing on the radio, *'I'm mad about the boy, and I know it's stupid to be mad about the boy, I'm so ashamed of it but must admit the sleepless nights I've had, About the boy ....'* Dinah Washington, a classic, and it couldn't be more appropriate to her situation. The last few nights had been restless. Passion rising in her body roused her from sleep. Her green tea did nothing to dampen her growing ardour, and he pervaded her every dream. She yearned for his tender touch and passionate embrace.

"*...Will it ever cloy, this odd diversity of misery and joy? I'm feeling quite insane and young again. And all because I'm mad about the boy.*" Dinah continued her song. The words resonated around her brain as she reached for her phone. She needed to find the joy and stop the misery.

"Hello. It's me. I wondered if you would like to meet up again. I'd like to thank you for the wonderful evening I had on Saturday." She swallowed her nerves and practiced yoga breathing to keep calm. "You would. Wonderful. See you tomorrow at 2pm. My choice you say. Okay. Bye John." A wide smile spread across her face as she floated around the kitchen. She pinched herself.

I did it. He wants to meet me again.

She rushed up the stairs, two at a time, into her bedroom.

What am I going to wear? And he said it would be my choice where we go? Oh I know. The museum.

Her clothes scattered over her bed as she tried outfits, one after another. The prefect outfit presented itself, and she hung it up, ready for her date the next day. She paced around the house, into the kitchen, through the hallway, into the conservatory, until she visited each and every room. Not knowing what to do with herself, she needed an escape from the misery the joy of a second date brought. That song again. She jumped into her car, arrived at Beth's in record time, and barged through the backdoor, into her friend's kitchen.

"Beth. I did it."

"Oh, Hello. I didn't expect to see you. Did what? What did you do? Calm down. You sound out of breath. What have you been doing?"

"I couldn't sleep for days, just thinking about him, you know. Then I heard Dinah Washington on the radio, and so I called him and we're going on a date tomorrow. I'll take him to the museum. Do you think he will like that? Oh gosh, what if he thinks it's really boring? Should I go paint balling or something else instead? What do you think?" Emma's words tumbled out in an excited rush.

Beth grinned at her. "Hey, slow down. I only got half of that. What was that about Dinah Washington? And you said you're going on a date, with John? Great. What are you going to do; you said something about paint balling. Emma, there is no way you can go paint balling. Why don't you take him to the Impressionist art exhibition you want to see at the museum? He would love that, I'm sure."

"Yes that's what I said I'm going to do. Beth, I felt so nervous calling him but afterwards it felt so liberating and powerful. Ooh, it felt good. Oh, I'm sorry for turning up so unexpected, but I had to tell you in person." They clung on to each other, and jumped around the kitchen like the school girls in the song, in the flurry of their first affair.

Chapter Twenty-two

Emma checked her watch every few minutes. "Would he come?" Doubt raced through her mind as she stood on the steps to the museum. She tapped her fingers, her gaze drifted to the brochure stand. Some leaflets looked haphazard; the poster for the current exhibition didn't stand in the perfect centre. The corner sprung up as the tape holding it down gave way. She checked her watch again, 2.05pm.

Where is he?

The museum lobby reflected in the glass panels and contained teachers trying to control a rowdy party of school children, but no one else. She frowned.

What if he stands me up? Was I too forward?

A tap on her shoulder turned her around, and a big smile beamed across her face at the sight of him. "You made it. I thought you'd stood me up."

"What, and miss a second date with a beautiful woman. No way. It's great to see you." His eyes crinkled as he grinned.

"Ok you can put me down now. I quite like breathing. It helps me live my life you know." She teased as he released his bear hug. "Do you like museums? I didn't ask if you did."

"I don't often get chance to visit, but when I do I like the peace and tranquillity they bring. Shush. Everyone is so very quiet in museums aren't they? Isn't it all hushed whispers and the rest?"

Emma put her finger to his lips and whispered, "We don't want to disturb the exhibits, do we? Behave yourself please, or I'll have to reprimand you."

"Oh, that's what I was hoping for." A sly grin spread across his face and his eyes twinkled. He laced his fingers in hers as they entered the lobby. "Two for the Impressionists, please, and I'd like a guide book as well. Which way do we go?"

Sparks flew from his fingers up her arm and landed in her groin. Her skin tingled from the magnetic pull between them. Her breath quickened.

How am I going to concentrate on art when he is so close to me? This was a mistake.

The museum guide indicated up the stairs and to the right. John guided Emma through the party of school children, towards the exhibition. At the top of the stairs, he turned to her. "Now I guess it's time for you to take over. Isn't this your field, if I'm correct in my research?"

She wiggled her fingers free. "Yes. I love art. I have a first degree in Art History and a Masters in Fine Arts. What research are you talking about? Are you investigating me?" She poked him in his ribs.

"It's amazing what a Google search on someone's name can reveal. It's pretty simple really. You have a website for your art workshops at The Warehouse, all your contact details are there as well as your bio. It looks fantastic, actually. I may go along to one, if it wouldn't be too much of a distraction. You probably noticed in my flat that I like to collect art and I could do with some new pieces from unknowns. You never know if they are going to make it. If they do then you're quids in and if they don't well, it really doesn't matter as you've got a great piece of art you love. Strut your stuff, pretty lady."

Emma stifled a giggle at his assessment of the heady world of art collections. The clarity of his point of view refreshed her. "Come on then. Let's find Matisse. He is my favourite, then Degas, Renoir, Pissarro and of course, everyone's darling, Monet. You need to be as quiet as a mouse though." She pushed him through the door into the main exhibition room. With the dimmed lights the silence in the room bore down on them like a shroud of darkness. Emma caught John's eye and they both exploded into fits of laughter as they burst back through the door. "I told you to behave yourself. Why did you make me laugh so much?" Tears streamed down her face as she sat on the bench, breathless.

"I didn't say a word. I was waiting for my personal tour guide to start her commentary but here I find myself. Back at the start. I think I'm going to make a complaint to the museum. You just can't get good staff these days. I wanted a serious tour but all I'm getting is a frivolous but beautiful woman leading me astray." He sat beside her, took her hand in his, and drew a few letters on her palm. He leaned forward until his hot breath caressed the corner of her mouth. "You smell great."

Shivers ran down her back and butterflies flew around her stomach. Her groin tightened in anticipation. "Let's get out of here. I can't look at art when you do that." The smell of his body and his breath on her skin sent a shudder through her, burning her core.

"Really. So tell me what else would you like to do, pretty lady." His eyes pierced into the depths of her soul.

"I think you know exactly what I'd like to do, Mr Smithfield." A low groan escaped her as he continued to draw letters on her palm. "What word are you writing?"

"I'll show you later." He smiled, pulled her over to him and placed his lips over hers. She reached up behind his neck, spread her fingers in his hair and pulled him closer.

"Excuse me. Ahem. Excuse me." A gruff voice interrupted their embrace. The imposing figure of the museum security loomed over them. "This is a museum not the back row of the cinema. Please desist or take it outside. Have some respect. There is a school party here as well."

"Oh gosh. I'm sorry. I think we're about to leave. Very sorry for our minor indiscretion." Emma flushed as she stood and pulled John up from the bench. "Let's get out of here. Come on."

The fresh air hit them as they hurried out of the museum and leaned against the stone pillar to catch their breath. One look and their laughter returned. John wiped his handkerchief over Emma's face, streaked with mascara. She took it from him and blew her nose. "Seriously?" He laughed even more. "You can keep that now. I'm glad you feel so comfortable with me already, but please no lady aromas."

Her hands flew to her face. "Oh shame. Please forgive me. I'll make sure it's washed, ironed and returned in pristine condition."

"Don't worry. I'm only joking. Keep it. I have plenty. You look like you need it more than me. I've had a really good time not appreciating the art exhibition in the museum. Come along. Let's go to mine. I have something to show you."

At his flat, he demanded she sit on the sofa and wait for him. He disappeared and emerged some time later with a canvas. Emma gasped as he turned it around. Leicester Square (Londres) La Nuit by Monet. "Oh my god. Is that—" Words escaped her.

"Yes it is. It actually belongs to my father. When he marketed the development he hung it in the lounge, to create an air of opulence. You know it's all about impressions, so an impressionist painting seemed appropriate. Most buyers thought it was a fake but there were one or two, like you, who knew exactly what it was. He left it here when he gave me the flat. I mentioned it to him but he just said not to worry about it. It's a gift along with the flat." John ran his fingers around the edge of the canvas.

"That's amazing. I knew it was part of a private collection but I thought somewhere in Paris or New York. Not here in the town where I live. You know Monet painted that in around 1900 to 1901. It was sold by Christies in New York in 2005, for 800,000 US dollars. Wow. That was your father. Thank god I'm sitting down." Emma leaned over to take a closer look at the painting. She reached out but withdrew her finger before it reached the canvas. "You can't leave it here you know. If anyone knew, it would be stolen in a heartbeat. It's one of France's national treasures actually. You need to keep it very safe. Please don't tell me it was propped up against the wall in your spare room."

"No I have a large safe and it was inside. But yes I should return it to my father's house. He has an air-conditioned art gallery with laser security. It's very James Bond. I'll put it away. I wasn't being boastful you know. I just thought you would appreciate it. Our own personal exhibition as we didn't get to see the one at the museum."

A thought pricked Emma's subconscious, about James Bond and the spy store, but she dismissed it for another time. She followed John to the spare room and as he closed the door, she wrapped her arms around him. She could wait no longer and her lips found his. His tongue probed and danced a slow erotic dance around hers. She melted into his passionate embrace. He scooped her up and they fell together on to the bed. All their laughter vanished as the air became serious between them. They looked into each other's eyes, no words necessary. His strokes sent shivers down her neck and she quivered in delight. Heat spread through her and pooled between her legs. She pushed him down and kissed his eyelids, his nose, his neck, his throat, his ears, his chest. His nipples hardened into tight balls as she sucked and nibbled them with a gentle bite. He groaned, "Don't stop. This is heaven." Her kisses continued down onto his erection. Her tongue searched out the most sensitive spots around the head and savoured the tip. Wet and salty. He pushed his fingers through her hair, pushing her down on him; faster and harder, until he moaned and her mouth filled with his salty sweet essence. His eyes closed as he relaxed into his pillows. "Thank you. That was amazing." He turned over and held her against him, caressing her neck. His hardness returned. His hand traced across her shoulders, down her back and his fingers explored her core. Hot, wet and swollen. He nestled between her legs and rolled her underneath him. She pulled him down with her nails running farrows into his back as her passion rose. Her legs wrapped around him as her hips rose in a sweet invitation. She moaned as he filled her. Her soft flesh tightened around him and he began his rhythmic movements. Her hips moved in unison as she clutched his buttocks pulling him further inside her. He buried his head in her neck, let out a low moan and shuddered. Hot moisture spilled inside her as waves of her own ecstasy carried her away past anything she had experienced before. Eventually, John rolled to the side and wrapped his arm around Emma, pulling her on to his broad chest. He stroked her hair and planted a kiss on her forehead. "Wow. Just wow." She snuggled into him and let her eyes close, as her breathing returned to normal. She floated away savouring every moment of the euphoric high just experienced.

A shrill sound in the background woke them; John jumped, and scrambled around for his phone. "Yes I'm here. What happened? Okay, I can be there in about 20 minutes okay. No don't worry everything is okay. I had a long afternoon meeting with a potential client but nothing's going to come of it. See you soon." He cupped Emma's chin and nuzzled her neck. "I need to go. I'm sorry. Something has come up at work that needs my attention. Make yourself at home. If you want to leave you can, just pull the door, but I'd love it if you stayed. I'll make it quick, baby."

Emma sighed, a sinking feeling in the pit of her stomach. It all seemed too familiar. Work always came first with guys, whoever they were. "It's okay. Don't worry. I'll let myself out. I have a few errands to run, in any case, so it's not a problem. You can call me if you want." Her eyes couldn't meet his. She studied the geometric pattern hidden in the linen curtains to distract her mind and the roller coaster of emotions steaming through her body.

Nothing's going to come of it. Isn't that what he had just said? What a fool I've been.

She buried her head in the pillow, curled into a ball and turned away from him. A silent tear trickled out of the corner of her eye. A sadness sat heavy on her heart.

He leaned over and kissed her forehead. "I won't be long. I'll see you soon, pretty lady." He left.

The shower refreshed Emma as she attempted to wash him out of her body and soul. Tea tree and cucumber replaced his scent on her skin but his essence remained in her soul. The urge to explore his home and discover his life no longer piqued her interest. She closed the door behind her, making sure it locked itself. She had no wish to be held responsible for anyone being able to enter and steal the Monet. An overcast dusk replaced the bright afternoon and the river meandered dull and grey to match her despondent mood. She trudged down The Esplanade and passed 'Spy High.' That would have to wait for another time. She needed to get home to her peace and solitude. She needed to think.

Chapter Twenty-three

The long lens glinted then disappeared in the cover of the trees as the light faded and turned to a dull grey dusk. Julian had captured enough and seen as much as he could stomach without feeling sick. His emotions on edge, he could barely concentrate on his work. As he secured the lens cover in place, he took one more look across the river and saw her emerge from the building. He flicked the lens cover off and zoomed in. She hunched her shoulders, head down, with her arms wrapped around her body, protecting herself from the cold but it seemed more than that, from what he knew of her. She had a dejected air about her.

What happened?

He had seen John leave earlier, drive off at speed, but he hadn't expected to see her appear. He expected her to wait until her lover returned. As she turned to cross the road, he zoomed in on her face. A heavy feeling came over his heart, as he saw a tear and a look of sadness in her eyes. He didn't want her to be with another man but he also didn't want her to be sad. If his rival made her happy, then he would be happy.

Their afternoon spent at The Museum had been so joyful, he could hardly bear to observe. Each touch and kiss, Julian witnessed, pierced his heart and burned his emotions, raw. He had been so wrapped up in their antics when he followed them to Riverside Drive; he had had to swerve out of the way of a mother and children crossing the road. He had said a silent prayer to the god of style and trendy decor, for the long undressed windows, providing him with a clear view into the flat. The long lens provided perfect detail on their every move, including the painting, and judging from her reaction, it didn't strike him as being an ordinary painting. Once he downloaded the shots he would investigate further. He puzzled over her current dejected state which did not make sense to him, and wondered again what had happened.

He held his breath as she hesitated outside 'Spy High' and released when she continued. No ambiguity remained. She knew about the MemQ device, and clearly wanted to find out more. He contemplated how he would retrieve it. It would be a challenge without giving his game away. He would wait for further instructions from his employer. His pocket vibrated. "Hello. This is Julian. How can I help you?" A number he didn't recognise flashed up on the display.

"We need to meet. You know the quarterly report is due or had you forgotten? I heard about a few developments which sound very interesting, to say the least."

Julian stopped, and caught his breath. He had not expected to hear from his mystery client for quite some time. He checked the date on his watch. "There is another month to go and there is really nothing to report. I am intrigued about the interesting developments you mention. As far as I can see it is business as usual. He paid for me to continue to follow his ex-wife. My associate, who works for him, has nothing to report. I checked in with her a few days ago."

"I need to disclose something important to you. It has bearing on the situation. When can we meet?"

Julian heard urgency in his client's voice. "I am in the middle of something right now but I can meet you later tonight if that suits. The usual place?"

"Yes. Don't be late. Don't be seen. Don't be followed. Understand."

"Yes. I do. 11pm." No response, the phone went dead. He frowned.

That's strange.

He continued walking but Emma had disappeared.

Damn.

He activated the MemQ app on his phone and searched for her location. The pin travelled fast. He zoomed in on the map. He knew her next move. Home. That is where he needed to be as well, to gather his thoughts for his unexpected meeting that evening.

#####################

The house didn't welcome her as she expected. Something had triggered the alarm, the outside sensor flashed blue and the siren pierced the air. Her pulse quickened and a sick feeling settled into the pit of her stomach. She fumbled and breathed deeply in an attempt to remain calm as she dialled the alarm service number.

"Hello. It's Mrs McKenzie. The alarm has been triggered. Can you send someone please?"

"Yes we received the notification a few minutes ago. We informed the local force and they have dispatched someone already. Where are you? Are you in danger?"

"Thanks. I've just arrived home. I'll stay in my car outside the house."

"Yes but make sure you close the windows and lock the doors. If the intruder is still in or around the property then you do not want to put yourself in danger."

"I'll drive down the lane, away from the house. Thanks again." Her hands shook as she turned the key in the engine and manoeuvred out of the drive. Sweat stung her eyes and scant relief came when she parked on the lane outside the house. Her mind overran with different scenarios.

What or who will the police find? Maybe it is a false alarm. Maybe the place has been ransacked.

She jumped at the tap on her window and shrank away from the dark face looming through the glass. Another tap; this time more persistent.

"Are you Mrs McKenzie? I'm Constable Parker. Are you okay?" She lowered her window and the dark face peered in, thrusting an ID badge in her face.

"Oh gosh. Yes I'm okay. Do you want my key? I just returned home and found the alarm going off. What are you going to do?" Her words tumbled out in a rush of relief. She started to open her door.

"No stay here. It will be safer for you. I'm here with WPC Jones, who will stay with you whilst I investigate." The friendly face of WPC Jones appeared from behind Constable Parker.

"You'll be safe with me, Mrs McKenzie. Don't worry. We'll sort everything out for you."

"Thank you very much. I do hope Constable Parker will be okay. Does he need the alarm code to disable it?"

"No he has it from the security alarm company. They sent it through when they alerted us to the incident." Emma inhaled deeply and let her eyes close. A calm secure sensation replaced her nervousness. She trusted the police and let them do their job.

The piercing shriek of the siren stopped and silence returned to the neighbourhood. She squinted to see over the hedge but the dark moonless night obscured any movements. The security light outside the house flashed before going out as Constable Parker entered. She clicked the indicator lights on and off, on and off, as the minutes ticked by.

"Ma'am. Can you come and take a look at something, please. The house is secure. Constable Parker has checked and no-one is there. There has been some vandalism though." WPC Jones opened the door to the car and indicated to Emma to follow her.

Nerves flew through Emma.

What vandalism? Oh god. To think someone has been in my house.

She felt sick to her stomach. Constable Parker met her in the doorway.

"There doesn't appear to be anything missing. It is either an idle act of vandalism, kids playing around. We get a little of that at this time of year. They are bored at school you know. Or someone is sending you a warning. A brick was thrown through the kitchen window with a message attached." He indicated the evidence bag sat on the kitchen table. Emma read the message.

BE WARNED. YOU ARE IN DANGER. KEEP YOUR FRIENDS CLOSE BUT YOUR ENEMIES CLOSER.

She trembled and sunk into one of the chairs.

What does this message mean? What danger am I in? What enemies do I have?

Her hand shook as she read the note. A shiver ran down her back. Her nerves tingled in dread and a strange metallic taste formed in her throat. She coughed and swallowed. "Where did you find this?" As she spoke she saw the broken window and glass scattered across the floor. "Oh. Someone threw it. What does it mean?"

"We were hoping you could tell us? Do you have any enemies? Do you know what danger you may be in?" A barrage of questions came from Constable Parker. Emma raised her arm to defend herself. "I, I have no idea."

WPC Jones shot a look to the constable who retreated from his line of questioning and took up guard by the door. She placed her hand on Emma's shoulder to reassure her, "If you don't know, then don't worry. It may be just a prank from kids you know. We'll take a look around the garden tomorrow when there is more light. Will you be okay tonight? Are you on your own?"

"Yes I'm on my own but I really don't feel comfortable staying here tonight. I'll stay at my friend's. Can PC Parker board up the window please and would you help me sweep up the glass, if that's not too much to ask." Emma nodded at the PC standing by the door, and whispered, "Thank you."

"Oh don't worry about him. He is just doing his job although he can be very officious at times. I am certain it's kids playing a prank. We have an idea who so just try and forget it happened. Why don't you call your friend and tell her you'll be on your way shortly, once we have this sorted out. I take it the broom is in the pantry."

"Yes, thanks so much."

Beth waited for Emma on her doorstep. "Oh my god, girl. What happened? You said something about a brick and a message. This makes no sense to me. Why would anyone want to hurt you? Do you think it's Andrew playing games but that sounds a bit too malicious even for him. Maybe it's kids."

"That's what the police think. Kids messing around. They said a couple of other houses in the area had had the same thing happen so I don't think it's anything to worry about, but it's a little unnerving. I don't feel comfortable staying there. Thanks hun. Really appreciate it." Emma hugged her friend.

"I can imagine. Oh and wasn't it your museum date today? Tell me all about that. Did you have fun?"

The date with John had paled into insignificance, after the adventure of the brick and the police, but Beth's question brought the reality of how the afternoon ended crashing back. "We had fun at the museum, well of sorts. We didn't really look at the exhibition to be honest, we were laughing too much and almost got thrown out. We ended up back at his place, and oh he has this amazing Monet. An original. Just there in his spare room. Well, in a safe in his spare room. But Beth he got a phone call, and I overheard him saying that he had a meeting with a client and nothing was going to come of it. I felt so upset. How could he say nothing's going to come of it, I thought he liked me so much and we could have a relationship, but I guess I was wrong. He dashed off to work. All guys are the same. Work always comes first. I don't know if I want to see him again if he is going to dash off at every opportunity." Emma's shoulders drooped, and she played with the spoon in her tea.

"Maybe there is a reasonable explanation you know. He seems like a decent guy from what Tony says. What work does he do? Don't wear out my cup with that spoon." Beth removed the spoon from Emma.

"You know. I have no idea what work he does. I didn't even ask. In fact, come to think of it, I don't know that much about him. We laugh and joke a lot about stuff we see but haven't really spoken about our lives."

"Hun, before you go jumping to conclusions you need to find out what his conversation was really about. Maybe he had to make up an excuse for work. He couldn't exactly tell them he spent the afternoon in bed with you could he. Come on. I know this is pretty new to you, but I would say you need to talk to him. Promise me you'll do that. I like him for you, Emma. He makes you smile and your eyes shine whenever you mention his name. He is good for you. Don't let a misunderstanding ruin things."

"I guess you are right. I'm just not used to the ins and outs of dating someone again. It's all so new to me." Emma yawned. "I'm going to go to bed, Beth, I'm worn out to be honest after this eventful day. Thanks again for being there for me. Love you."

"I love you too. You know that, anytime. Good night."

####################

Julian arrived early and parked out of sight of the Old Lion. He stood on the corner and huddled into his jacket. He wished he had worn his fleece. The dull glow from the street lamp didn't provide much light and he didn't have time to set up for long exposure night photography. A group of people, mostly men, hung around outside the pub, smoking, laughing, drinking. No one he recognised. Although he had never met his client, he had an uncanny knack of recognising them. He couldn't explain it. He felt something and he had always been right. He focused on the activity outside the pub, when a rough hand grabbed his collar and dragged him into the back seat of a car. He struggled to free himself and wriggled onto the seat.

A voice sounded through the partition in front of him. "I'm sorry about that. I didn't want to meet in the pub. It's too busy. Terry can be a little rough on people sometimes, but I wouldn't want it any other way. I'm sure you understand. You realise who I am don't you."

"Not really. I don't know who you are. I just receive the instructions in the mail and the money in my post box. To be honest, I have no idea who you are. I must admit I usually like to meet my clients. This is highly unusual." Julian straightened out his jacket and settled back into the seat. "But I will respect your privacy, although if we have to meet again, I would prefer that Terry didn't man-handle me quite so much. A polite request to follow him would have been sufficient."

"Yes I understand. Again, I'm sorry. I wanted to bring you up to date with a few developments. Do you know who John Smithfield is?"

Julian inhaled sharply. He had not expected to hear that name in this conversation. He concentrated. "Yes I am aware of John Smithfield. How is he relevant to you?"

"He is my son."

Julian gasped. That changed everything. Six degrees of separation narrowed to three. Bryan Smithfield, ex-business partner of Andrew McKenzie, ex-husband of Emma McKenzie, current lover of John Smithfield, son of Bryan Smithfield. He liked connecting the dots but this went beyond anything he could have imagined. "Oh, I see how that could be interesting."

"I presume you are aware of Mrs McKenzie's relationship with John?"

"Yes. I am aware of it." Julian chose his words with care to protect his other client's confidentiality and Emma.

"It needs to be stopped. It will only get in the way, when I reclaim what belongs to me."

Julian stomach lurched. He knew when men like this wanted something they would stop at nothing. "What, er, how do you propose to stop it?" He coughed as his voice broke with emotion.

"Tell McKenzie about it. Everything. Tell him she is in love with the boy. Tell him she is his lover. Tell him they can't keep their hands off each other. He will know what to do. His jealousy will guide him."

"Okay." Julian could barely speak. Blood rushed through his veins and his chest tightened as if his heart would explode any minute. The walls and roof of the car closed in on him. He needed to get out of there. "Anything else?" His hand on the door handle reaching for escape.

"No. Report back to me next week, when it's done."

Julian tumbled out of the vehicle into the cool night air. He leaned against the wall, head down, eyes closed.

Was that a dream or a nightmare? How can Emma's lover be Smithfield's son and why didn't I put two and two together. Why didn't I realise Smithfield was the client, who asked me to keep an eye on McKenzie? Everyone knows he and McKenzie only keep up appearances for business. My judgment is being clouded by her beauty. I should have worked that out. What would McKenzie do now when he told him about his ex-wife and her lover?

His stomach turned over but this time he relinquished control and vomit sprayed over his shoes and the pavement. Cold sweat crept down his back like a snake making its way towards its prey. Betrayal of the worst kind lay ahead and he, like a deer frozen in the headlights, felt unable to stop the oncoming wreckage.

Chapter Twenty-four

Winter sun flooded the studio, past floor to ceiling windows. No long shadows until late in the day. The scent of oil paint mixed with white spirits filled the air with inspiration and creativity. Emma loved it. She escaped into herself and with her summer break over and the studio renovations complete, she welcomed her new students. The studio burst with chatter about famous artists, new techniques, new paints, new ideas. A melting pot brimming over with creativity. She organised everyone into pairs and paired up with one of her favourite students. Alison. In her second term and quite brilliant. She challenged Emma, making her think about her life being an extension of her art. Alison's philosophy ran along the lines of you painted what you wanted in life. You painted it happening. Emma didn't quite believe in that but happily played along so Alison's skill could develop. The excited chatter dulled into a murmur as the artists went to work. One sitting, one painting or drawing, using free medium. As Emma sat for Alison, her thoughts ran over the events of the past few weeks. Had she painted these scenarios into her life somehow as Alison suggested? She promised herself she would look back at her abstract paintings to find meaning. Her thoughts consumed her so she only vaguely registered the door to the studio creaking open. A hand snuck around her waist and the familiar lemon musk awakened her senses. Her groin tightened. Her eyebrows knitted together. She jumped off her perch and spun around, pushing the hand away from her. John laughed. "That's the reaction I get after just a few days, pretty lady. Have you forgotten me already?"

"What are you doing here?" She objected. "How dare you intrude? I am giving a class." She regained her composure as she felt the eyes of all her students on her. She checked her watch. Five minutes to go. "Okay everyone. That's enough for today. Same time tomorrow. Thank you and remember life is inspiration all around." She turned back to John, "So, what are you doing here?"

"I had to come to see you. You ignored all my calls. I even called the house. I must have left a zillion messages. I think I filled up the machine because it can't take any more messages. Don't you check them? And your mobile just goes to voice mail. Are you trying to avoid me? Tell me what did I do if you are? I had such a fabulous day at The Museum, and afterwards was amazing but you just left. I expected to find you there when I returned but, no note, no messages and unavailable. What happened, Emma?"

"I'm with a client but nothing's going to come of it." She quoted and glared direct in his eye. "That's what's wrong. I thought we had a good thing going but nothing is going to come of it. I left because I heard you say that, and it hurt me to be honest." Her voice broke and revealed her rising emotion.

"Oh babe. That was nothing, really. I had to lie to my boss so I could take the afternoon to meet you at The Museum. I was desperate to see you. Something came up at work that I needed to go and sort out, that's why I left," he pulled her close to him and wrapped his arms around her, "sweetheart, I had an amazing time and want to continue seeing you. You are incredible. I've never felt like this about a woman before. I'm serious. You are beautiful, funny, intelligent." His finger hooked her chin upwards and his lips found hers. His tongue explored and danced around her mouth, pulling her tongue, he nibbled and sucked the end. Her legs gave way, and she clung onto his arms for support. Heat rose within groin and her core became wet at the thought of him.

How can he have such an effect on me?

"I'm sorry. I thought, well you know what I thought. I'm not used to dating," she whispered, "not here." His hand slid down her trousers and his fingers met her wet folds. His thumb found her nub and stroked and caressed until she moaned in delight. His fingers explored inside her as she arched her back and cupped his hand against her breast. She let her head hang back, closed her eyes and groaned in ecstasy. She floated to places she didn't know existed, and she couldn't get enough. She held his hand against her, she needed more. "I need you inside me."

"Not here." He kissed the words into her ear.

"Please." She begged him, pushing her hand into his trousers. He stopped her.

"No. Come for me." He bit her neck; his fingers continued stroking with growing intensity until she shuddered in submission to his demand. She sat back on her stool, her face flushed with satisfaction. He smiled. "I love it when you come. I want to make you come until you beg me to stop," his eyes crinkled as his smile broadened and lit up his face, "so what about another date?" His question broke into her dream. "What about I choose this time? Laser tag. It's great fun."

"I don't even know what laser tag is? A video game or something." She wrapped her legs around him, and pulled him close. "I'd like to play other games with you, John. I'm sure they are as interesting as laser tag."

He laughed, "Not here, I said. Laser Tag is kind of a virtual reality game. You suit up and shoot at the opponents with laser guns. Tag you get hit. The suits count the hits. It's pretty simple really. Great fun. I'm going on Saturday with a couple of friends and would love you to come along as well." His fingers ran up and down her back, under her shirt.

His touch took her breath and voice away and her whole body tingled in anticipation. Her nipples hardened and rubbed against the lacy fabric holding them in. "It sounds great. I'm in. But won't your friends think I'm ancient."

"No way. Tony is coming and bringing your friend Beth. Dave is coming along with Ally. In fact, I think Ally attends your art class. I don't know her very well but I may have seen her here today. I hope that's okay for you, and there are a couple of others. You'll meet them on the day. I'll pick you up around ten, okay. God, you're beautiful. I want you so badly but not here. I like to savour the moment. It heightens the feeling and makes me feel alive." His mouth reached hers before she could respond and drew her into a deep sensual kiss, sending shivers down her back into her core. A fire burned inside her wanting more of this man than she had ever wanted before.

"Take me home." She nibbled his ear and kissed his neck. "Take me home to my house. I need you."

John released his grip and led her out of her studio. She motioned to the janitor to lock things up as they passed his office, on the way out. "Follow my car. It isn't far. Stay close."

"Okay."

At the house, she pushed him against the door as it closed. He laughed. "Not here. Let's take a few minutes and relax. I don't know what I did to you back there but it seems I turned a switch or something. Can I take a look around the house?"

"Of course. Where are my manners? Please make yourself at home. Would you like a drink?" She composed herself, and ventured into the kitchen. A wooden panel replaced the window that had been broken earlier, and the police tape remained.

"What happened here?" John asked. "I can guess a window was broken as it's boarded up but what's the story with the police incident tape. Kinky decorations. Don't tie me up with it will you? That would be hard to explain." He twisted some of the tape around his wrists, and offered them up to her in mock submission.

"Now there's an idea. No. Someone, kids probably, threw a brick through the window. There was a note which said that I'm in danger, to keep my friends close and my enemies closer. I don't have any enemies I'm aware of so I guess it was just a prank. That's how the police are treating it. I've been staying at Beth's place for the past few days which is why you couldn't get hold of me. I've had my phone on silent actually, just in case the person who threw the brick wanted to call me. I didn't get any calls. I think it's okay now." She pulled him towards her. "Tea or me?" She grinned.

"Tea first, then you. Wow, that is quite a story. I guess the police are used to dealing with this kind of thing, but if you need more security or a security check on what you have in place, then let me know. The guy who set up Spy High is a good friend, and an expert in surveillance. He used to work for MI6. A real James Bond." He spun her around, and pointed her in the direction of the kettle. "Polly, put the kettle on, let's all have tea. Come on, pretty lady. I'm gasping for a cup of tea actually. I like mine green with no sugar."

"So do I. I'm interested in your friend. I found a usb drive thingy in my handbag when I was on the cruise just before I met you. It's got a flashing light so looks a bit unusual. I thought it was something that Anthony had given me to hold, but I checked with him and he says not. It's so strange. Hang on. I'll find it for you." She reached for her handbag, and pulled out the MemQ device. "Look" She offered it to John for a closer look.

He lowered his voice to a whisper. "Here wrap it in foil to stop the transmission, if it is what I think it is. Put it back, and yes take it to Ben. He will take a look at it for you. I believe it is a tracking device that can record sounds as well as pinpoint your position with a 200 metre range. Ben has some which are similar. In fact I think they are all coded so he may be able to tell you who purchased it and when, if it was purchased from his store. It's part of the regulations."

"Oh I'll go and see him. I passed the store when I left yours the other day but I just couldn't go in I was so upset." She turned, and poured the hot water on the tea.

"Oh baby, baby. Come here. I hate to think I upset you." He pulled her towards him, hugged her and kissed her forehead. "Now where is my tea?" He picked up one of the cups and walked into the conservatory. "This seems like a relaxing place to drink tea. Please do come and join me, Mi'lady." He gestured, his hand swooping down from his head to his waist as he curtsied.

She giggled, and followed him. She curled up on the sofa next to him. Her head rested on his shoulder. She appreciated his gestures, and a warm secure sensation washed over her. "This is nice. I like you a lot, John. You do know that don't you?"

"Yes, pretty lady. I do too. More than I probably should. You make me feel at home, I think is the right word for it. I feel you understand me and you make me happier than I've been in a long time." His arm snaked around her shoulders.

"That's good to hear. Tell me what do you do for work? You told me your father is a property developer, and I think he knows Andrew or is a business colleague at least. Isn't his name Bryan?"

"Yes. I am an architect for Smithfield, Jones, and Taylor. They were the architects on the Riverside Development where I live and many other projects of course. I think even on the building where your husband's business is. Does he own it, the building I mean?"

"Yes, of course. That's where I know your father from. He was the lead architect on that project, but that was years ago. You must have been pretty young. Well, we all were back then. Time flies." She snuggled further into his arms. Bliss.

"Yep. They do know each other. They had business together at the beginning of the millennium but they haven't had any for quite a while. I think they had a disagreement or something. I don't know. It was maybe something to do with a shipment but I'm not sure. I think it was around the time of the height of the Iraq War. My father isn't just a property developer, and architect you know, he is a bit of a wheeler and dealer. If there is a deal to be done he will do it. That's how he made most of his money. I can't be certain, because it was ten years ago, and I was in and out of the business, I was still studying but I think he had some deal going with some guy in Paris but it was something to do with information and the war. Anyway, I try and keep out of these things. I keep my head down and work hard. I'm one of the best at the firm, actually. Even though many think I only got the job due to my family connections. That simply isn't true. I got a first at University and was the valedictorian for our year group. I worked very hard, whilst all my friends were partying, I studied and drew and designed."

A cold shiver ran down Emma's back, as if someone had walked over her grave. A sense of foreboding pricked her. She reached up and kissed him quiet. "Shush baby. Don't talk any more. I understand. Let's enjoy the peace and quiet of the night. Look at the beautiful moon. We should go out into the garden. Come on." She dragged him up with her out into the garden. The moon cast a bright light over the house and garden. Its luminance reflected on the pond. "This reminds me of that first night, walking through the park. Remember. I can't believe it was only a few weeks ago. I feel like I've known you forever." She shivered as the sense of foreboding strengthened.

He pulled her close and wrapped his shirt around her. The heat of their bodies entwined. She reached up to kiss him, and he scooped her up and carried her back inside. "The moon is beautiful but it's freezing. I want to look at your beauty, baby, and feel your heat. Come here." He pushed open the door to the guest bedroom and fell on the bed with her. Her heart raced with the anticipation of what he promised but also with the knowledge that the last people to use this room were Andrew and Luisa. She intended to erase that memory, and create new ones that evening.

He ran his hands under her shirt, and found her taught nipple. She moaned, as he inched the shirt over her head. Her breasts, released from their lacy constraint, spilled into his hands and he sucked in a breath as the delicious flesh yielded in his hands. His lips found one soft pink nipple as his thumb circled around the other. Her groin tightened with each circle and teasing bite. Moisture pooled between her legs, and she imagined him sliding in and out of her. Desire roared through her like an inferno. She whispered. "Don't stop."

"Don't worry, I'm not going to." Fire raged through her body as his fingers slid between her legs finding her burning desire. Blood surged through her veins, and her breath quickened. Her eyes closed as she succumbed to the unfamiliar lust consuming her. The amount of pleasure she received from his smallest touch scared her. Unable to hold back, her face flushed as her orgasm ripped through her body. Intense and powerful. Muscles ached and burnt with lust, she went limp for a moment. Dazed she reached for John craving him inside her.

Emma ripped his shirt off, and ran her hand across his hard torso. His nipples, hard and erect, begged for attention. Her tongue flicked around one then the other. He let out a low moan as his erection strained for release. Her fingers traced the outline against his boxers, teasing and playing, until he freed himself. She admired him. Dark, thick, erect with a pearl of fluid peeping from his slit. She quivered at the sight, and a trail of warm fluid slid down her leg.

He filled her mouth as her tongue danced, savouring the pearl at the tip, up and down the length. His strong fingers twisted around her hair, and he pushed himself further into her mouth. Emma tasted his sweet salty wetness, and slowly released him. She moved down to his balls, circled her tongue around, and sucked them into her mouth. His grip around her hair tightened, sending a sharp pain over her skull. The balls contracted inside her mouth. A low moan escaped him. He cupped her chin, and pulled her back on to him, harder now. He pushed his hips into her, gyrating until a gush of hot liquid spilled out of her mouth, down her face, onto his groin. He lay back, spent but the look in his eye told her he hadn't finished.

He rolled over. He found her nipples again, sending electric impulses down her back. She ached for him. John breathed into her ear, "Let me show you what you've been longing for."

She tried to speak but could only manage, "Oh god, yes." His words left a pulsating sensation between her legs. Their fingers entwined, as his soft lips found her core. He swirled his tongue over her swollen nub, still sensitive from earlier. Pleasure mounted inside Emma like a roller coaster, inching to the highest point on the ride. Like the cars, she balanced on the edge, holding on until the perfect time. His tongue explored inside her soft swollen lips. She ran her fingers through his hair and gasped to catch her breath.

She rolled her head back, closing her eyes. He transported her to another world. Her hips rose upwards, as she quivered and shuddered as one orgasm after another tipped her over the edge, in an all-consuming heat. She found ecstasy once more with her lover.

"Do you want me to stop?"

"God no." She pushed her hips towards him.

"Do you want me inside you?" He rolled her over, pushed her shoulders down, and pulled her hips up.

Sweet anticipation swirled through Emma. "Oh God, yes." He slid into her soft wet embrace, and she gasped with the double ecstasy of pain and pleasure. He rode her, gently at first, but then building into a crescendo. He stopped for a moment, leaned over and stroked her back, then began again. She raised her hips higher, begging to feel more of him inside her.

They moved to the floor, and she bent over, pushing herself on to him. Heat seared through her body. He drove deeper and deeper into her. He ran his hand over her back, and slapped her pink cheeks. She screamed with pleasure, and quivered. Multiple orgasms rocked her body. He held her hand as waves of his own orgasm washed over him and through her. He savoured the moment and pulled her up. They lay on the bed, in each other arms. No words between them, just contentment.

Chapter Twenty-five

I run after her, past the shops on The Esplanade until she reaches the crossing. I grab her arm, and pull her towards me. She recognises me from the cruise ship, and takes me for a coffee to reminisce. She is friendly; happy to see me. There are no questions about why I have been following her so no awkward explanations. She tells me she wants me to protect her. I swear to do so forever. Her husband appears in the shop doorway, and points a gun at me or is it her? A shot rings out and—

He woke up. He always did. Julian stretched and pulled the sheets under his chin. He didn't cherish the meeting he would have that day. The clock showed 6:30 a.m. Time to move. His heart jittered as he jumped out of bed. He didn't know if he had moved too quickly or if the day's events had started to prey on him already.

The shot of caffeine buzzed through him. His senses on the alert. He would need all his wits about him today. 7:45 am. Time to go. He had a stop to make before his meeting with McKenzie, and he didn't want to be late for either.

Spy High had all the makings of James Bond. Voice control opened the door. Customers needed to call first to get the voice code. It changed every day. Once activated the doors disappeared into themselves and closed. Lasers swept the entrance like a sophisticated security system. He hesitated before he broke the red lines and smiled at the clever marketing idea. Julian waited at the counter for 'B' as he had called himself over the phone. He appeared behind Julian.

"Sorry for the dramatics. It's all for show actually, but the punters love it. You said you were a PI, and you had a message for me? That sounded very intriguing."

Julian spun around. "Hello. It's all very James Bond. Did you know him? I heard you used to work for MI6. I don't suppose you can talk about it though can you. Official Secrets Act and all that." He reached out his hand. "I'm Julian Cunningham, Private Investigator."

'B' shook his hand, "I'm B, but you can call me Ben Forde. B is just a tease. Adds to the mystery. So Mr Cunningham, what's this message you have for me?"

Julian checked around. No one else entered the store at this hour of the morning. The Esplanade had few people; the street and office cleaners, some returning home from the night shift, some starting work. "Do you know McKenzie Associates, and who they are?"

"Yes. Who doesn't in this town? I guess McKenzie is a big deal around here. Why?" Ben gazed at the floor, his confidence appearing to drain at the mention of McKenzie.

Julian wondered if Ben used an old MI6 trick. "Well it appears a device that was purchased from this store has come into the possession of Mrs McKenzie. She doesn't know what it is or what it could be used for, and he would like to keep it that way. He suspects she may visit you with the device to find out more about it. Do not tell her what it is, under any circumstances. He wants you to swap the device out for a regular USB device loaded with movies. Any movies, but no blues, stick to action adventure, drama." Julian raised his voice. "Once the device is in your possession, then you are to call me to collect it. Do not look at any of the data on the device. Do you understand?" The counter shook as his hand slammed down for emphasis. He had tricks up his sleeve as well.

"Yes, sir. What is the device, may I ask? So I can prepare a lookalike USB." Ben picked up the stack of leaflets that had been on the edge of the counter. He concentrated on stacking so all the edges lined up.

"MemQ. White with a green light. Do you have something similar or identical? I am sure she has inspected it closely, and will see any differences immediately."

'Yes I have a sample MemQ, used for display purposes. I can easily fit a USB into it. I can't guarantee how long the light will flash for though, as the battery is integrated into the tracking chip on the live version. The display version has a mini cell battery which cannot be replaced. I can get movies from a torrent site. No sweat." Ben raised his eyebrows. "Anything else, Mr Cunningham, or is that all? You can leave your phone number." He pushed a notebook towards Julian.

"No that's all. Remember though, if you think you could make something out of this by somehow blackmailing McKenzie, then think again. He owns the building you are currently leasing, and can make life very uncomfortable for you indeed. If, on the other hand, this works out well. The device is retrieved and Mrs

McKenzie is none the wiser, convinced it is a USB drive full of movies, then he is sure that something can be arranged about the high rent you are currently paying to occupy this prime spot on The Esplanade. He understands how difficult things can be when you are starting out in business, and he would be inclined to assist you." Julian scribbled the number of one of his pay as you go phones on the notepad. He regretted not giving a false name, and wondered how Ben had ever made it through MI6. He appeared so sheepish, especially at the mention of McKenzie's name. He promised himself he would look into him. Maybe he didn't make the cut or maybe he had excellent acting skills. It didn't matter. He had delivered the message and had other meetings to attend. "Good bye, Ben. I hope I made myself clear. Good luck with this task, and with your business."

"Goodbye. I will call you once it's done. Press the green button to let yourself out." Ben vanished into the back of the store. Julian exited onto the street, full of shoppers looking for early morning bargains from the side stalls. He pushed his way through the crowd gathered around the hawker, selling china or something similar, no doubt fallen off the back of a lorry, and found the bench by The Green, opposite the tall glass building.

Deja vue. Only this time, more like Ground Hog Day, where time repeats itself over and over. He closed his eyes, and shook his head, trying to clear his thoughts, only they became as grey as the sky reflected in the glass. Once more betrayal left a sour taste in the back of his throat. This time he couldn't begin to guess how it would play out. He knew, from monitoring her conversations, she cared for John, maybe she loved him. He couldn't be certain. He should have been happy his actions would clear the way of any obstacles to her love. But he hated himself, and the job he loved held no joy today. He dragged his feet across the green and stopped outside.

The entrance hustled and bustled with employees arriving for their days work. He lost himself in a sea of faces until one shone out above the rest. Luisa. As she passed close, she hissed, "What are you doing here?" She smiled and greeted her colleagues, but whispered to him. "Make it quick."

"I have a meeting with McKenzie. I need to see you as well. There have been developments we need to discuss. Usual place, tomorrow." He didn't listen to her reply. He knew she heard and would be there. He walked towards the lift. He knew she would hang back and check that no-one had seen them speak. Luisa was a professional.

McKenzie welcomed Julian into his office. "I must say I was intrigued when you said you had an important update. What has happened? I thought everything was business as usual with Emma. The art, the yoga, nothing much else. You had mentioned the Smithfield boy but because of the age difference, how old is he again, thirty or something, I presumed it had fizzled out. She hates that whole cougar thing, you know." He sat behind his imposing desk, and offered Julian the chair facing him. "Drink or is it too early. Let's get coffee. Susie, be a doll and get two cappos for us will you. Sugar on the side. You know how I like it. Thanks."

"I'll get straight to the point, Mr McKenzie. She is falling for Smithfield in a big way. She has stayed at his house several times and is his lover. He has stayed over at hers. He seems to have awakened a passion within her, and she can't get enough of him, from what I have observed. Night and day. I think the expression is—at it like rabbits, sir." The expression on Andrew's face darkened as he slammed his fist into the desk. The coffee cups jumped and hot steaming liquid spilled over.

"I had not expected this. This is not part of the plan. I will have to handle this myself. Smithfield, Jones, and Taylor. Yes. Perfect." He muttered to himself, no longer cognisant of Julian, who remained quiet in the chair, observing.

"You are correct. He works as an architect for Smithfield, Jones, and Taylor. I presume the Smithfield is his father; however, I think he got the job on merit. He got a first from Bristol in Architectural Studies. He is quite brilliant actually." He waited for the reaction, but Andrew seemed oblivious as he flicked through his rolodex.

"Aah. There it is. I knew I had the number." He dialled. "Good afternoon. This is Andrew McKenzie. I'd like to speak to Taylor please. It's a matter of urgency so I suggest you interrupt his meeting and put me through." He gestured for Julian to leave, and then returned to his phone call. "Taylor, McKenzie. How are the plans coming along for the East Side building? Good, good. I need something spectacular, and I have just the man over this side of the pond. He is Smithfield's son. He needs a promotion and a relocation. I want him as the lead architect on my building. He has perfect credentials. I will get my lawyers to sort out all the paperwork but you need to get things moving with your HR people over there. Next week. Good, good. Perfect, couldn't be sooner. "

Julian dawdled gathering his papers, and making his way out of the office. He needed to hear the rest of the conversation. "Haven't you left yet? Good work. Thank you. Continue. I'll see to it that you are rewarded for this." Andrew hurried him out of the door, and slammed it closed. The secretary raised an eyebrow as Julian passed her desk.

Secretaries know too much these days. I wonder how much she is privy to.

He needed another coffee. He knew he had set a chain of events in motion that could not be stopped.

He ran his hand down over his face and pulled his chin, before the wave of nausea hit him.

What have I done? I hope this isn't as bad as I think it may be.

Going down in the lift, he caught sight of his reflection and turned away to concentrate on the decreasing numbers. Anything held more interest than the face of betrayal.

Outside, relief came and breathed deep trying to refresh his body and mind. The air felt crisp but not refreshing. A stale odour hung around and followed him like a stray dog following the rubbish collectors, feeding on scraps. He had a lot of time to kill. He monitored Emma, and the blip showed up at her art studio. She would be there for the rest of the day. A yawn came from nowhere fuzzing his thoughts. He decided to return home to escape into sleep for a few hours.

Buzzz, buzz, buzz, BUZZZZ. The noise sounded louder and louder until he hit the stop button. 8:00 pm flashed on the display. He jumped off the bed, tripping with the sheet tangled around his leg. The cool water of the shower refreshed his body until he shivered and reached for the hot button. The fresh scent of palm oil and eucalyptus cleared his mind. He felt ready to face the night. 8:45 pm. He needed to move otherwise he would miss her. She didn't wait around for anyone. He knew that. That's what protected her.

"You made it. Just." She growled at him. "It's good to see you again. I was surprised at the office today. You should have warned me you were coming. What if I'd have been with him? I don't think we could have disguised ourselves. He reads body language very well." She moved closer to him and wrapped her arms around him. "It IS good to see you. I missed you."

He pulled away. She no longer held any attraction for him. "Yes it's good to see you too, Luisa. I can't do this you know. But that isn't why I need to talk to you."

"Oh. What happened to you? I thought, well you know what I thought. Why the sudden change of heart? Oh, my god. Don't tell me. Please don't tell me you've fallen for her. Julian. After all we've been through and all our promises to each other. Come on. You can't do this to me when we are so close to finding out the truth. Come on, baby." She curled her fingers around his neck and pulled him close. She peeped from under her long lashes. "One last time, baby. You know how much you mean to me. I knew this would happen. I can understand. It happened to me, you know that. But baby, baby. I need to feel real love after all that false love. After all I've done to get close to him." She brushed her lips against his. His body awakened and his groin pulled tight.

"I need to discuss business with you first before anything. I don't even know what I think anymore. Yes, you are right. Woman's intuition I guess, but I can't stop thinking about her. Every waking hour. I betrayed her today. She is in love with Smithfield, but he is sending him away. New York, I think. You know he gets insanely jealous, right? You need to be careful. I gave you up to him. I know you are doing it for your cause, but be careful. He has connections. He has changed someone's whole life with one phone call and they don't even know it yet." He turned away from her. "I need you to make friends with the secretary. We need to speed this up a bit. Others after the same thing are getting impatient and there is no knowing what they will do. I suspect the secretary, Susie, knows much more than she lets on. Tap her for information. We know he sold the information. Our sources in Iraq confirmed that. We need to find the trail. Every transaction leaves a trail. Where did the information come from and how did he get the information to Iraq? That will give us the evidence we need. I am convinced Susie will know." He inched away from her. She overpowered him and he needed some distance.

She moved closer. "Good idea, Julian. I know Susie, pretty well actually from my own surveillance. I'll take her to lunch. I'll tell him she needs sweetening to keep quiet. You seem stressed. Let me sweeten you, but there's no need to keep quiet." She linked her arms around his neck and pulled herself up, wrapping her legs around his waist. He breathed her overpowering scent, and hardened.

One last time, for old time's sake. God, she is amazing.

He spun around, and sat her on the kitchen counter. One hand moved her damp panties to the side, whilst the other unfastened his trousers. She offered no resistance. She pushed her hips towards him and pulled her feet into his back bringing him closer. He slipped into the moist warmth, his head spinning into nothingness as the stress of the day vanished with each thrust. It didn't take long. He released his tension, and pent-up emotion, and pulled out. He held on to her. "Sorry. I didn't think it would end like this. You are amazing and deserve to find out who was responsible for your brother's death. I know it's hard for you, but I can't mix his business with your pleasure and especially knowing what you are doing to find out information. You are a strong woman, Luisa. Stay strong and we will find out."

"I understand, you know. I think I saw it coming. She is beautiful and strong as well. You deserve her, Julian. She would make you happy. Just bide your time. She will find you. Mark my words, one day you will be there in the right place at the right time. I feel it. I will do anything for my brother. He did everything for me. He saved me from Iraq and the regime over there. He sacrificed everything he had for me. I am in his debt and need to repay it, and I will. I will bide my time as well. Everything comes to those who have patience." The former lovers wrapped their arms around each other. Her heart pounded against his chest and brought him comfort. He hoped his did the same for her.

Chapter Twenty-six

"Hey pretty lady. I was wondering if you would show up. I'm glad you did." John scooped Emma into his arms, knocking the breath out of her. Lemon musk sent shivers down her back and moisture pooled between her legs.

How am I going to keep my hands off him today?

She untangled herself and grinned.

"Great to see you. This sounds like fun. I'm looking forward to it. It's something different for me."

"Let me introduce you to the gang." He waved towards a noisy group waiting to enter the main hall. "Everyone this is Emma. Emma this is everyone. Sorry. You'll pick up their names, and you already know Ally. Tony and Beth couldn't make it in the end, something about helping her to hang some artwork." Emma grinned as she knew exactly what Tony and Beth would be doing.

"Hi everyone. Good to see you, Ally. How's the painting coming along?" Something surreal crept over Emma. To see someone outside of where she knew them felt like a dream. She only knew Ally as Alison, her 'A' student. A brilliant artist who conceptualised ideas from life on her canvases. Emma wondered if Laser Tag would be the next subject.

"It's coming. You know how it is. Shall I call you Emma or Mrs McKenzie? This is very strange don't you think, and such a coincidence meeting like this. I couldn't believe it when John mentioned he was bringing a new friend and that it was my art teacher. It's cool though. It's nice to see you here as well. You look happy. Recently I've noticed you've looked sad or stressed over something. It's not my business of course but your face lights up when you smile. If it's due to John, then you go, girl. He is lovely. A real gentleman and you're very lucky to have found him. It's obvious he likes you a lot. I've never seen him like this before." Ally hugged Emma. "It's great to have you here. Are you ready for Laser Tag? Have you played before? It's fab."

John's friends welcomed Emma into the group. No airs or graces. Just a group of people of all ages meeting to have a good time. She had wondered if she would be the oldest there and the odd one out but it turned out she fitted in perfectly and her age seemed insignificant. One of the group hung back and stared until she smiled in his direction. His eyes escaped her gaze. He turned away. A shiver ran over her and brought a sense of foreboding, which she dismissed as nerves.

"Come on let's get you suited up. A small should fit you. It needs to fit snugly but not so tight that you can't breathe. Do you know how to use an air rifle?"

"Not a clue. Sorry. I hope I'm not going to be useless at this."

"I'm sure you won't be. It's simple. That's the safety which you keep on when you're not in play. That's the trigger which fires the laser. One pull and a laser shot appears, keeping your finger on the trigger gives you a laser stream. You'll work out which you need when. We play in pairs. You're with me. The vest has sensors which light up when you're hit. They keep count automatically, but we don't play for points we play for fun." His lips met hers and he held his breath. He exhaled and a sad look passed over his face.

"Is something wrong? I—"

His finger pressed on her lips. "Nothing, pretty lady. You are so beautiful you know I'm in love with you. Come on. Let's play." He pulled her into the arena before she had chance to respond.

Lights strobed and colours flashed. Loud music assaulted her ears. She could barely think. "Duck. Over here. Come on." Ping. One of the lights on her vest lit up. "Fire back. Don't just stand there." John pulled her behind a shield. "Come on. You need to be quick. Once you see someone, just fire." He pushed her out, and she fired, scattering lasers all around. Everyone ran for cover. Ping. Another spot lit up. "You only have one left then you will have to take a time out for 3 minutes to reset. Come on, Emma, you don't want to get hit. Start firing back." She ducked behind a black foam barricade and peeked out. Someone approached. Ping. Her first hit. Adrenaline rushed through her body. She pushed herself into the wall and crept to the end. Ping. Another hit.

Yes. This is fun. I can do this.

Ping. And another. She crouched with her head down. Lasers whizzed overhead, looking for a larger target in the distance. She fired. Ping. A loud curse came from the darkness—someone had been hit three times and had to take a timeout. Neon colours broke the darkness surrounding her. A movement at her back spun her around. John. "Well, I see you got the hang of things. You've got three good hits and two timeouts. Well done. Come on this way." She followed him, keeping close to the walls. Ping. Another light illuminated and her laser froze.

"I've been hit three times. I need to take a time-out. I'll see you in a few minutes."

"Okay, baby. See you soon." The dark arena swallowed John as Emma made her way to the rest area. She collapsed into a seat, and gulped down a bottle of water. The friend who avoided her earlier, sat at the table.

"Are you Emma McKenzie?"

"Yes. Sorry I didn't catch your name. You must be one of everyone. John was terrible at the introductions." She shook his hand.

"I'm Ben. I thought I'd seen you around."

"Really. I don't recognise you. What do you do?"

"I own Spy High." Emma's eyes widened and her mouth fell open. "Are you okay? You look surprised."

"I almost came into your shop a couple of days ago. I have something that I need you to look at."

"Okay. What's that? Do you have it with you?"

"Yes. Hang on. It's in my handbag in the locker. I'll go and get it. Actually, maybe it would be better to do this after the game. My three minutes is up and I'm sure yours is too. "

"Oh it's not a problem. It's pretty quiet here, and it may be busy afterwards, once everyone has finished playing. We may end up caught up in the melee. You know."

"Oh okay. But I think John will be wondering where I am. I don't want him to get worried."

"It will be okay. I'd like to look now, if that's okay with you." Emma heard a quiet firmness in Ben's voice as he spoke. She retrieved her handbag and handed the MemQ device to Ben. He turned it over in his hand, and inspected it under a magnifying glass he pulled out of his backpack. "Well it looks like a regular USB device but the flashing light is interesting. I won't know more until I've analysed in on my laptop. Is it okay if I keep it overnight? You can pop into the store tomorrow to pick it up. Why did you want me to take a look at it?"

A sneaking suspicion crept over Emma at Ben's eagerness to keep the device. She felt sure he knew exactly what the device was but didn't want to tell her for some reason. "Erm. Okay. I wondered about the flashing light. I haven't seen a USB with a light before. Why can't I bring it to the store tomorrow, and we can take a look at it together. It isn't going to take you that long is it?"

Ben's eyes glanced up to the left before he corrected himself. "Again, I prefer to work alone on things. Sometimes these things can take time and I don't want to waste your time. Don't worry. You'll get it back."

"Okay. I guess if that's how you work. What time tomorrow?" The suspicion grew stronger. She had a feeling that something wasn't quite right but she couldn't put her finger on it.

John burst in to the rest area, breathless. "Hey I've been looking for you all over. I wondered what happened to you. Don't tell me Ben is trying to work his James Bond suave magic on you. I should have warned you about him. He used to work for MI6."

Emma shot a look at Ben, who took a step back and kept quiet. "Oh, he has been nothing but a gentleman. Very sweet," she turned to Ben, "Thanks so much, Ben. And thanks for everything. Tomorrow at 10 am you said. That's perfect. I'm not teaching tomorrow until 2 pm so that gives me plenty of time to come in."

"Okay. Thanks Ben, but remember she is mine. Emma, I've been hit, and wanted to find you. I missed you. I don't want to lose you, ever." He gulped back his bottle of water. "This is great fun but if you want we can duck out. In fact, let's do that. The others won't mind at all. I think a few of them will be pleased to see me go, and you, by the looks of your hit rate. Have you seen your score card? It's great. 20/30 hits. Ben, you can let everyone know we've gone okay." Ben high-fived John and returned to the game.

Emma, relieved Ben had disappeared, turned to John. "Really. I had no idea. I knew I got a couple of hits but not so many. People merge into the background and it's hard to know if I hit a wall or a person. But, yes let's escape. I'd like to spend some time alone with you. Your friends are great but it's you who I want to spend my time with."

"Come on then. Let's go." Her hand slipped into his, and an electric charge ran up her arm. Oh, sweet anticipation. Heat flushed her face, and the familiar tingle returned to her groin. She pulled him into her, and her lips met his. She explored his mouth, biting his tongue, and weaving around. He whispered, "Not here."

The low sun cast long shadows through the skeleton trees, as they strolled through the park. Refreshed by the crisp air, after the heat inside the Laser Tag arena, John gripped Emma's hand. A sigh came from deep within him. Not for the first time. During Laser Tag, she had caught him looking at her with a wistful expression on his face. He seemed to have forced a smile but Emma had got the feeling something was wrong. His grip tightened on her hand. Another sigh. He stopped at the bench where they sat on their first date.

"Emma. I need to tell you something."

Her stomach sank, and her eyes closed, "What is it? I noticed something was off with you during the game." Her nerves filled with dread. The river meandered by, dark and grey, as the sun disappeared behind the clouds.

"I've been offered a promotion. It's what I've been working towards for a long time." Her heart sang. She had this wrong. This sounded like good news.

"That's fantastic. Congratulations. I'm so proud of you. You work so hard. What's the promotion? Don't tell me they made you partner, so it's Smithfield, Smithfield, Jones and Taylor now." Her giggles flooded out with relief.

"Well, yes it is good. I have worked hard and no they didn't make me partner, but they did promote me to Lead Architect on one of our flagship projects." His voice filled with sadness. He swallowed hard. "It's in New York."

The world caved in around her. Her thoughts crashed into oblivion.

New York. Did he say New York?

She squeaked, "You mean New York in America?" Hoping she had misheard and there happened to be someplace else called New York, with a large architectural project.

"Yes, baby. New York in America. Yes. 3,000 miles away. Yes. Across The Pond. I don't know what to do. I don't want to lose you. I think I've fallen in love with you but I know this is the big break I need in my career. It has taken so much hard work to get here, and I just can't give up now." He wrapped his arms around her as her tears splashed on to his jacket. His sadness spread over her, and they sat in silence, holding each other. No words.

Chapter Twenty-seven

"It worked out perfectly. She seemed a little reticent to hand over the device but she did in the end. I convinced her I'd work on it overnight and she's going to come into the store tomorrow to discuss what I found. She is coming at 10 a.m., so if you come in the afternoon to collect it then she should be out of the way by then. Give me a call back when you get this message. It's Ben, by the way." Ben hung up and pulled the MemQ out of his pocket. He smiled. That had been much easier than he thought. She had given it up without too much resistance, although he had noticed a look cross her face when she had handed it over. Her eyes had half closed; a sign of suspicion. He doubted if she trusted him completely but he didn't think she had any alternatives.

He inserted the MemQ into his laptop USB port and downloaded the data from it into an encrypted folder for future reference. Maybe it would be useful, but for now he needed to concentrate on creating a copy of the USB with music and movies. No blues the PI had said. He smiled as he thought about the PI and the softness he had heard in his voice when he had spoken about her. A dead give-away for his feelings. A common phenomena.

Her aura had captivated him at Laser Tag; beautiful with a hint of innocence and naivety, but he had also seen something more than that. Something determined; an inner strength. She contemplated whether to give him the MemQ. She insisted on coming the next day to pick it up. She knew more than either she realised or let on. Random thoughts shuffled through his mind as he set up the copy USB. Like the card game, Patience, his mind sorted the thoughts into a logical order and when all the suits stacked up, he would be ready. Ready for what? He didn't know yet but when it happened he would.

####################

"Hello, Mr Forde. Can I come in? It's Mrs McKenzie." She jumped, as the doors disappeared, and she tiptoed over the red lasers sweeping the floor as if she expected an alarm to be triggered at any moment.

"Hello. Don't be worried. The lasers are just for show. There isn't an alarm or anything. It's a marketing idea really, to try and sell high tech home security systems. I'm glad you came by. Would you like a coffee or tea? It's pretty early still." Ben led Emma into an area in the back. He busied himself making coffee, without waiting for her response. He knew what she liked already.

"Well they are pretty impressive. I thought they were real and all sorts of alarms would be triggered at any second. Coffee would be lovely, black with one sugar please."

"There you go. Coffee, black, one sugar." Ben sat beside Emma on the sofa. He turned towards her. "I have the USB here for you. It just has music and movies on It. Mainly action and drama movies and EDM music. Where did you say you found it?"

"Oh. Is that all? I must admit I was expecting something more exciting than that." She laughed. "I went on a cruise to the Med and purchased a new handbag, when I swapped over handbags, I

158

found it amongst all the junk I tipped out of my old bag. It looked important so I didn't want to throw it away. I discussed it with my son but he said it wasn't his and to be honest I believe him. I just don't know how it would have got into my handbag. It's a real mystery." She cocked her head on one side and stared at Ben. "So you don't have any clues or ideas as to how it could have got into my handbag, and are you absolutely sure it's just a USB stick with music and movies? There are no hidden codes on it? John told me you used to work for MI6, so I'm sure you're an expert in decoding hidden codes aren't you?"

Ben shuffled in his seat and moved away from her. "Yes I used to work for MI6, until stress got the better of me. I love the toys though and hoped there would be interesting data on the drive but no, just EDM and movies. Sorry to disappoint. I have no idea how it came into your possession if you don't know." He held out the USB to her. "Here take it. All you need to do is plug it into a USB port on a laptop or speakers or even on a smart TV if you have one, then a folder will appear and you choose the music or movie you want to watch. Simple really."

"What is EDM? That sounds mysterious." She took the device and rolled it over, examining it.

"Electronic Dance Music. You know club music. The stuff young people listen to. I'm afraid it's not my taste at all and I doubt it would be your taste either, but if you say you have a son at uni, then it may be something he would listen to."

"Well I didn't say my son was at university, you said that, but he is in actual fact. He is studying architecture at Bristol. I don't know. Maybe one of his friends gave it to him for safekeeping and he popped it into my bag last time we saw each other and he forgot about it. It's a real mystery. Anyway thanks for taking a look at it for me. You have quite a place here."

Heat rose in Ben's face as he realised he'd slipped up, but an opportunity for escape presented, "Yes. Thanks. I also offer home security checks. John mentioned that you may be interested in one. He said something about a recent incident at your house where you had to call the police?"

Emma sighed. "Yes. I would like something like that to be honest. Some kids, I guess, threw a brick through my kitchen window. There was a note tied to it which said, 'Keep your friends close but your enemies closer.' I'm not exactly sure if that meant something or it was all just a prank. The police seem to think it's a prank but I'm in two minds. There have been so many unexplained things happening recently that I am beginning to wonder. Anyway that's just my paranoia talking really. When can you come to do the check?" She wrung her hands as she spoke.

"Whenever you are ready. Just give me a call, or we can set a time now if you like. I can come on Monday if you like. Oh, John leaves Monday doesn't he? What about Wednesday then?" Her eyes glazed over and she pulled a tissue out of the box Ben offered. "Sorry, I shouldn't have mentioned him. That was insensitive of me." He held her hands in his and whispered, "It will be okay you know." A twinge of remorse pricked his conscience.

"Ok. That may be a good time. It will take my mind off him leaving. Thanks again. I need to go. I'm sure you understand."

"Yes of course I do. How is 10 a.m. Monday?"

"Perfect. Thanks. Good bye."

####################

"She suspects something is going on. I've offered her a security check so I can get the bugs planted then and we should know more soon. I'll take a good look around when I'm there, although I doubt she will leave me on my own. I don't think she totally trusts me yet. I should be able to put her off the trail. If anything she may be holding the paper trail we need. I'll report back when I know more." Ben hung up. Contact had to be kept brief at all times. His employer wanted results with no complications and he intended to deliver.

The door sounded and the lasers started up their dance. He peeked out through his spy hole. Julian. He had come to pick up the USB. The real one with the data.

"Hello. Ben. Are you there? Hello."

Ben emerged from the back. "Hi. Good to see you again. Glad you got my message. Here is the MemQ. Did you say that you had something for me in return?"

"Yes. I have a new contract for you from McKenzie. The rent on the property has been waived for the next six months, after that it's 50%. I hope that is agreeable."

Ben reviewed the contract. Exactly what he needed. It had information on McKenzie and more importantly his lawyer. Perfect. This would go in the case file. "Thanks. This is perfect. It was a pleasure doing business with you. Anytime you need anything else then just let me know."

"Thanks. As long she doesn't suspect anything, I think we are good."

"No she has no idea about anything. She is a nice woman, and I guess she just wants to get on with her life. You seem quite attached to her. That happens when you have been following someone for a while."

Julian concentrated on the pattern on the floor. "Yes, she is lovely. Her husband is incredibly jealous and wants to know her every move. He arranged for her boyfriend to be promoted overseas, out of the way. It's a shame. I know she will be upset."

Ben recognised the signs that Julian didn't want to give too much away, and couldn't look him in the eye. His body language betrayed him. He had fallen for her.

This was an interesting development. I wonder if I can make use of him to find out the information I need.

"I'm sure she will get over it and move on. She seems like a strong woman. I suspect she is much stronger than either of us think. Well, it was nice meeting you Julian. Enjoy the rest of your day." Ben moved towards the door and showed Julian out. He needed some time to analyse the information from the USB and contemplate the events unfolding.

Chapter Twenty-eight

The MemQ sat in the centre of Julian's dining table, staring at him, or so it appeared. Like the eyes on some paintings, he felt it followed his every move and he couldn't escape its presence. It overwhelmed him. He didn't know what to do. Hand it over or listen to the recordings on it first. His task had been to retrieve the device, follow Emma and report back on her movements. He had done everything asked of him and now a tiny device sat on his table holding the most intimate details of her life; her conversations with her friends and her lover. A sick feeling rose in his gut when he thought of her with her lover. Could he stomach listening to what the device held?

He swallowed as he picked up the device and inserted it into his laptop. He downloaded the information and searched through the dates on the files. He clicked play on the one recorded the day they went to the museum and John showed her the painting; that had intrigued him. He listened and skipped over sections when they were in the museum. It sounded like they were larking around, then her tone of voice caught his attention. He listened intently.

'Oh my god. Is that—'

'—Yes it is. It actually belongs to my father. When he marketed the development he hung it in the lounge, to create an air of opulence. You know it's all about impressions, so an impressionist painting seemed appropriate. Most buyers thought it

was a fake but there were one or two, like you, who knew exactly what it was. He left it here when he gave me the flat. I mentioned it to him but he just said not to worry about it. It's a gift along with the flat.'

'That's amazing. I knew it was part of a private collection but I thought somewhere in Paris or New York. Not here in the town where I live. You know Monet painted that in around 1900 to 1901. It was sold by Christies in New York in 2005, for 800,000 US dollars. Wow. That was your father. Thank god I'm sitting down. You can't leave it here you know. If anyone knew, it would be stolen in a heartbeat. It's one of France's national treasures actually. You need to keep it very safe. Please don't tell me it was propped up against the wall in your spare room.'

'No I have a large safe and it was inside. But yes, I should return it to my father's house. He has an air-conditioned art gallery with laser security. It's very James Bond. I'll put it away. I wasn't being boastful you know. I just thought you would appreciate it. Our own personal exhibition as we didn't get to see the one at the museum—'

The talking stopped and he heard rustling, some laughter, and John's voice again.

'Don't stop. This is heaven.'

Heavy breathing followed John's words and Julian stopped the recording. He couldn't bring himself to listen to anything else and said a silent prayer of thanks that nothing visual had been recorded. The painting intrigued him and he wondered why Bryan Smithfield, known for being a high stakes gambler and keen sports betting man, would have an art gallery in his house with such a valuable painting. His instincts screamed at him;

Follow the painting.

He followed his instincts.

####################

"I want you to have it. Please. Look after it for me. You appreciate it so much more than my father. He gave it to me as a gift. I doubt if he actually realises its value and if he did I'm sure he would just put it back up for auction. In fact I'm not even sure he purchased it in the first place. I seem to remember someone gave it to him as part of a business deal or something. I don't know and to be honest I don't get involved in his business at all. Just some of the property development and architecture because that's my passion. He knows that. He is very supportive in that respect." John hugged Emma and nestled his face into her neck. "I'm going to miss your smell. Come with me."

"What? I wish I could and I couldn't possibly accept the painting. I'd be paranoid about it. It's so valuable." She stroked his face and cupped his chin in her hand. "If you really want me to have the painting, I will, but I'll just be looking after it for you whilst you are away. You understand that. We will need a contract to say so, otherwise there could be issues. I wish you didn't have to go. I will miss you too. I like you more than I realise and maybe I am in love with you too. It's been a long time since I felt this way over anyone." She kissed him; deep and sensuous. Her tongue hungrily explored his mouth. A fire raged in her groin made worse by the flood of moisture between her legs. She whispered as her tongue explored his ear. "I really am going to miss you. You are funny and make me laugh. You are incredibly sexy. I have never felt so much passion over anyone. Not even Andrew when we first met. I can't believe it. At first, I fought it but now I want to devour you each time I see you."

"Oh god. Me too. I will miss you so much. Let's sort out the papers for the painting. I'll write something down for you and you can take it to your lawyer to get a seal or whatever. That's the easiest thing I can think of. There is an envelope with the paintings papers and authentication mark. I'll give that to you when you leave." He groaned. "Don't stop. I need you. I need to feel you once more before I leave. The painting can wait." He pushed her on to the sofa and pulled her blouse over her head. Each kiss tingled on her skin and heat rushed through her body. He cupped her breast in his hand and swirled his tongue around her hard nipple. She moaned, and wrapped her legs around his hips. He unfastened his pants and pressed against her thin panties, and she pushed her hips into him, eager for him to enter her. He pushed her panties to the side, and slid into her warm soft core. She gasped. Shivers ran over her body, and her nails furrowed deep into his back. She arched towards him. His hand supported her back as she pushed onto him. She grasped his hair and pulled him closer as her lips met his. Heat and passion overwhelmed her. Waves of orgasm crashed through her body, as she reached the heights of her escape from reality. Her tongue pushed deep into his mouth as he pushed deep into her core. She moved in sync with his rhythm; the momentum rising and falling as he held back then pushed forward. He shuddered and groaned. A flood of warm liquid exploded inside her as he collapsed on top of her spent. She wrapped her arms around him and shifted to his side.

"Come on. Let's go to bed. You're exhausted from all the sorting and packing. Let's sleep." She pulled him up from the sofa and into the bedroom. Sleep came easy to them, entangled in each other's arms.

He untangled himself from her as the bedside clock buzzed and the blue numbers flashed 5 a.m. "I need to make a move. My flight is in a few hours. I've checked in online already so I just need to turn up but I don't want to be late. You know what the traffic can be like. Thanks for offering to give me a ride to the airport. You needn't have you know. It may be hard saying goodbye there. I can easily call a taxi."

"It's okay. I actually find airports exciting and I'm hoping the excitement will replace the sadness of the goodbye, at least for a while. I wish you didn't have to go, but it's a fabulous opportunity for you. We had a great time together and you've helped me along my journey to no end. I'm very grateful to you in so many ways. You made me wake up and start enjoying my life again. John, I don't believe long distance relationships work, and I think you feel the same if you are truthful with yourself. We would never see each other and probably end up resenting each other in the end. I don't want that. It's best to end on a high. We'll remain friends but if you meet someone else then that's okay, you know. I don't expect you to stay home in New York, waiting for me. Big city, bright lights, all yours to enjoy." She swung her legs on the edge of the bed and reached for her robe.

"You know me so well and thanks. It was an unexpected adventure with you Emma. I loved every minute of it but you're right. I'll always remember you and don't forget I'll be back for the Monet." He pulled her back on to the bed and nuzzled into her neck. "Once more for the road?"

"No if we start now, you know you'll miss your flight. Go and take your shower. I'll sort out the bedding and the rest for your housekeeper."

"Aww. But you're right." He jumped off the bed and headed into the bathroom.

A sadness sat heavy on Emma's heart as she stripped the bed and tidied up. She wiped away the tear from the corner of her eye. She wanted to be strong. She didn't want to breakdown. Not here. A familiar lemon musk scent wakened her senses as he emerged from the bathroom. She dashed past him. "My turn. I'll make it quick."

####################

A large unassuming parcel, wrapped in brown paper, rested against the door. "Is that what I think it is?"

"Yes and here are the papers. Inside I've written a letter, authorising you to be the custodian of the painting for the foreseeable future, until I return to the UK. I hope that's going to be okay." He handed her a fat manilla envelope. "I know you'll look after it well. Come on let's go."

Elevator music blared out of the radio on the way to the airport. Neither one inclined to talk or change the station. Emma concentrated on driving, giving him an occasional glance. He stared out the window, at the passing cars on the motorway. She had no wish to interrupt his thoughts and didn't have anything to say that would make things better. A bitter taste, started at the back of her throat, had made its way into her mouth. Her swallow neutralised it.

"Would you like some gum?" He read her thoughts.

"Yes please. Thanks. You okay?"

"Not really. I'll survive I guess, so will you."

"Yes." The music changed to the news; bombings around the world, the right wing reaction to the increase in gay marriages, racial tension, somewhere, probably in America. No good news. Each news item blurred into the next. She found no words.

"We're here. Look it's best if you just drop me off outside Departures. I'm flying BA and it's chaos you know. I've only got about 90 minutes before the flight, so just time to drop my bags, dash through security and board. I'll message you just before we take off okay. Emma, I—" She pressed her finger to his lips.

"Don't. Don't say it. Just go." Tears streamed down her face as she pulled the handbrake and released the boot. He pressed a finger under her chin, lifting her face until her teary gaze met his. He whispered. "I love you."

"I know." She turned away from him. "Go. Please."

He pulled his case from the boot, and she turned for one last look, but lost him as he disappeared into the crowd pushing through the doors to the departure lounge.

"Oy Oy. You can't stay there. Move along move along Missus. Come on, now. If you've unloaded then move along. Keep it moving." A harsh voice cut into her thoughts as the traffic police passed by, controlling the chaos of drop offs outside departures.

"Oh. okay. Sorry." She mumbled as she turned on the engine and drove off. She pulled up in the nearest lay-by, just outside the airport. A few deep breaths, in and out. Inhale. Exhale. Her nerves calmed. The knot in her stomach released. She tuned the radio station into a jazz station for the morning show and drove off into the rush hour traffic. Bumper to bumper, she crawled along. Each foot taking her nearer home, but further away from him.

<PING> 'About to take off. Thanks. Love you always. Xxx'

'Safe journey. Love you too. Xxx' <SEND>

A single tear rolled down her face and splashed on the phone. She squeezed her eyes to clear her mind and wipe away moisture. She knew one chapter in her new life had ended and whilst sadness rolled over her now, she didn't intend to let it hang around for long. She had come too far to turn back now. The road ahead cleared, and the traffic started moving. She turned up the radio, and put her foot down. She would soon be in the comfort of her home, and she knew exactly what she wanted to do.

Chapter Twenty-nine

"He left this morning on the first flight to New York. In fact he should be arriving at JFK in about an hour's time. She drove him to the airport but is now back at her art studio. She doesn't have a class but she is painting. I observed her before coming here. I also have the USB device for you. The guy at Spy High came through. It turned out he was a friend of Smithfield and when they all went to Laser Tag, she asked him about it then. He convinced her it was just a music and movies drive. She collected the dummy drive from him the next day. You were right she had begun to suspect something but hopefully this has put her off the trail." Julian shuffled his papers.

"That's excellent news on both counts. Do you have the drive?" Andrew leaned over his desk, holding out his hand.

Julian dropped the device into his open palm. "Yes here it is. You do know how it works right. You just pop it into the usb port on the laptop and the data will download. It is categorised by day so you just click on the day that you want to listen for. I've done some analysis of the data and it's pretty mundane really. She likes to talk to the cats, but I guess you knew that already. There are a few interesting days, when she visited Smithfield. He gave her a painting, a Monet that his father gave him with the apartment. She was very excited about that of course, being an artist. She was his lover, the recordings confirmed that. I don't know how she is now that he's left. What's next, Mr McKenzie?" Julian looked his employer direct in the eye; willing him to say he was free to go, willing him to release him from his contract.

"Thanks. This looks easy enough. I'll call you if I get stuck with it. I want you to continue following her. I'm concerned about her, to be honest. I think she fell for Smithfield more than I realised. Make sure she is okay, and not planning on doing anything stupid. She shouldn't because she isn't like that but you just never know. If she's upset she will make a beeline for the art studio or her friend Beth. She will want to talk. Do you think it would be possible to plant another listening device on her or is that too risky?" Andrew inserted the device into the USB port and clicked away.

"I think it may be too risky. I can take photos of her movements but to plant something strange on her so soon after her discovery of this one may raise her suspicions. I'll take a look at what Spy High has. Maybe they have other more innocuous devices, such as a pen. I'll let you know." Julian gathered his papers and rose. He shook Andrew's hand and left. The overpowering scent of stale cigars, whiskey and Poison perfume followed him into the lift. His nose twitched and he swallowed the vomit rising in his throat. The fresh air provided welcome relief as he left the building.

The bench on the green gave him the best view of the building. He waited. He knew she wouldn't be late.

Her hand slipped into his. "I'm glad you came. I miss you. How's the new love interest?"

He squeezed her hand. "Unobtainable and frustrating. Have you found out any more information?" He moved away from her.

"Don't sit so close. You are supposed to eating your lunch alone, remember."

"Yes but I'm cold. I'm trying to keep warm. This country has the worst winters of anywhere. Grey and miserable. At least winter in Iraq is cold but the sun still shines." She moved closer to him and held his hand again. "Susie is a minefield of information. She knows everything and actually hates him. He treats her like a slave. She was happy to chat to me over our lunch. In fact we had a few lunches."

He turned to her. "Make sure he doesn't suspect anything. Does he know?"

"Oh yes he knows. I told him he needed to be nicer to her, and she would do more for him. He liked that, but he doesn't do nice so he asked me to be nice to her instead. Look he gave me a black Amex card to use for my expenses." She waved the black card in front of his face.

He grabbed her hand and pulled it down. "Stop. You're drawing attention to yourself, and me. Tell me what you found out from Susie."

"Sorry. Well she knows I am his lover and also works there so she was wary at first, but I told her that I wanted to get to know him better and thought she could help me. I asked her if he had ever shown unusual behaviour as that could be a key to his personality traits. I also told her I used to be a psychoanalyst. She has no clue and won't check. Anyway, she said that around 18 months ago there was an unusual art deal that agitated him. He seemed very concerned about the fine details and wanted all the paperwork, which she normally dealt with and filed away once the deal went through. She doesn't know where the paperwork is, but she did say that she thinks the art deal went through and the shipment was handled by Mrs McKenzie's art gallery."

He shivered, and pulled his scarf close around his neck. "I don't think she has an art gallery. She has an art studio where she teaches."

"Are you cold? There is a fresh breeze here. Let's walk to warm up. We can still talk. Come." Luisa pulled Julian up from the bench and pushed her arm through his. His legs, stiff from sitting, tingled as they strolled around the green.

"I'm okay. Continue."

"Okay, well the art gallery closed down a few years ago. Susie didn't know why, just that it was something to do with him. She said Mrs M had stormed into the office in quite a rage one day, which surprised everyone as she was usually such a sweetheart. She always remembered the birthdays, and came into decorate the office at Christmas; you know the kind of thing. Anyway, Susie thought she was angry because he had taken over this particular shipment, and she didn't like him interfering. She also remembered that the art was shipped to an address in Paris as she had to send a telex to someone called Princess. She thought that was a strange name which is why it stuck in her mind." A smile began to form on Luisa's lips. "But you know who that may be, don't you?"

"Oh you don't think it's—" Julian spun around to face her. "We need to get that paperwork. If the art was shipped to Princess Naya then we need to confirm that and follow it up. This could be the lead we've been looking for."

Luisa's grip tightened on Julian's arm. "I know Malik and Naya were lovers, and she would have done anything for him. Maybe the shipment contained something for him. I'll push Susie to try and find the paperwork. This shipment took place a few months before they murdered my brother. I am convinced McKenzie had something to do with it. I'll work on him as well. Sorry."

Julian rested his hand on hers and squeezed her fingers. "Don't be. It's okay. We'll survive this you know. As friends though not lovers. It's best. You are an amazing woman, Luisa and don't ever forget that. I hope Malik, god rest his soul, knows that, and is watching over you. He knows what you are doing for him."

"I know. Thanks for helping me. You are a good man and you deserve happiness as well. How are things going with the ex Mrs C. Or shouldn't I ask?

"It's okay. She asked for another maintenance payment from me. I'm hoping that's the last. It's for fifty thousand this time. To be honest it's the only reason I've kept the job with McKenzie trailing his wife. He is very generous. If I didn't know better I'd say he was trying to reduce his cash assets. Maybe he knows something we don't." A non-weather related shiver ran down his back as he laughed. A foreboding feeling; following the painting could lead into more trouble than he may be prepared for. If his suspicions proved correct, there were some very dangerous secrets being held by some dangerous people, and he wasn't sure if he had the courage to uncover them.

Chapter Thirty

Home—a welcome sight after the early morning and the long drive from the airport. The rich scent of freshly brewed coffee awakened her, and the sun streaming through the blinds in the conservatory lifted her spirits as she contemplated the task ahead. She admired the Monet propped against the wall. The colours leapt out as the rays of sun bounced off the canvas. She loved it. She couldn't leave it there as it would fade in the UV light but she could wallow in its glory for a few days before she hid it.

She emptied the papers from the envelope onto the table; certificates of authentication from Christies and Sothebys, a history dating back to Michel Monet in Giverny. She reached into the desk drawer, and pulled on a pair of white gloves. Ancient papers demanded care and attention. She sorted them into chronological order, soaking up the history of the painting. From Giverny to Paris, Basel to Brussels, Geneva back to Basel, London to Paris and finally; her eyes closed and her head shook in disbelief when she read the final entry. *'2013; Private sale; Andrew McKenzie; London, GB.'*

Is that a mistake? How on earth did that happen without me knowing? Am I dreaming?

She opened her eyes and reread the entry.

Wait, what the hell, I own a Monet.

She shuffled through the rest of the papers, and one fluttered to the ground. She retrieved it: *'Deed of Gift...Painting by Claude*

Monet....Purchased by Andrew McKenzie gifted to Bryan Smithfield on this date, 1 June 2013....'

She examined the document. It looked genuine. She recognised Andrew's signature, and the other signature was Smithfield's. The lawyers seal glinted in the corner.

Why would he purchase a piece of art work without telling me? What else don't I know? I know I don't own a Monet.

She leaned back in her chair, and surveyed the papers spread across the table. Her fingertips formed an arch, and her thumbs twiddled backwards and forwards as she thought.

Why would Andrew give Smithfield such an expensive gift? They only knew each other as business acquaintances. I remember Andrew spitting feathers over Smithfield many times. There was no love lost between them. So why such as expensive gift. Was it payback for something? Or payment for a business deal?

Everything was about business with Andrew, and probably the same with Smithfield. They had similar traits which was why they despised each other so much.

What now?

She gathered up the papers and returned them to the envelope.

The attic. Her archive from the art gallery lived in storage in the attic. The last document had piqued her curiosity, and her gut instinct told her more discoveries awaited in the attic.

What am I looking for and what will I find?

Her nerves tingled, and her stomach tied itself in knots with anticipation. She climbed the ladder into the attic. She shivered as the sharp damp coldness hit her. She pulled the light cord, and coughed from the dust that settled in the back of her throat. Boxes and boxes of archived records from her art gallery sat beside boxes of memorabilia of happier days, when Anthony was young, and she and Andrew only had eyes for each other. She ignored the memorabilia. That could wait. She pulled down one of the boxes, and stood back as spiders scurried away to new homes in dark corners, and the dust settled.

Bundles of papers burst out of the box when she opened it. Filing and paperwork had never been her thing, and when the gallery had closed down she had just bundled everything together and stuffed it into archive boxes. She sighed at the prospect of a long day ahead. The first bundle held receipts from the closing party she had held to thank her faithful supporters. She flicked through it. Nothing interesting.

Wow did I really spend so much on champagne and canapés? I can't even remember them now.

She smiled and returned the bundle to its position in the box. The next bundle held receipts from a trip to Amsterdam to attend the annual art auctions. Nothing of note. She flicked through bundle after bundle; boring receipts, invoices and miscellaneous paperwork that she had no idea about, but kept just in case. The first box proved fruitless, and the mountain of boxes in front of her loomed large.

Another box sent another cluster of spiders scurrying and more dust. Her eyes itched, her throat tickled, and a sneeze exploded from her nose.

This is going to be harder than I thought. All this dust.

More bundles in the second box. That looked promising. The first bundle held the bill of laden and invoices from a shipment to Australia, the second a shipment to the USA, and then BINGO. There it sat. Staring her in the face. A bundle of invoices, shipping dockets, a bill of laden for a shipment to Paris. She thumbed through it. Yes. That was the shipment Andrew had insisted on handling himself, and that she had been so angry about at the time—at him taking over and controlling her business. This is what she had been looking for. Her eyes watered with the dust, and her breathing constricted. She craved fresh air, and an antihistamine. She stuffed the discarded bundles back into the box, and secured it back into position.

The fresh air streaming in through the open kitchen window provided welcome relief as did the antihistamine for her coughs and sneezes. She had no idea the attic had so much dust. She would have to get Maria to clean it one of these days. A cool glass of water refreshed her dry throat.

'DING DONG.'

She jumped at the sound of the doorbell. She scooped up the papers spread over the kitchen counter, and stuffed them into the nearest drawer. The clock showed two p.m. She remembered the appointment for the security check with Ben from Spy High.

'DING DONG.'

"I'm coming. Hang on."

"Hello, Mrs McKenzie. I hope I'm not interrupting you." Ben offered his hand.

"No. Not at all. It's a pleasure to see you, and I'm pleased you could make it so soon after our meeting." She waved him in. "Please go through to the kitchen."

"Thanks. This shouldn't take too long. I can see you already have an alarm system in place. I'll check that it works and is set up correctly. Do you have any paperwork for it?" Ben perched on one of the stools by the breakfast bar.

"Err. I, I, I'm not sure exactly. Andrew, my ex-husband used to look after all that kind of thing." Heat rose in Emma's face as she lied to Ben. Andrew had no idea about house alarms. She dealt with all household things and knew exactly where to find the paperwork for the alarm—at the bottom of the drawer where she had stuffed the papers from the attic. She had no intention of searching through that drawer in Ben's presence. "I'm sorry. That sounds a bit disorganised doesn't it? I do know that if the alarm goes off then City Alarms gets a notification, and if I don't punch in a code within 45 seconds they in turn notify the police, who respond immediately. We have their Gold Service Level." She opened the kitchen door. "It's a little stuffy in here don't you think. I hope you don't mind. I know it's cold outside but the winter air is refreshing." She took a deep breath, and felt the colour of her face return. She smiled. "Where would you like to start, and please, excuse my manners, would you like a coffee or tea? The kettle has just boiled."

"No thanks. I'm fine. I'm not much of a coffee or tea drinker to be honest. Just a glass of water will be fine. Thanks. I'd like to check the alarm points around the house then I'll look at the locks on the windows and doors, then discuss any other security concerns you may have. If that's okay. I like to work alone if you don't mind. It's distracting if the owner of the house follows me around asking questions so I keep the Q and A session to the end. I'll explain everything to you once I've finished. Is that okay with you?" Ben stood, and took, what looked to Emma like a testing device, out of his backpack. He placed his hand on her arm. "Don't worry everything will be fine."

"Thanks. That's good. I'll be in here in the kitchen reading the newspapers. I didn't get chance earlier today."

Ben disappeared from the kitchen and a variety of pings and electronic sounds floated on the air as he busied himself with his security check. She breathed a sigh of relief.

That was a close call. I wonder if he noticed my blush. I wish I could control it. I hope he gets through this quickly. I really want to find out what those papers say.

She turned the pages of the newspaper but the words blurred into each other. She couldn't concentrate. Her fingers tapped on the counter, one after another like practising scales on a piano, in an attempt to calm her frayed nerves. As she stared into space, a slight movement in the garden caught her eye. She focused.

What was that? It seems larger than a dog or cat or is it my imagination playing up.

She peeked out of the door for a better view. Nothing moved in the garden, and the bare branches on the trees and bushes didn't leave many places to hide.

My imagination running overtime.

She closed the door and returned to the newspaper. The words continued to blur and her concentration failed her. The knot grew in her stomach. The finger tapping annoyed her instead of offering relief. She stood, feet apart, pulling the tension down her shoulders, through her arms and into her clenched fists. Nothing worked.

"Ben. Ben. Are you okay? How it is going? Would you like that cup of tea or coffee now?"

"I'm okay. Thanks, Mrs McKenzie. I won't be long." She heard him call from the main bedroom. She paced up and down the kitchen, fists clenched, then unclenched, then clenched again. She tidied away the dishes from the draining board. She emptied the dishwasher. She straightened the herbs and spices and sorted them in alphabetical order. She categorised the cook books in size, from tall to short, making sure all the titles faced the same way.

Why did the French have to be different and put their titles running from bottom to top? How annoying. How on earth are you supposed to read that? It makes no sense.

"Hi.

She jumped.

"Oh. Sorry if I startled you. I've finished. You have a very good security system already in place actually, so there isn't much I can add to it to be honest. All the windows are alarmed and have high quality locks. You need to be careful where you keep the keys for the window locks. I noticed in some rooms the keys were kept on the window sill. That makes it pretty easy for an intruder to find. Apart from that, everything looks good. The alarm system works well. I triggered it and called City Alarms to let them know I was testing. They are very responsive. I commend your husband for such a good job. You should try and get the papers from him, however, just in case. I presume he no longer lives here if you are separated or divorced?" Ben placed his backpack on the kitchen counter. "I wouldn't mind a glass of water if I may."

"Oh, yes of course. Thanks. I, err, he, my ex-husband that is, made sure the alarm system was one of the best before it was installed. Here you are." He gulped down the water. "Oh you seem thirsty would you like another?"

"Yes, please. There was a lot of dust around the upstairs landing. Have you been in the attic recently? The hatch seems to have been disturbed. If you don't mind me asking. It's part of my job to notice the unusual, rather than the usual, if you know what I mean."

"Well. Yes I was looking for some old school photos for my son. He wants to post them on Facebook, I think it is. I don't do social media really, but he said there is an alumni group for his school." Emma cut herself off before her lie grew into something she couldn't contain. "That's good that the security check worked out. I don't have any questions for you now but if I do I know where to find you. How much do I owe you?"

"Nothing. It's already paid for."

"Oh who?"

"John paid for it before he left. He said he was concerned that someone had thrown a brick through the window and he didn't think the police were doing anything about it. Is that true?" Ben remained on his stool. Emma felt his eyes watching her every move, and it made her uncomfortable. She needed to wrap this up.

"Oh that. It was nothing. The police found some kids who were pranking around. Gave them a good telling off. The parents are to blame I guess. Not much for kids to do these days. That was very kind of John. I'll thank him next time I speak to him. If you've finished then I'll see you out. It was a pleasure, Ben. If I think of any questions I'll call you or visit the store. Thanks again." Emma ushered Ben to the door, and waited on the step until his vehicle turned down the lane. She gave a sigh of relief. Now she could return to her research.

The hot green tea refreshed, and calmed her nerves. She reviewed the papers, once more scattered over the kitchen counter. She prayed for no more interruptions. She needed to concentrate, and only a few hours of daylight remained. She sorted the papers into an order; the bill of purchase to her gallery, the bill of sale from her gallery to the client, copies of the certificates of authenticity, the bill of laden, the shipping invoice, invoices for packaging and carriage. She remembered the sale—to Princess Naya—an Iraqi princess living in Paris. She had escaped the war and made a new life in Paris. She ran an art gallery for her rich Middle Eastern friends, and had been one of Emma's best clients. The strict Sharia laws had forbidden the Princess to travel out of Paris, and so she had used Emma's gallery to purchase the art her friends requested. She had held most of it in Paris until the war ended. Emma knitted her brow as she read the papers. Nothing unusual sprung out, so why had Andrew been so keen to handle this shipment, especially when he knew nothing about shipping art. He had delegated most of it to his secretary who had passed the file back to her once the transaction had completed. She massaged her temples. A dull pain poked into the back of her neck and worked its way up. The beginning of a migraine. She reached for a beta blocker and realised she had forgotten to purchase more on the way home from the airport.

Damn. Beth could help.

"Hi."

"Hey girl. How are you? Didn't you take him to the airport this morning? How did that go? Are you devastated?" Beth fired questions down the phone.

"Actually I feel better than I thought I would. I guess it is what it is, you know. I can't do anything about it. Hey do you want to come round for dinner? I could do with a good chat and I've got a few things I'd like to go over with you. Can you come soon and pick up my prescription for beta blockers at the chemist? I'll call them and tell them I asked you to collect it. I feel a migraine on its way. Thanks, hun."

"No problem. Do you want me to pick up anything else for dinner? Steak, salad, Prosseco." Beth laughed.

"Yeah. That sounds great. Make it fast though, otherwise I'll be out of it, and you'll be cooking and drinking by yourself."

"Hey. I'm on my way. You know me. I'll be there in a flash. See you soon."

Emma pressed her forehead against the cool glass of the conservatory window. The robins chased each other around the bird bath, and a squirrel ran across the lawn and up the nearest tree. The crack of a branch startled the birds, and they disappeared into the dusk. Her eyes widened and her hearing sharpened. Was someone there? She thought she had seen something earlier but wasn't sure. She heard a crack as if someone had trodden on a dead branch. The leaves rustled beyond the hedge. Maybe the wind or a cat hunting for small prey or maybe a person. The outside security light triggered and bathed the garden in bright light. Nothing. No cats or dogs or squirrels or birds. Nothing. Her imagination played tricks on her again. She rubbed the back of her neck. The dull pain throbbed.

"Hiya." Beth let herself in and found Emma. "Here, you look terrible girl. Take one of these, and here's a glass of water. Come on. Come into the kitchen. It's warmer there. I think that will be better for you. It's freezing in here. Ooh, look. That cat just set off the security light. Maybe you need to get them adjusted so the cats don't set them off."

Emma leaned on her friend, and appreciated the warmth of the kitchen. Beth set about making their supper. "Tell me. How was the sendoff? I see he gave you the Monet. Wow. Isn't that something? It's a real shame he left. He is lovely, and I've not seen you smile so much in ages."

"Yes it was well, it was emotional, but you know. I don't feel as bad as I thought I would. I cared for him, but I'm not sure I loved him. It's easy to fall in love but real love with a person doesn't happen overnight. It takes time to grow and develops as you get to know that person. You know that right."

"I know. It drives me crazy when these guys tell you they love you after the second date. They hardly know what love is really.

They love the booty but do they love you as a person, warts 'n all. I doubt it very much. So you're okay with him leaving then?" Beth handed Emma another glass of water. "Drink this. No Prosecco for you tonight my dear, not with those horse tablets you've taken."

"Thanks. I needed that. It's true. I never appreciated it until now. He was amazing in bed though. I never thought sex could be so good with someone. Wow. I'll miss that, but I guess I'll survive. No there's no guessing. I will survive and it's made me stronger than I was before. I know I can do this on my own and have fun at the same time. I think we caught the migraine just in time. It's subsiding."

"Great. So what else do you have to tell me? You mentioned something on the phone that sounded mysterious. What's going on?" Beth served up the steak and salad. "Would you like dressing? There's balsamic and olive oil or lemon juice or Caesar."

"Balsamic and olive oil please. Thanks. That looks good. I just realised I don't think I've eaten all day and I had an early start taking him to the airport." Emma took a bite of the steak. "This is delicious. Well, there're a few things. The first is that Andrew purchased the Monet in a private sale about 18 months ago."

"What? Andrew who? Your Andrew? That despicable man you used to be married to." Beth almost choked on her steak, rested her fork on her plate and stared at Emma. "What are you saying?"

"Sorry to shock you. I am saying that with every painting of value there is a certificate of authenticity which lists the provenance of the painting. Who owned it, and where? So the Monet's provenance starts with his son, Michel Monet, in Giverny,

France, where they lived, and then documents everyone who purchased it until the present day. The last person to purchase the painting was Andrew McKenzie in a private sale in 2013. But that's not all. There is a deed of gift attached to the provenance, which states that Andrew gifted the painting to Bryan Smithfield, also in 2013. Bryan Smithfield is John's father. He hung the painting in the show house, and then left it there for John when he gave him the house as a birthday gift. Maybe he doesn't know the value of the painting or doesn't care. I don't know, but I do know that if Andrew purchased the painting privately in a sale it would be at least one million US dollars, as it was last sold at auction in 2005 for $800,000 US dollars. I haven't found any financial records showing what he purchased it for, so that's just a guess but an educated one. I know how the art world operates."

Beth's mouth hung open. She stopped eating. "Oh. My. God." She took a breath and stared at Emma. "But that doesn't make sense. Why would Andrew purchase a painting like that without telling you? You had an art gallery. You have all the connections in the art world. Surely he would have asked you to purchase it for him? Unless he didn't want you to know anything about it. It must have been part of some kind of shady deal. Maybe he purchased it to pay off Smithfield, who is a real shady character you know. Do you know him? The rumours are that he deals in anything with anyone. No scruples or integrity. It's only a matter of time before someone catches up with him. I think his wife left him a couple of years ago. She couldn't take the heat. Didn't John mention anything to you?"

"No just that he works for his father's architectural firm, but his father isn't involved. He is more of a sleeping partner. He said he thought his father was proud of him but not too much more about him. I got the impression that John didn't get involved with anything else in the business just the architecture which seems legit. I know Smithfield from various functions but nothing more than that. Just small talk nonsense that you forget as soon as you turn your back. But there is more, well at least I think there is. I had some suspicions, and so searched my archive files in the attic, which is probably why this migraine is coming on - there was so much dust up there and spiders. Ugh. Anyway, remember that time I told you that Andrew insisted on handling one of my shipments and it made me angry, well, I found the paperwork for that. I don't know. I have a gut feeling that there is something going on that he didn't tell me about, and I have some information but I'm not sure what exactly." Emma drained her water and poured another glass.

"So what did you find in the shipment paperwork?"

"That's the thing. Nothing but I'm sure I've missed something. After dinner can you help me go over it again? I'm sure there is something I'm missing."

"No problem. That bastard. I hate him even more for dragging you in this, whatever this is. It's not good. I can feel it in my chakra. We will need a serious reset session after this."

The food energised Emma; she left Beth reviewing the paper trail for the shipment as she loaded the dishwasher and made tea. "So Emma, I don't understand something here. Maybe I'm being blonde but why were five paintings purchased by your gallery and but six paintings were shipped?"

"What? Show me." Emma left the tea cups on the counter and dashed over to Beth who held out two pieces of paper.

"Look. Here is the purchase information for the paintings. They are all Impressionist, if I'm not mistaken—you have influenced me over the years you know. But look on the shipment note, there are six paintings listed, and one is by Picasso. The others are by Pissarro, Manet, Monet, Renoir and Cezanne. Picasso isn't an Impressionist is he? Why would his painting be listed on the shipment note?"

Emma grabbed the papers from Beth. "No that doesn't make sense. I couldn't possibly purchase a Picasso even if a client wanted, and 'Nude, Green Leaves and Bust,' I know is owned by a private collector who gave it to the Tate Modern on a long term loan. Maybe it was a copy that was shipped. Many people do copies and Picasso often used regular house paint, so with skill you can easily create a Picasso that is almost as good as the real thing. I wonder if Princess Maya knows about this. She must realise the Picasso is a copy. The original last sold at auction for US$106.5 million. The sale broke records. I'll call Princess tomorrow. She'll be pleased to hear from me. We always got along well."

"Incredible. There is definitely something going on. But Emma, please be careful. Maybe you should let sleeping dogs lie. You don't know how dangerous some of these people are and what they will do to protect their secrets."

"Oh Beth, you read too many of those spy books. Real life isn't like that. That's just fiction. Although I did have a real life 007 here earlier today."

"Ooh, who? Tell me more."

"Ben from Spy High. He is friends with John, and he came to do a security check on the house. He spent ages doing it so I thought he was going to find all kinds of things wrong but when he finished he said everything was in order and he couldn't improve it."

"Okay. Is he handsome, attached, works out? Did you check him out?"

"Beth! No I didn't. He is okay looking, a bit geeky if you know what I mean. He looks like he needs a good haircut, and a wardrobe overall, so I bet he is single. You are incorrigible." Emma collected the papers back into the bundle and returned them to the drawer. "Come on. I'm sick of playing private investigator, let's go watch a movie. Your choice, as long as it isn't Top Gun again."

"But I love Tom Cruise in that film. He is so, well just so, you know." Beth grinned, and dragged Emma into the lounge in front of the large flat screen TV. "It's like the movies here."

"If you want a Tom Cruise film what about that Jack Reacher film. He was pretty good in that. Did you read the Lee Childs book?"

"Forget Lee Childs, give me Tom Cruise. Come on, fire up Netflix."

####################

Julian breathed warm air onto his numb fingertips to bring them back to life.

Why did I always have surveillance jobs in the dead of winter? Never summer.

He had seen enough; the Monet, two lots of paperwork, Ben planting his devices—probably under the guise of a security check—Julian had photographed him unscrew the receiver on her telephone, unscrew smoke alarms, put devices behind mirrors, and under console tables. He wondered about Ben's interest in her. He knew he still worked for MI6, a source within the ministry had confirmed that, but the question why the interest in Emma bugged him. Pins and needles shot through his leg as he stood from his position behind the hedge. He shook it out as much as he could in the confined space, and thankful for the cover of the evergreen hedge and bushes surrounding the garden, he scrambled back to his car, parked out of sight down the lane.

Chapter Thirty-one

"Good Morning, Susie, is Mr McKenzie in his office? I have something important to discuss with him about the upcoming merger project I'm working on."

"Oh, good morning, Luisa. No he hasn't arrived yet. He had a meeting at Smithfield, Jones and Taylor, but he should be here soon. Would you like to wait in his office or leave a message for him?" Susie beamed at Luisa, perched on her desk.

"Did you ever find out what happened to that paperwork from the shipment of paintings? You said you were going to look for it for me."

"Yes. I remember I gave the paperwork to Mrs McKenzie for her gallery records, because the shipment came from her gallery. Mr McKenzie told me that would be best otherwise it would look strange, an art shipment from here. Do you want me to ask her for them?" Susie reached for the telephone.

"No. Don't call her. It's okay. I just wondered, don't worry about it." Luisa placed her hand on Susie's to stop her making the call.

"Okay. Why don't you go into his office? Would you like a coffee or tea?"

"No thanks. When he gets here we don't want to be disturbed." Luisa closed the door behind her as she entered Andrew's office.

She sat behind his desk, and swung around on his large chair, as the chair returned to the desk, a white piece of paper poking out from under the drawer caught her attention. She moved in for a closer look. The hidden catch sprung the drawer open, scattering papers on to the floor beneath. She scooped them up, skimming each one for any information of interest. Her eyes rested on a bank statement from 2013. A payment for £1,000,000, a direct transfer into an account. She scanned the information into her phone. That could be interesting. Such a large and unusual payment. Susie buzzed the intercom. "Just thought I'd let you know, Mr McKenzie is on his way up. Would you like that coffee now?"

Luisa scrambled out from under the desk, and pushed the intercom button, "Thanks for letting me know but no coffee." She stuffed the papers back into their hiding place and waited by the window.

####################

Andrew entered the office and stopped in his tracks at the sight he met. The sunlight shone through Luisa's thin blouse, outlining her full breasts. Her nipples strained against the tight material. The buttons on her blouse gaped. He smiled and walked towards her. "This is a nice surprise. You look radiant, my dear." He popped the first button and released her breasts into his hands. He nuzzled into her cleavage and kissed her hard. "I want you. Now."

She writhed under his touch, and slid out of his hold. Her fingers ran over his head and around his neck as she passed. She pushed him onto his chair. "Sit and stay." She commanded. "I have something to ask you." She sat on the chair she had positioned earlier. Her breasts protruded from her blouse as she leant back.

She hitched her skirt up and opened her legs to reveal her naked dark core. She cupped one breast in her hand and reached down between her legs with the other. Her eyes closed and her head leaned back as she twirled her finger around her nipple. The fingers on her other hand moved in small circles, around and around. Her hand glistened with her wetness.

She mesmerised him. He stood and took a step towards her. She stopped her show. "Sit and tell me about the art shipment, or you won't get any more."

He could barely speak. "What do you want to know? God you are beautiful. Do you know how much I want you?"

"Everything." She sucked her juices off her fingers, and swirled them around her breast. Her tongue ran around her lips, moistening them. "Do you want to watch me come for you?" She whispered.

He moaned. "You know I do."

"Tell me."

"There was an extra painting, a fake Picasso I needed to send to Paris. I used the art gallery as a cover up. Show me."

She opened her legs wider, and pushed her fingers inside. Her thumb twirled around, playing, teasing. "Why?"

"A microchip of information had been painted into the fake. I needed to get this to Tariq in Paris." Andrew's eyes closed, and his breathing quickened. He unfastened his pants, and released himself. "Please."

"No. Why did Tariq need the microchip? Look at me. Look how wet I am. Look how hot I am inside; I'm waiting for you to fill me. Do you want to be inside me? Why did Tariq need the microchip?"

Andrew could barely talk. "He wanted to pass it on to someone, but I don't know who. That's everything I know. Come here."

She hitched her skirt up and slid over to him. She turned and hovered over him. She teased. Lowering then raising herself. A little more each time. Each time his moan increased until she slid all the way down and savoured the moment. She quivered as her orgasm rushed through her. She rose up and swivelled around on him. She leaned back. He sucked her breasts, and his hips rose, pushing himself farther into her. She held his back and pushed down on him, then up then down in a rhythmic movement until she felt him shudder and his heat spilled inside her.

####################

She slid off him and poured two large measures of whisky. She needed to blur his memory of her questions and knew that the whisky would help. "Knock it back. Down in one." She threw her drink down her throat and waited for him to do the same. "Another?" She refilled his glass. He drained it again. He coughed as the harsh liquor burned his throat.

He leaned back in his chair. Satiated. "Now that is what I call a good morning's work. Luisa, you are one amazing woman. I don't know what hold you have over me but whenever I see you I lose control of my senses. It's like you cast a spell on me."

"My darling. I know. I feel the same, but I need to go and finish my work on mergers and acquisitions." She kissed him on his forehead, turned and left his office.

####################

Back at her desk, Luisa made a quick check of her co-workers. Most busied themselves with the daily barrage of emails, spreadsheets and telephone calls; others were away from their desks, presumable on the early lunch shift. She reached for the telephone. She pressed 9 for a secure outside line and dialled a number in Paris. As it rang, she hoped it was still in service.

"Âllo. Comment ça va?"

"Bonjour, puis je parle à Mademoiselle Naya, s'il vous plaît?"

"Luisa, is that you? It's been such a long time. How are you my darling?"

'Naya. Yes it's me. I am wonderful. I keep meaning to call you but I'm so busy these days. How have you been keeping?"

"Well you know how it goes. It must be worse for you. He was only my lover but he was your brother. I miss him every day. He was such a beautiful person, but he would want us to live our lives you know."

"Yes. I miss him as well. I'm looking in to some things connected with his death and wanted to ask you something. Is that okay?"

"Of course my darling. Anything to assist you. Are you a private detective now like Clouseau? I hope you are better. You know the Pink Panther always defeated him every time."

"Ha ha. Not really. It's just for my own knowledge to be honest. There are some things I need to know. Do you remember the art shipment you received just before his death?"

"Oh yes, from Mrs McKenzie. She is wonderful. Do you know her? It was a large shipment and my clients were very happy with the paintings. She always worked very hard for me. I was sad when she closed her gallery. What about the shipment? Everything was in order with it. You know my cousin, Tariq. He actually handled that one for me as I was ill at the time. I had the terrible Parisian flu and couldn't move for several days. He very kindly accepted the shipment and made sure all my clients received their paintings. Everyone was very happy. In fact, he will be in London next week. It is strange but Mrs McKenzie also called me about this same shipment. She wanted to know how many paintings I received. She said her paperwork showed she sent 6 over to me, but I think only five were received. I told her to meet Tariq and discuss it with him. Maybe someone made a little mistake at her gallery."

"Thanks. That's interesting. Do you have any idea when and where she is meeting Tariq?"

"Yes he mentioned he would meet her next Wednesday around mid-morning by the Italian Gardens in Kensington. I will let him know to expect you as well. He will be in awe of all you beautiful ladies wanting to meet him."

"Oh there's no need. I just wondered that's all. It's nothing really. In fact, forget I even asked. I thought Malik had something to do with the shipment, but I was mistaken. Thanks for your help. I appreciate it. One of these days I will visit you in Paris. It will be wonderful to see you again."

"Yes that would be wonderful. It's been good catching up with you Luisa. Take care of yourself my darling. Until we meet again. Goodbye."

Luisa hung up. She typed an email to HR requesting a day's leave next Wednesday. She Googled Italian Gardens, Kensington and found a map of the gardens which she printed out. If she knew Tariq, he would meet Emma in The Pump House, at the far end of the gardens, and she intended to meet him first.

####################

Andrew closed the door after Luisa. He returned to his desk, sat, head in hands. He closed his eyes as he contemplated his next move. He knew she wasn't exactly who she said she was. He knew she chased something and from her questions earlier, which he remembered despite the whisky she had poured down his throat, she had given her game away. She needed to be stopped before she got closer to the truth and discovered dangerous secrets. He kicked himself for being so weak under her influence. He prided himself on being ruthless and powerful in business, but a beautiful woman and sex made him weak, and he lost all control. He loved her but also hated her. He sighed. He knew what he had to do and it would not be an easy task. To let go of someone so beautiful who brought him so much pleasure in his grey life. He reached for the telephone.

Chapter Thirty-two

"Hi Luisa. Sorry we couldn't meet today, but I wanted to know if you found out any more information." Julian shivered by the pay phone.

"Not much, only that the paperwork was returned to the gallery. He didn't want it to be held in his office for some reason. What's next?"

"I'm not sure then. I'll try and find the paperwork and take a look. I took some close range photos outside her house but I'm not sure if that was the right paperwork. I need to have a closer look at them. I'll continue following her, maybe something else will come up. Mr M wants me to report back on her movements. I'm not sure if it's just about his possessiveness or it's something else."

"Are you still in love with her?"

"Yes. I am. It is a double edge sword—it's a joy to watch her but anguish to report on her movements to Mr M. I just don't know what I'm going to do to be honest. I can't go on like this much longer."

"Don't worry. Things will work themselves out. They always do. Remember I'll always be here for you, whatever happens."

"Yes I know, and I appreciate that. I'll always love you. Take care."

"Me too." He heard the phone click, and go dead. He hung up. A hint of warmth began within him as he wrapped his arms around himself. His ear tingled as he rubbed it back to life.

What am I going to do? Am I still in love with her?

His mind worked overtime on Emma, the Monet, the art shipment, Andrew, Luisa, John and Bryan Smithfield on his way home, as he tried to puzzle it all together. Maybe the photos from last night's surveillance would reveal some of the missing pieces. He had work to do and put his confused thoughts about Emma out of his mind as he concentrated.

####################

Emma left her house early. She knew the drive to the station could take extra time at this hour of the morning with the London commuters. She did not relish the thought of a packed train with standing room only, but she did not want to be late for her meeting with Tariq. He had mentioned something on the phone which had been interesting. He had handled the art shipment for his sister, but when she had questioned him about receiving six paintings, he had been very quiet and mumbled not here and something about people watching him. He suggested they meet at ten a.m. in the Kensington Italian Gardens Pump House.

Emma pushed through the crowd boarding the train. She had reserved a window seat and relief ran through her when she found it. Grumbles of travel weary commuters increased as the train rumbled out of the station; complaints about the bad weather; the rising price of fuel and train tickets, the poor management of the privatised train companies drifted past her, as she watched the countryside flash by, then change into the high rise buildings of the London suburbs. The view plunged into darkness as the train descended into the underground, and then out again under Paddington Station's impressive wrought iron arched roof. The crowd hustled and bustled to leave the hot airless train, pushing her forward towards the door, when a face in the crowd caught her attention.

Wasn't that the guy from the cruise? The one who sat next to me on the excursion.

She searched the crowd but the face disappeared. Her imagination playing tricks again.

The tube map blurred into a multicoloured maze. "Excuse me. I need go to Lancaster Gate, can you help me?"

"Yes love, you need to take the Circle Line westbound to Notting Hill Gate, then the Central Line eastbound to Lancaster Gate." The ticket inspector opened the barriers for her. "That way, love. Enjoy your day."

How do people do this each day? It is bedlam, pure chaos. Everyone going in different directions. Everyone crowding on to the trains as they arrived in the stations.

Mind the gap. Stand clear of the doors. Mind the gap. Stand clear of the doors. Over and over, like a record as each train arrived and departed.

The fresh air welcomed her as she exited the barriers at Lancaster Gate. She looked around for the street sign.

This should be Bayswater Road. Oh yes it is. Oh wait. I recognise that car. LU15SA. The blue Jag XK. The woman that was with Andrew. Why is she here? Her brow knitted as she puzzled over the car. *Maybe a coincidence?*

The station clock stuck ten; she hurried across the road and into Kensington Gardens. According to her map the building on the right should be The Pump House, and the waterfalls and gardens in front should be The Italian Gardens. Beautiful. Winter flowering shrubs and well-kept lawns created a peaceful scene.

####################

Julian exited moments behind Emma, and recognised the Jag, parked opposite the station. He frowned as he called her. No response. He left a message. "Luisa, call me as soon as you get this message."

####################

As Emma approached, she saw two figures; a man and a woman stood by the entrance. The woman threw her hands up as the man pointed at her. Emma held back. She didn't want to intrude on anyone's argument. The brown skin and black hair of the man made her suspect it was Tariq, but she didn't recognise the woman, although on a second look she realised she bore an uncanny resemblance to herself; a similar handbag, coat and hairstyle. Emma sat on the nearest bench to observe and wait.

A shot rang out, and a flash of metal whizzed past. She jumped, and stifled a scream. The woman collapsed, blood seeping from her head. The man bent down, checked her pulse, and ran off in the direction of the nearest exit. Emma froze to the spot, until curiosity made her turn and look up. The glint of a glass disappeared into the rooftop of the nearby building. Her heart pounded as she ran to take cover in the tube station. Frenzy began around her, the transport police ran out to investigate. "Shooting incident in The Italian Gardens. The parks police have been notified. The ambulance is on its way."

She looked back at the scene where a small crowd gathered around the woman, one man bent down and appeared to administer first aid, but she knew it was too late. The woman was dead. Shot dead. The man removed something from the woman's coat pocket then disappeared into the crowd. She raised her eyebrows in disgust. People stealing from the dead. They had no shame. A cold shiver ran over her as realisation dawned.

That bullet was meant for me. The woman was disguised to look like me. Why?

She swiped her card, and disappeared back into the tube network. If that bullet was meant for her, then she had no intention of staying around.

######################

Julian bent down and checked Luisa's pulse. Nothing. He placed her scarf under her head, kissed her forehead. He removed her phone from the coat pocket. He had no wish for the police to look into her phone records and find his last message to her. That would only cause complications. The police arrived and cleared the crowd. "Sir, please stand back from the body. Sir."

Julian stood. "Sorry I am trained in first aid and wanted to assist. She has no pulse. She is dead. The bullet was a direct hit into her head it looks like."

"Okay, sir. Thank you. We'll take it from here. Did you see anything or anyone?" The policeman took out his notepad.

"No I didn't. I was walking in the park, heard a shot and saw the woman collapse. I don't know her. I am just visiting London for the day. Do you need my details?" Julian offered as he stepped away from Luisa. He felt bile rising in his stomach. He needed to leave before his emotions took over and gave him away.

"No we don't. Thanks for your help. Enjoy your day in London." The policeman turned back to the body as he radioed for backup of an ambulance, and the forensics team.

Julian breathed deeply as he walked away. The cool air calming against his emotions in turmoil.

I only spoke to her yesterday and told her I loved her. Why didn't she tell me she was meeting someone in London? It looks like it was the same person that Emma was supposed to be meeting. What if that bullet was meant for Emma? Luisa was in disguise with a similar coat, handbag and wig.

Julian sat on the nearest bench. Head in hands. He couldn't believe what had just happened.

Luisa. My beautiful Luisa.

He blew his nose and wiped his face. A moment of clarity struck him. He needed to find Emma.

Is she okay? What happened to her?

He swiped his card, and disappeared back into the tube network.

####################

Emma trembled with fear on her way back to Paddington. She entered the westbound instead of the eastbound platform of the central line. She retraced her steps and then took the circle line travelling east instead of west. She remained on the train. The long way round. Time to be anonymous and think. If anyone was following her then they would be going the long way around as well. The carriage had the remains of commuters, who had missed trains or started later, and a few tourists, but no one else of note. She reached Paddington Station as her train departed. The information board flashed; the next train had a one hour delay. She took refuge in the nearest coffee shop, and ordered a double espresso and croissant. She chose one of the tables on the concourse where she could watch people passing by and maybe recognise a familiar face. Her coffee arrived, and she spilled most of it before she drank it. Her nerves on edge, she placed her head in her hands. Tears streamed down her face. Her shoulders slumped.

Who was that woman who looked like me, and had just been shot?

Her thoughts blurred into one. Her stomach lurched, and she ran into the nearest restroom. Her stomach emptied until only the bitter taste of bile remained. The tiled walls gave cool relief as she leaned back. She splashed water to refresh her face and emerged.

"Can I have a glass of water please?"

"Are you okay? I have your handbag here. I picked it up when you dashed into the bathroom. You should keep an eye on it."

"No I'm not okay. I'm not okay at all. I need to sit quietly and think. Thanks for my handbag. How much for the water?"

"Nothing. It's tap water. On the house. If you need to talk just ask. All kinds pass through here. Part of a baristas job is to be a good listener, when I'm not making skinny lattes with caramel."

"Thanks. That's actually very kind of you. I appreciate it." Emma took her water and handbag and returned to her seat.

####################

Julian dashed into Paddington Station relieved to see from the information panel that the next train back had been delayed by an hour. He found her sitting at one of the cafe tables. Her head rested in her hands and her shoulders shook; crying, probably in shock. He resisted his urge to go and comfort her. He slammed his fist into the wall.

How could this happen? What happened?

He retreated into the station pub. "A double whisky and a pint of Guinness, please."

"This early, mate? You okay?" The bartender set up the Guinness, and turned to pour the shot.

"It's been a rough day so far. I need something strong to take the edge of."

"You want to talk about it? I see all sorts passing through here. Part of a bartender's job is to be a good listener. That's four-fifty, please."

Julian handed over a five-pound note and emptied the whisky shot as he waited for his change. The raw heat burnt his throat and ricocheted around his stomach. He swallowed the rising vomit.

"There you go, mate. You want another whisky, you knocked that back quick? You sure you're okay?"

"No I'm not okay. I'm not okay at all. I need to sit quietly and think. Thanks."

"Anytime. I'm here all day. Just holler."

Julian took a seat by the window with a view of the station concourse and Emma at the cafe. He drew a sad face in the froth on top of the Guinness. Tears slid down his face, splashing on to the wide windowsill. Sorrow surrounded his heart.

She's gone. How can she be gone? So alive one minute and now so dead. Should I go back for her? What about Emma? What if she is in danger? Why was Luisa dressed like Emma? She must have found out something. Why was she meeting the Arab, who is he? Why didn't she tell me? Damn you Luisa and your determination and stubbornness. Look where it got you. You should have left it alone.

Chapter Thirty-three

The train rumbled into the station. The screech of brakes woke Emma. She blinked as she orientated herself and jumped out of her seat as she saw the station name. She grabbed her handbag and dashed off the train as the door closed behind her and it pulled away.

"Ooh, you only just made it, love. This is the airport express. The next stop is an hour away. You were lucky." The ticket collector opened the barrier for her.

"Yes. I fell asleep. It's been a tough morning. I'm glad to be home."

"Well, I hope the day turns out better for you love. Drive safely." The ticket collector closed the barrier.

Emma found her vehicle in the car park. Her hands shook as she opened the door and took a few deep breaths before she started the engine. A shiver ran over Emma as thoughts about the events of the day, pervaded her mind.

What would have happened if I had gotten there earlier? That woman had dressed to look similar to me, was that a coincidence or did she mean to do so? How would she know about my meeting with Tariq? Did she know Tariq already? Who was she? Was she the same woman who drove the blue Jag XK?

Her knuckles whitened as she grabbed the steering wheel to calm her nerves.

She drove out of the station and down the High Road, as she turned the corner; she slammed on her brakes to avoid a dog. The

ABS groaned trying to prevent the tyres from skidding on the icy road. A loud metallic crunch pierced her ears as the car crashed into a fire hydrant. Water sprayed everywhere. Emma opened her eyes and gasped for air.

What just happened? Where am I? A burnt chemical smell invaded the little airspace between her and the expanded airbag. Her mouth tasted of blood. Steam hissed from the crumpled engine. She struggled to release the seatbelt constricting her breathing.

Is that fuel I can smell? Oh god, I need to get out of here? I can't move.

She opened her mouth to shout but no words came out, just a whisper. "Please someone help me. Please." Her throat constricted with the acrid smell. Her breathing laboured. She pulled the seat belt buckle but the crash had locked it in place. She whispered again. "Please."

Her door opened and a hand reached over to release the buckle. The airbag hissed as the air released, and she felt herself being pulled out of the car. She gulped the fresh air into her tight lungs. Each breath bringing back life and energy into her body.

"Do you hurt anywhere?" she heard a voice in the distance.

"I don't think so. My mouth."

"Let me take a look." She opened her mouth.

"Oh you bit your tongue. Nothing to worry about. You'll be okay. Does anywhere else hurt?" The voice came nearer and had a kind gentle tone.

"No. I can wiggle all my fingers and toes. Look." Emma wiggled her fingers and toes and burst out laughing. Her giggles came in floods, uncontrollable. "I'm sorry. It's not funny, but look I can wiggle."

"Don't worry it's the shock. Do you have a number for a breakdown service? We need to get the car out of here and the police will need that once they arrive, which should be soon."

"Here look on my phone. It's the AA." Emma handed the stranger her phone, and continued giggling and wiggling.

####################

"Can you tell me what happened please, Ma'am?" The policewoman sat beside Emma and took her hand. "I know you are probably in shock and the paramedics are on their way but do you have any recollection of what happened?"

"A dog ran out so I braked because I didn't want to hit it. I love dogs. It looked so sweet. Did it live?" Emma looked at the policewoman; a tear ran down her face. "I hope I didn't hit it."

"No there isn't a dead or injured dog here so it must have run off. You probably did more damage to your vehicle and the fire hydrant, though. I hope you have good insurance." The policewoman took Emma's details. "Do you have a friend who can take you home? Is there anyone you would like me to call once the paramedics have checked you over?"

"Oh yes. No. My good friend Beth is away at the moment. She is visiting her parents in Yorkshire. I'm divorced and don't want you to call my ex husband. Err, I think I'll be okay." Emma stood but sat again as the blood rushed to her head.

"Don't worry. I'll make sure she gets home. I'll take her for a cup of tea so she can calm down first." The kind voice offered.

"Can I take your details please, sir? Just in case." The policewoman took out her notebook.

"Julian Cunningham. I'm a consultant. I work nearby and saw everything. I pulled her out of the vehicle. She looked like she was unable to breathe. I know the airbags can be life-saving but restricting. Here is my card with all my details. Just call and I'll be happy to give a statement. I've already called the AA to remove the vehicle, and I think Mrs McKenzie should be okay. I'm sure she will be in shock but there doesn't appear to be any broken bones or other damage."

"Thank you, Mr Cunningham. We appreciate your quick thinking on getting her out and calling the AA. Very commendable. We may be in touch, but for the moment it looks like a matter for the insurance company." The policewoman put her notebook away and returned to report to her partner.

"Mrs McKenzie. I'm Paramedic Sahil. Please look into this light. Look this way. Now look that way. Hold out your hand. Touch your nose with your forefinger. Can you stand? Good. Please walk five paces forward, turn and walk five paces back to me. Okay. That's good. I'm going to listen to your chest now. That seems to be okay. How are you feeling?"

"I'm okay. I am a little shook up and worried about my vehicle, but I'm okay. Nothing broken. Thank god for the airbag. I feel very tired now. I think this kind gentleman has offered to give me a lift home." As Emma turned towards Julian, a hint of recognition registered in the back of her mind.

"That's good. I can't find anything wrong but would suggest that you take it easy for the next few days. If you have someone who can come and look after you all the best. If you feel anything is wrong then please make sure you visit your local GP and give them this card which says that I saw you and details under what circumstances."

"Thank you. You are very kind." Emma held Julian's arm for support. Her legs trembled.

"I think the police will wait for the AA and take over the rest of those arrangements so would you like to go home immediately or would you like to go for a coffee or tea or even something stronger." Julian placed his hand on hers to reassure her. "Everything is under control."

"Oh, a coffee would be nice actually. I'd like to sit somewhere but I don't want to be alone. You are very kind. Thank you." Emma kept her hand on his arm as they crossed the road and entered the nearest coffee shop.

"What would you like?"

"I'd love a green tea, please. No sugar. Leave the teabag in. Thanks."

Julian made her comfortable in an easy chair near the window and went to order their drinks.

Emma sunk into the chair.

What a day. First the woman got shot, then this accident. What is happening?

"Thanks. The tea looks perfect. What are you having?"

"A double espresso cappuccino. I need the caffeine. I'm Julian by the way." He held out his hand.

"Wow. That's far too strong for me. The green tea revives and refreshes me. I'm Emma. Don't I know you from somewhere? You seem very familiar. Did I see you on the train earlier today?" Emma studied Julian.

"Maybe. I had an early meeting in London today, but it was cancelled due to unforeseen circumstances. I think I may have met you before, but I'm not exactly sure where." Julian concentrated on his drink. He made a well in the froth, and poured in the sachet of sugar.

"Okay. But I think you were on the Norwegian Cruise around the Western Mediterranean earlier this year weren't you? I remember meeting you a few times. Once at the sushi bar, then again on one of the excursions, and somewhere else, but I can't remember just now. Each time you said something, then disappeared. Wasn't that you?"

"I doubt it. I wish I could afford to go on a cruise. It sounds wonderful. I do have a face that everyone says seems familiar. It happens all the time. I get mistaken for so many different people. Once a woman mistook me for a former lover. She hounded me. I couldn't go out for days for fear she was watching me. And when I finally emerged, there she was. She followed me all over, and wouldn't believe who I was, until I showed her my driving license. Then she said I'd had a false one made to escape her. "

Emma smiled at his story. "What happened?"

"Well, finally her husband found out what was happening, and came to see me."

"Oh, wow, and—"

"It was a bit awkward, but I managed to convince him I wasn't her ex-lover, and he went away happy. I didn't hear from the woman again, but do sometimes wonder what happened to her." Julian sipped his drink, which left behind a frothy moustache.

Emma pointed. "You have something on your lip. That's an amusing story. So I guess I mistook you for someone else. Sorry. I promise I won't hound you. I would like to repay your kindness though. Would you like to go to dinner one evening? My treat." Emma warmed to Julian. His gentle nature made her feel safe and secure. Her shoulders relaxed as the tension flooded out of them. She smiled.

Julian's eyes sparkled in the light; his mouth twitched as a smile formed. "Yes I'd like that very much. Thank you. You don't need to, you know. I'm sure anyone would have done the same."

"But they didn't, and you did. I have a good feeling about you, Julian. Maybe fate made sure you were in the right place at the right time. Who knows? But I'm glad you were there for me." Emma squeezed his hand. "Thank you."

"Anytime, Emma. I would have done anything." Julian lowered his voice. "Come on let's get out of here. Let me take you home. You need a good rest after everything that's happened today."

Emma stared at him. "You mean the car crash right. Nothing else."

"Yes, the car crash. Why? Did something else happen?" Julian avoided her stare and tidied away the coffee cups and used napkins.

"Err yes, oh no. It's nothing. I went down to London today, and my meeting was cancelled so I had to come back. I guess I'm tired from the travelling, and am feeling stiff from the crash. Home sounds good. I'll direct you. It's down The Lane. Do you know it?"

"Yes. I know." Julian checked himself. "No, I don't know it. If you can direct me, that would be great. Thanks."

Chapter Thirty-four

The sun streamed in through the crack in the curtains, and as Julian woke, his face broke into a wide grin. He hugged himself, jumped out of bed, and laughed as he danced around the room, into the bathroom. Lightness filled his soul.

I can't believe I actually met her. She wants to take me to dinner.

He brushed his teeth, but gagged on the bitter taste of the antiseptic cream he had mistaken for toothpaste.

Pull yourself together. Seriously.

The sharp mouthwash cleaned his mouth, and he organised himself. His mind jumbled at the thought of her, and his nerves tingled. He leaned over the sink, and the cool water brought calm relief. Twinkling eyes, and a sparkling smile replaced the usual weary face that stared back at him from the mirror each morning.

Nothing could spoil today.

The letter box rattled as the postman delivered the mail; bills, junk mail, and the daily newspaper, with the headline spoiler of the day—*LOCAL WOMAN SHOT IN LONDON*—Luisa. His legs gave way, and he stumbled onto the kitchen stool. His head lolled into his hands. Luisa.

Why did you push so hard to find out? You didn't listen to me. I wanted to play it safe, but you wanted to find out what happened and now look what happened to you.

His coffee cup rattled as he slammed his fist down. Heaviness sat on his heart. He read the article, which didn't reveal much. The journalist's theory of the woman being in the way of a shot aimed at the unknown man of Arab origin who had reportedly met with her in the Italian Gardens seemed plausible. The police had no leads. He sent a small pray of thanks for that. No one had recognised him, or seen him remove the phone.

Oh, the phone. Let me look through the phone. Who was the last person she called?

He pulled out her phone, and tried a few different combinations for the lock code. Nothing.

What code would she use? Come on, Luisa. Tell me. I want to help you.

A moment of clarity, and he tapped in the date her brother died. Bingo. The phone sprung into life.

PING, PING, PING, text messages flooded in. Friends asking what happened; if she had had an accident like they had heard— He scrolled past them until he found a message from someone called Tariq.

<Naya told me you called her. It's too dangerous. I think I'm being followed. Do not meet me. If you know Emma McKenzie tell her not to meet me.>

What does that mean? Who is Tariq? Do I really need to get involved in this? He must have something to do with Naya. Who was the shot for? Emma or Luisa. Luisa had disguised herself to look like Emma so anyone looking through a scope from a distance at her back wouldn't be able to tell the difference. Was the shot for Emma? If so who and why?

He pushed the newspaper aside, and jumped up. He needed more intel, and he knew who could provide exactly the right information.

The laser show annoyed him. He strode through the red lines dancing all around the entrance to Sky High.

"Ben, Ben where are you?" The key-rings jumped in their display stand as he slammed the newspaper on the counter.

"Hello. What's wrong? What can I do for you? Is everything okay?" Ben emerged from the back holding a hot drink.

"Did you see the newspaper? Do you know who that was? The woman who was shot." A rush of questions tumbled out from Julian.

"Hang on. Slow down. What newspaper? No I haven't seen it today. Let me take a look." Ben picked up the newspaper, and read. "Hmm, okay, aha. Oh, that's interesting."

"What do you think? Did you know her?" Julian stabbed at her picture. "She worked with McKenzie. I know you're MI6. I know you're on to something."

"Well, you seem to know more than I do?" Ben raised his eyes from the newspaper. "Yes I am working for MI6. I can't reveal everything, but I can tell you that there are some dangerous people involved. Who are you working for, Julian? One or two masters? Isn't that a conflict of interest?"

Julian offered his hand to Ben. "Yes I do know things as a private investigator, as you know things being MI6. I think we are on similar trails don't you? I'll be honest with you. This is a long shot I'm taking, and I hope that I'll get something in return from you. The woman who was shot, worked with me on a project, but she had her own personal agenda. She was ex-Iraqi secret service, and was investigating the death of her brother, but I actually think the shot was meant for Mrs McKenzie.”

“Interesting theory, and very similar to mine. It’s an unusual situation, but I can work with you. It appears we’re on the same page. Obviously you’ve checked me, and you must know that I’ve checked you out. How did you meet Luisa, if you don’t mind me asking? Were you ever in the service?” Ben indicated for Julian to take a seat in the reception area at the side. He turned the sign on the door to ‘Closed.’ “No interruptions.”

“I used to be in the police force until I had health problems and was forced to take early retirement. I hire myself out now as a PI. Mostly adultery cases, you know. Men not trusting their wives, and vice versa. I take whatever comes my way, to be honest. That’s how I met Luisa. She contacted me to investigate some leads in the UK she had on her brother’s death and we, well, we ended up as lovers.” Julian sipped the hot tea Ben produced.

“I’m sorry she died like that. It’s a shame. Were you still lovers?”

“No. We ended it. Well, she ended it to avoid complications. What about you? What are you following?”

“Okay. I see. Well, I’m chasing a paper trail, err—”

“Oh, you mean the painting shipment?”

“Yes. What do you know about that?”

“Not much.” Julian concentrated on his tea. He didn’t want to give too much away just yet. He wanted to let Ben talk.

"Well, I know there was a microchip painted into one of the paintings. The Picasso I suspect as that is the painting McKenzie, Andrew McKenzie, that is, added to the shipment when he took over the arrangements. I need to see the paperwork to prove it but that's at Mrs McKenzie's house. I've bugged out the house—"

"I know. I was on surveillance when you did that. Look, I have photographs to prove it. I guess they would come in handy if ever—" Julian pulled up the photos on his iPad. "They are backed up."

"Julian. If we're going to work together on this, then we need to trust each other. You are right, the photographs would prove that I bugged the house in a covert operation, but how would you explain you being there, taking photographs of a woman in her house. Another covert operation."

"Yes, we need to trust each other. I won't use those photographs, but I do have detailed photos of the paperwork, if that's of help. The photos are high res and show all the documents clearly. Six paintings were sent in the shipment. She only has gallery receipts for five paintings."

"We need that paperwork. Photos aren't good enough. Any ideas how we can get to it without breaking and entering? You seem to know her quite well. How long have you been following her?" Ben returned the iPad.

"About six months, maybe longer. In fact, she had a car accident yesterday, right after the shooting. I was there, and kind of rescued her. I pulled her out of the car from behind the airbag. She wants to take me to dinner so she can say thanks. I'm hoping to win her trust, and then maybe I can get the paperwork. It will take some time though. Do you have that?"

"Nice one." Ben high-fived Julian. "Smart move. I think it would be very good for you to get closer to her. I think she is in danger. She may know more than she realises, and I know there are others after the shipment paperwork for what it proves, and the provenance for the Monet. I believe she is holding the Monet for Smithfield's son."

"Yes she is. What's the story on the Monet then? I've seen it in her house, and know Smithfield gave it to her before she left but that's all."

"It proves that McKenzie purchased it, and gave it as a deed of gift to Smithfield senior. I don't think the son has anything to do with things. Smithfield senior sold the microchip to McKenzie, and McKenzie purchased the Monet as a way of a payment for him, but what is more important is who McKenzie passed on the microchip to, and what did he get in return? That's the trail I'm following."

"And that brings us back to Luisa. The woman who died. She believed her brother was assassinated in Iraq, and this had something to do with the microchip. She followed the trail to London. Emma, err, Mrs McKenzie, met with an Arab man, maybe an Iraqi, called Tariq, to find out more about the painting shipment. I think she is innocent in this, and just wanted to rectify an anomaly on the art shipment. Luisa knew Tariq handled the painting shipment, and also wanted to find out more about the extra painting, but I doubt if she knew about the microchip. She would have told me. I'm sure of that. Her brother and Naya,

Princess Naya, were lovers. The Princess had arranged the shipment from Emma's gallery." Julian pushed his hand through his hair, stood and paced the floor. "I believe Emma is in danger, and the sooner I can retrieve the paperwork the better. She doesn't deserve this at all. She is kind, sweet, loving, and generous." He returned to his seat.

"You sound like you have quite a thing for her. Be careful. Don't mix business with pleasure in this game. Remember what happens to the Bond girls. Good luck my friend." Ben stood, and walked over to the window. "Anything else?"

"Smithfield asked me to observe McKenzie, and I subcontracted that job out to Luisa. She worked the honeypot routine very well. She provided a mine of information, and I think she fell in love with him. I don't suspect him in her death at all, although who knows what he would do, if he thought she had found out too much, and the net was closing in. Last month, Smithfield put the heat on me. He wanted to move things to the next level, and push McKenzie for information. I asked Luisa to do the same, and look what happened to her." Julian's head rested in his hands. His shoulders sunk under the weight of her death.

Ben placed his hand on Julian's shoulder. "Come on mate. It's not your fault. If she was secret service then she understood that consequences of the work she was in, and the game she played. It's part of the training. Even if you say she was ex, you never really leave. It stays with you. Obviously, you cared for her as well. I'm sure she would be proud to know that you're continuing what you started together, but it's hard I know. I've been there. Don't mix business with pleasure. Ever."

"It's comforting but it's going to take me some time to come to terms with what happened. How do you do it?"

"Time. It's the nature of the job. You never forget but it gets easier, especially if you catch the bad guys. So let's work together on that." Ben pulled Julian up from the chair, and slapped him on his back. "Come on; time to get back to work. Let's work out what else we know, and you can concentrate on your new lady friend to see what she knows. That's something to look forward to."

Julian grinned. "Yes that is very much something to look forward to. Where do you want to start?"

Ben pressed a button transforming the reception area in to a full surveillance, and incident room with flip charts, monitors, photographs, documenting the characters involved, and everything he knew so far. Julian patted himself the back. He had come to the right place. His confidence rose as the light at the end of the tunnel began to shine.

Chapter Thirty-five

"Mr McKenzie, two gentlemen from CID are here to see you."

Andrew's eyes widened, his heart raced. "Send them in, and organise refreshments." He stood to greet the police. "Good morning. This is an unexpected visit. What can I do for you?"

They shook his hand in turn. The younger stood back letting the older take the lead. "I'm DI Smith, and that is DI Jones. Do you know a Ms Luisa Fakre?"

"Maybe. I know lots of people. Some only on a first name basis. I do have an employee here called Luisa, but I understand she is taking a few vacation days at the moment. I can check when she is due to return. To be honest, I'm not sure what her surname is." He pressed the intercom. "Susie."

The police cancelled the intercom button. "Wait a moment, please."

Andrew raised his eyebrows. "Oh. Is something wrong?"

The intercom buzzed. "Did you want something, Mr. McKenzie? The refreshments will be here shortly. "The detective shook his head. Andrew buzzed back. "No everything is fine, and I don't need the refreshments after all."

Smith motioned to Jones, who pulled a series of photos from an envelope, and spread them on the desk. "I'm sorry, but we have reason to believe that the Luisa who works here is the same Luisa Fakre who suffered a fatal shot to the head last Wednesday. Do you recognise the person in the photograph as being your employee?"

The colour drained from Andrews face. He stumbled back into his chair, and gasped for air as a piercing pain stabbed his heart. "Yes. That's her. What, what happened?" He loosened his tie, as beads of sweat appeared on his forehead.

"Are you okay, sir? Here's a glass of water. Do you need any medication? We know this came as a shock to you. We had to confirm who she was. She doesn't appear to have any relatives in the UK. We can give you a moment if you need it, but we would like to ask you some more questions before we go, sir."

Andrew lifted his head from his hands, and composed himself under the detectives' calm authority. "No. I don't need anything. Thanks for the water. It was a shock seeing her like that. She worked on special projects for me, mainly in Mergers and Acquisitions. I don't know much about her but we probably have a Personnel file on her. References, that kind of thing. You're welcome to take a look."

"Yes, that would be helpful. As far as we know, she was in the wrong place at the wrong time. Witnesses said she had met a Middle Eastern looking man, who ran off after the incident. We are analysing the CCTV from the station, and other buildings but to be honest it is not promising. We know she worked for the Iraqi Secret Service, but left Iraq around 18 months ago, after her brother was assassinated. It is not clear if she was still on active duty but working over here, maybe as a honeypot or she was trying to make a fresh start. Any information you can provide on her will be useful at this point."

A cold shiver ran down Andrew's back. He swallowed to keep his composure, and clasped his hands in front of him, to prevent any giveaway signs. He knew the police had expert training in reading body language. His mind sharpened. He needed to play this straight as the employer, without giving anything away.

"Honeypot?"

"Where a female agent traps a male suspect using sex. Did you have an intimate relationship with the deceased woman?"

Colour rushed back to Andrew's face. "Me? Not at all. That would be totally unethical. I am the owner of this business. I would never take advantage of any of my employees, however beautiful they were." A sigh escaped Andrew.

"The file if we may, sir?"

"Of course. Susie, please bring in Luisa Fakre's personnel file. "

Susie entered. "It appears to be missing. I was looking for it last week when Ms Fakre applied for her vacation days, but I'm unable to locate it. We keep all the files in one place. It's not there. I've been through every section to make sure it wasn't misfiled when we had the temp covering my assistant's leave. It's nowhere to be found."

"Have you looked everywhere?"

"Yes I have, Mr McKenzie. I assure you it's nowhere to be found. May I ask why you need it?"

"The police have informed me that Ms Fakre was shot last week. Can you send an email around to all personnel, please? We will close business tomorrow as a mark of respect for your colleague. Thank you."

Susie gasped and blinked back tears. "She was always so lovely. In fact I'd only just got to know her. I, I'll send the email."

DI Smith closed the door behind Susie. "That's rather unfortunate or maybe too convenient? Can you think if Ms Fakre had any close friends here or did she have any enemies that you know of?"

"I barely knew her. I have no idea. It's unfortunate about the file. I'll ask Susie to look again, and we can find out who temped here. Anything to assist. I'll let you know."

"Well, thank you. It's always good for to us receive help from members of the public. We may need to return to interview other members of your staff, but it may be best to allow them time to get over the shock of what happened to their colleague. Thank you again for your time this morning, Mr McKenzie." DI Smith shook Andrew's hand whilst DI Jones collected the photos. Andrew closed the door behind them and sunk back into his chair.

"Hold my calls, Susie, and cancel anything else scheduled for this morning."

He reached for the whisky and poured until the amber liquid reached the top of the tumbler. No time for short measures. His lips and throat stung as he drank. His stomach burned and retched in protest. He drained the glass and poured again.

What happened? How can she be gone? Just like that. She was here last week and now I'll never see her again. Did I do this? Am I responsible? Please no. Not Luisa. Anyone but Luisa.

His head hung heavy on his shoulders. A sigh escaped and tears rolled down his face. He reached into his briefcase and pulled out a photo of her; full of life and joy. He stroked her face, kissed the photo, then held it to his heart, and closed his eyes. He wanted to feel her life force.

This must be a mistake. This could not be Luisa. Not my beautiful, beautiful Luisa.

He realised he loved her; more than anyone he had ever loved. His cheeks coloured as he thought—even more than Emma. He needed someone to hold him but he had no-one.

Luisa always made things better for him. She would know what to do.

He reached for his phone and pressed her number before he caught himself. Emptiness grew in the room. He could not escape. His head pounded. He closed his eyes in an attempt to dull the growing pain in his heart.

"Mr McKenzie. Mr McKenzie. Wake up." A light touch on his shoulder woke him.

"Susie. What's wrong? What happened? Oh." His hands ran over his face as he remembered. A sharp pain increased behind his eyes. "Tell me I'm dreaming. Tell me it isn't true." Susie's face told him otherwise.

"I brought you a strong black coffee, Mr McKenzie, and a ham and cheese Panini. You should eat and drink something. You'll feel better. I've sent the memo to the staff, but to be honest, everyone is in shock. HR wants to know if we can close for the rest of the day and tomorrow. No one can concentrate on any work today."

"Err, Yes. Please do that. Send the phones to the messaging service. They can handle today and tomorrow. I understand, and Susie, thanks. I appreciate it. I really do."

Susie squeezed his arm. "It's okay. I realise how much she meant to you. She was a beautiful woman and kind." The hot drink and food eased the pain behind Andrew's eyes. The cool water rinsed away the salty trails down his face. He composed himself. He had a phone call to make.

"What happened? You were only supposed to scare her away. Not kill her. My god."

"It wasn't us. We only do what is asked. We had planned to throw a brick like we did with the other lady, to scare her off. We were waiting for the right time."

"Oh, so maybe she was in the wrong place at the wrong time as the police think."

"What did you tell the police?"

"Nothing of course. I'm not so stupid. We will talk." Andrew hung up. His desk toys jumped as he slammed his fist into the table.

What now? Business as usual. I don't know what to think. Was she really in the wrong place at the wrong time? If she was Iraqi Secret Service, like the police think, then the net is closing. She hadn't mentioned a brother being assassinated, maybe she was chasing that trail, but why was she so interested in the painting shipment, unless her brother had something to do with the painting when it reached Paris and that's what got him killed. Was he the acceptor?

Andrew drew a thick black line across his desk calendar. Business as usual. He intended to let sleeping dogs lie for as long as possible.

Chapter Thirty-six

"Hey, I'm so glad you could make it." Emma kissed Julian on both cheeks and a shiver of excitement ran down her back. She smiled. "Come on. I reserved my favourite table. Luigi will look after us tonight." She grabbed his hand and pulled him into the restaurant.

"Hi Luigi. This is my hero. He saved me when my car crashed. You remember I told you him."

"Oh yes, Madam Emma. He is a hero. I have special treat for you tonight. You sit down, and Dani will bring the menu." Luigi turned to Julian. "She is my special friend you know. I love her. You are lucky, Mister Hero. Enjoy tonight."

Julian's grin widened. "I know. She is lovely. I absolutely intend to enjoy tonight." He winked at Luigi, who clapped as he waddled back to his kitchen.

Emma turned. "Come on. You look like you are making friends already. Luigi is wonderful. He always looks after me so well. Come, sit and let's choose something to eat. I'm starving and the kitchen smells wonderful already."

They sat at the table in the nook, by the picture window overlooking the river, and the town lights. Dani passed by with the menus and lit the table candle. "Can I get you something to drink? Emma, I know exactly what you'd like. Your usual bottle of Prosecco? And you, sir?"

"Actually, Dani, I'm going to have a G & T as an aperitif. What about you, Julian?"

"That sounds great, and yes we will have a bottle of Prosecco. Thanks."

"Are you okay? You look as if you are deep in thought?" Emma held her palm out for Julian. "It is so nice to see you again. I've thought about you a lot over the last few days. I felt a real connection with you after we had the coffee, and you drove me home after the accident. That was so sweet of you."

Julian took Emma's hand, and his thumb stroked her knuckles. "It was no trouble at all. In fact, it was an absolute pleasure. It's been a long time since I've had the company of such a beautiful woman. What happened with your car? Did you get it back?"

"Thanks for the compliment." Heat rose in Emma's face, and happiness flooded over her. "My insurance provides a courtesy car whilst mine is being repaired. Thankfully. I haven't taken public transport in years to be honest, not until last week." She swallowed. "I went to London to meet with a business colleague but saw a woman being shot instead. I think she met with my business colleague but he ran off before I met with him. I felt the bullet whizz past my ear, saw the woman collapse and the man ran off. It was awful. I thought I saw a guy with a rifle, what are they called? I'm not sure though as I took cover in the station. Sorry for off-loading all this on you as soon as we met. It's being preying on my mind. I'm not sure if I should go to the police, but I don't really know anything at all. I'm sure they've caught someone by now."

"Oh that's terrible." Julian took both her hands and squeezed them. "I read about that in the news. I think the article said the police didn't have much to go on; the woman was wearing a disguise and was originally from Iraq. It said she was in the wrong place at the wrong time. I thought she was so beautiful. Luisa." A heavy sigh escaped. He composed himself as Emma's eyes pierced into him.

"How do you know her name? I don't think it was in the newspaper article. I would've remembered it. Especially as I know who she was." She removed her hands from his and played with the beer mat. Dani delivered the drinks to the table, and took their dinner orders.

"Oh well, I, err, it was in the article. At the end." A crimson heat crept up Julian's neck finding its home on his cheeks. "I remember names and faces very well."

"Okay. I guess it was. Do you know who she was?"

Julian caught his response, as he realised the rhetorical nature of the question. "No, who was she?"

"The bitch was doing my husband. I walked in on them about ten months ago. It was awful. She looked like a porn queen, if you know what I mean. I don't blame her though; I blame my ex-husband. I divorced him. I can't stand liars and cheats. There's nothing worse. Don't you think?"

Julian crossed his fingers as he lied. "I agree. Cheats and liars always get caught out, Emma."

"Thanks. You are a good man. I can feel it. I think we'll be good friends." She leaned over the table, and hooked her finger under his chin, lifting his face, until his gaze met hers. "I don't think, I know we will. Maybe even more. I feel a connection between us. Do you feel it? You seem so familiar, as if I've known you all my life. Quite incredible." Julian reached for his drink, but shaky hands threatened to spill it. Emma placed her hand on his hand, and returned the drink to the table. "You seem nervous. What's wrong?"

"Nothing. As I said it's a long time since I've had a date with such a beautiful woman. I'm a little nervous. I usually mess up dates, so I stay away. Women usually don't go on second dates. That's when the excuses come out. I've heard them all from; a dog dying, and I saw her walking the same dead dog the next day in the park, to buses being hijacked in this quiet town, I don't think so, to the plain old 'I'm washing my hair.' At least I know where I am with that one. I don't know what it is, ever since my ex-wife left me for Adonis from the gym, oh sorry, I'm sure he is very intelligent, in his pants, certainly not in his head. Anyway they are still together, and I suspect I'm about to pay for more steroids for him or botox for her. Sorry to bore you with my tales of woe."

"Is this a date?"

"Do you want it to be?"

"Yes. I'd like that, and I'd like a second date with you, Julian. I won't make excuses about washing my hair or burying my dog." She laughed.

Julian exhaled.

Dani arrived with their food orders. "Thank you. This smells delicious. Give my thanks to Luigi. He always treats me so well."

"I will, Emma. Enjoy your food."

Emma swirled the pasta around her fork. She breathed in the aroma of garlic and fresh herbs. "I love Italian food. I went on a cruise earlier in the year, in fact just after my divorce, and the food was divine. I told you before, I thought I recognised you from the cruise. Are you sure you didn't go?"

"It wasn't me. Remember I told you that I often get mistaken for others. I have a familiar looking face. The food is very good. I haven't eaten here before, to be honest, but I think it may become one of my favourites, especially now you've introduced me to Luigi." Julian concentrated on his food, avoiding eye contact with Emma. Two lies in two conversations. "How do you feel now, after the crash? Did you have any whip-lash or other injuries? Sometimes injuries like that are hidden, and they take a while to appear. What about stress? PTSS is often delayed. Those dogs are a real nuisance, running out like that."

"I think I'm okay. My GP prescribed some sleeping tablets for me, nothing too strong but they seem to do the trick. You always feel better after a good night's sleep. Actually, it was only partly the dog's fault. My mind was on the woman who was shot. I had been thinking about her car. I'd seen it parked on Bayswater Road, and it was on my mind. I just don't know what she was doing there. I think my ex-husband purchased the car for her, although I don't have any proof. I know they were together for quite some time, as I found a hotel receipt for a trip to Paris last July. It's my dream car actually, so I was envious that he would purchase such a car for her and not me. But I can't dwell on that too much. I need to move on. I have found out a lot of interesting things about my husband recently, and I'm beginning to wonder if I really knew him at all."

"Such as?" Julian prompted, returning his fork to his plate.

"Well, he also purchased an expensive painting, an original Monet, but gave it away as a deed of gift to someone I thought was a business acquaintance, who I thought he despised, but it seems there was more to that relationship than I realised."

"Oh?"

"Yes. Do you know Bryan Smithfield? Well, Andrew, that's my ex-husband, gave him the painting, although it's in my care now. A long story, I won't bore you with the details, but Smithfield's son moved to New York with his work, and entrusted the painting to me, with all the paperwork, and a note authorising me to safe-keep the painting."

"I see. Are you still in contact with Smithfield's son? John, isn't it?" Julian pushed the food around his plate.

"No. I'm not. We agreed not to contact each other. Neither of us wanted to pursue a long distance relationship. It just gets too messy to be honest. I'm grateful to him for bringing me back to the living world, after twenty years of marriage. He was a wonderful tonic for my soul but no, I'm not in contact with him anymore. I guess if he returns to the UK, he will find me and reclaim the Monet. Aren't you eating? The food is delicious."

"Yes. I find pasta quite filling. It is very tasty. I wonder if I can take the rest home with me. I'll have it for lunch tomorrow. It will make a change from the M&S ready meals." He released nervous laughter. Julian arranged his cutlery in the middle of his plate, and signalled for Dani to come over. "Dani, Is it possible for me to take the rest of this home with me?"

"Of course. The portions are generous, even for big men. I'll package it up for you."

Julian reached out for Emma's hand. "Everything's going to be okay you know. It will all work itself out. Don't stress about your husband, if you're not with him. He isn't worth it, you do know that don't you?"

Emma laughed. "Yes I know. I decided that when I divorced him. If he can blatantly have sex with a woman in our family home, then it shows he has no respect for me at all. You, on the other hand, I like you a lot. Is it too forward of me to ask you on another date? I never used to be like this. I feel like I've rediscovered myself, and my confidence." A warm glow of happiness emanated from Emma as she smiled at Julian.

"Wow. Yes. I'd love that. You are a beautiful woman, Emma. I can't believe my luck. I must have been in the right place at the right time. Tomorrow evening? There is a wine tasting at The Museum. Would you like to go along to that?"

"That would be wonderful. I love wine, and I love The Museum. The last time I was there, I must admit I ended up distracted, and didn't get to see any of the exhibits."

"Great. Shall I pick you up around 5.30 p.m. then, or is that too early? The wine tasting starts at 6 p.m. and I don't like to be late."

"Perfect. Let's order dessert. I bet you have room for Chocolate Fondant. It's heaven." Emma filled their glasses with the last of the Prosecco, and raised hers. Julian followed her lead. "Here's to us, and new beginnings."

"To us."

Chapter Thirty-seven

The small clouds chased each other against the brilliant blue sky. Julian pulled his scarf around his neck, fastened the top button on his overcoat, and tucked his hands deep into his pockets. His face stung as the wind whipped mercilessly across The Green. On any other day, the reflection on the building would fill him with awe, but today, he couldn't bear to look. His stomach churned and his teeth ground, as he contemplated what he'd come to do. The right thing, but the right thing filled him with trepidation. He knew his employer could be ruthless and unforgiving.

Each strike of the church clock brought him one second nearer. Eleven. Time to go. He entered the building, looked around, and pinched himself.

She is no longer here. She is no longer anywhere.

He wiped a sole tear from the corner of his eye. Not a time for emotions. He needed all his wits about him. In the lift, he stood in a superman pose; legs apart, arms akimbo. He'd read, that standing like that for two minutes, opened up a channel of confidence. He needed that.

Susie buzzed into her intercom, "Mr McKenzie, Mr Cunningham is here for his eleven a.m. meeting with you."

Julian raised his eyebrows as he heard the growled reply. "Oh I'd forgotten about that. Better send him in."

"Good morning, Mr McKenzie. How are you? Please accept my condolences for the loss of your employee, Ms Fakre. I understand from the newspaper report she was an asset to the company."

Andrew stood to greet him. "Thank you. She was. It's a great loss of such beauty."

"Yes, she was." Julian exhaled.

"You sound like you knew her. Did you?"

"Well, a little. I'd encountered her in the lobby a few times, when I'd had meetings here with you, and of course her photograph, in the newspaper." Julian sat in the chair opposite Andrew, and took a deep breath, "Mr McKenzie, unfortunately I can no longer work on the project for you." He exhaled, and relaxed. He had said it.

"Excuse me. What did you say? It isn't your decision to make. It's my decision to terminate your contract."

"I have a conflict of interest, which prevents me continuing with the work. I'm sorry. Certain information has come to light, which I am not at liberty to divulge, but suffice to say, I need to terminate this contract. I believe there is a termination clause for both parties in our contract." Julian raised his eyes, and met Andrew's stare.

"I don't care. I need information on her movements. I don't understand what would be a conflict of interest for you. You work for me, and nothing should be more important than that. You understand, don't you? I can make it worth your while. You know that, don't you?" The papers on the table flew as Andrew slammed his fist down.

"I understand, however I am unable to continue working on the project. I do have some integrity you know. I appreciate the work that you have given me over the past months but I have to terminate. To be honest, I don't think Mrs McKenzie is aware of anything and isn't seeing anyone at the moment." Julian concentrated on retrieving papers from his briefcase, as his cheeks coloured. "Here is the last report on her activities. Nothing much. She went to London on a shopping expedition, and on her return had a small car accident. She wasn't hurt, but the car sustained some damage. The insurance dealt with it, as far as I could ascertain. She's driving a courtesy car, until her car is returned." A half smile crossed Julian's face, as he calculated the reaction to his news.

"An accident. Is she okay? Why didn't she tell me? Oh my. I'll need to call her to make sure she is okay." Andrew picked up the phone, and dialled her number but hung up. "I'll do that later. If you insist, I will accept your termination, but do not ever step foot in this office or building again. I never want to see your weasel face, or hear your rat's voice again. Do you understand? Now get out of my sight." He pointed at the door. "Get out, before I call security."

Julian scurried to the door, and disappeared into the lift. As he leaned against the mirrored walls, relief flooded over him along with a sense of freedom. As he exited to the street, he turned towards the building. The clouds darkened, and the building loomed larger than before. Foreboding replaced relief and freedom. He knew McKenzie liked to get his own way, and put those who crossed him in their place. McKenzie liked to be the boss, always in control. A shiver ran down his back, accompanied by a big splash of water as the rain started. He ran to his car.

Andrew closed the door behind Julian. He sat at his desk, head in hands, contemplating his next move.

What am I going to do about the PI? He knows too much. His reaction to Luisa's death was strange. He knew more about her than he let on, I'm sure. Oh Emma.

He dialled her number.

"Hello, Emma here. How can I help you?

"Hi Emma. I heard that you had a car accident last week, and I wanted to know if you are okay. Is there anything I can do? Why didn't you call me about it?" Andrew swung around on his chair.

"Andrew. Oh well. Yes I'm fine. I no longer need your help. Remember we are divorced, and I can, believe it or not, look after myself."

"Well, yes I know that, but I want to help you. How are you doing? Do you want me to come over, and give you a back rub like the old days?" He rubbed his hands together at the thought. He knew where it would lead, and what he needed to release the week's tension and frustration.

"Andrew. We are divorced. Stop it, please; otherwise I'll get a restraining order. Please don't call me from unknown numbers. Have some respect for my privacy."

He sat upright and stopped his chair spinning. "I do have respect for you. I have so much respect, if you would only let me show you. Please."

"No. You know I don't want to have sex with you. Ever. Again."

"Please baby. You know you miss me, like I miss you." His fingers drummed on the desk. "Please."

"Andrew. No. I am seeing someone else now. In fact, I have a date tonight so please leave me alone. I don't want to hear from you again. Goodbye."

His phone knocked over the floral arrangement, as it landed on the coffee table. Water gushed onto the floor. Andrew dashed to retrieve his phone. "Susie. Come and clean up this mess, and get me a new phone. This one is ruined."

###################

Andrew scanned the local listings, for events he thought Emma would be interested in attending. He knew her tastes, and from the reports the PI had been giving him, he had a good idea of where she went on dates; although the Laser Tag date struck him as being a little out of character. Wine tasting at The Museum. He would start there, and then trawl her favourite restaurants. He intended to find out who she was seeing. The PI had told him she didn't have any love interest, so someone was not telling the truth.

He sat in his car, across the street from The Museum. People smiled and laughed, as they entered. The wine tasting had been organised to promote a new wine shop in town, and judging by the crowds, looked to be a success. He wriggled down further into the seat, as Emma and her date approached. His eyes widened as he recognised who accompanied her. Julian Cunningham. The private investigator.

The liar. That's why he resigned. That's the conflict of interest. No wonder he was so adamant about the resignation.

A smile flitted across Andrew's face, as he planned his next move. No one got the better of him. Ever. Especially not a cheap PI.

Chapter Thirty-eight

"I am looking forward to this. Two things I love. Wine and Art. Thank you for inviting me." Emma turned to Julian, hooked her arm in his. A warm shiver ran through her as her lips touched his rough cheek. She swallowed. "I feel very safe and secure with you."

"The pleasure's all mine, you know. As I said, it's rare that I go on dates with women, so I should be thanking you for not washing your hair tonight, or walking your dog." Julian moved into single file, guiding her through the crowd on the steps of The Museum. "I have advanced tickets so we can bypass the queue, and go straight to the tasting."

"Okay. Any preference with what we start with? Red, white, or rose? New World or Traditional?"

"No. You choose."

"Okay, let's go New World Rose. Come on." Emma pulled him with her to the table with Australian wines. "Two Roses please. Thanks." She handed a glass to Julian, winked, and laughed. "You do realise we both need to spit rather than swallow, don't you?"

A slight heat rose on Julian's face as he grinned back. "Yes I realise. Sorry, maybe this wasn't the best date to bring you on."

"No. It's perfect. It's always good to see someone in a potentially uncomfortable position, such as trying to spit in a macho or ladylike way. I find it quite amusing really." Emma spat into the bucket. "That is very nice wine. I'm not one to talk about the scent of roses or virgins on a beach, and the rest of the Oz

Clarke flowery language. All I know is that I like the wine. I'm going to try the next one. Would you like some?"

Julian followed her lead and spat. "Yes. I know what you mean. What was the woman who used to work with Oz, Jilly something? She was always so flamboyant with her descriptions of wine. I never really got it. I don't want to drink wine that tastes of autumn leaves."

"Oh, you mean Jilly Goolden from BBC's Food and Drink. Yes, they were hilarious together weren't they? Ooh, this wine is lovely also. I think I prefer the first one though. What do you think?"

Julian took a swig of wine, swirled it around in his mouth, and spat. "I agree actually. This is too sweet. I prefer a drier wine. Let's try a couple of traditional Reds now. Come on." They found the Italian Reds. "Chianti Classico with a Sangiovese grape. My favourite to be honest. Baron de Barolo."

Emma swirled, and spat. "Yes. This is very smooth. Nice. Have you ever been to Tuscany?"

"Yes. It's beautiful. I went a few years ago on a wine tasting tour. It was fantastic. I'd like to go back though. Maybe we can go there together one day." Julian squeezed Emma's hand. "Would you like that?"

She turned her face towards his. "Mmm. Maybe. Let's see what happens." The hustling crowd pushed her into him, and the warm sensation returned. She liked this man. "Do you want to view the exhibits? It's getting pretty crowded here."

"Great idea. Aren't you an art expert? You can teach me. I have to confess I know a little about wine but not so much about art."

"Yes. Come on. This way to the Impressionists." Emma led the way into the heart of The Museum. "Through this door." She suppressed a giggle as she remembered the last time she had walked through the door. She held her breath in awe. She loved the Impressionists. She pulled Julian onto the bench in the centre of the room and placed her finger on his lips. "Shush. Look and absorb the beauty of the art work. I can't teach you, but if you open your eyes, and your mind then you'll feel it and understand."

"It's amazing. I never realised how paintings could draw you in before. You can almost hear the sounds and feel the scenes in front of you."

His shoulder rubbed against hers. Warmth flooded over her and her groin stirred. "You see. You don't need me to teach you. I'm pleased there is more interest in the wine than the art, otherwise we wouldn't be able to savour this moment." She turned towards him and kissed his cheek. Her eyes turned to the floor as she pulled away.

"Gosh. That was so forward of me. I do apologise."

Julian turned her head back. "Not at all. I've been thinking about kissing you all day. Can I kiss you properly please?"

Emma nodded and her lips found his. Her tongue explored his mouth, and set off an explosion of lust throughout her body.

"Wow. That's amazing. Thank you."

She pulled away and laughed. "Why are you thanking me?"

He swallowed, and whispered, "For that amazing kiss. I haven't been kissed like that in a long time. Come here." He lifted her chin towards him and kissed her again. "Emma."

"Yes."

"I don't want to move too fast if you know what I mean. I want to take my time to get to know you properly. I guess I'm a little old fashioned, but I see a lot of relationships today that start off in the bedroom, and end up in the courtroom. I'm not saying I want to get married or anything but you know what I mean. I like to get to know a woman; who she is, her hopes and dreams before moving on to anything else." His finger outlined the squares of wood on the bench.

"I understand. I couldn't resist. I guess it was the moment. I'm sorry if I acted too forward."

"No, don't be. I'm glad you did, and I meant what I said. I wanted you to know my feelings from the beginning. I like you very much, Emma and would love to have a relationship with you. A real relationship based on us getting to know each other first though. I hope you feel the same." His eyes met hers.

"I do, very much so." She whispered into his ear. "Thank you." She held his hand, and her thumb stroked his fingers. "It's refreshing to be honest, and I'd love to get to know you properly."

"Would you like to go for dinner at Luigis, again? I took the liberty of reserving a table there for 8.30pm, and it's 8.15 p.m. now. I think he'll appreciate a bottle of the Chianti Reservo from Barolo. What do you think?"

"He will love it, and I'd love to have dinner with you, Julian." Emma jumped up. "Come on. Let's get out of here, and get to know each other a bit better, over that bottle of Chianti. I'm sure Luigi will have a few tales of the old days in Italy to entertain us with as well."

Chapter Thirty-nine

"Hello. Is that Mrs McKenzie?"

"Yes. Who is this?"

"Francesca. I work for Mr McKenzie. I'd like to meet you if possible, to talk about a few things."

Emma frowned. "Well, I don't have anything to do with the business, so I don't know how I can help you."

"It isn't about work. It's about something else. Can you meet me for lunch tomorrow please? At Cafe Rouge on The Esplanade, noon. Please."

"Well, I guess, but this a mystery. I don't know who you are or what I can help you with, but I'll see you there." The phone clicked in Emma's ear. She didn't recognise the number displayed. She didn't know anyone called Francesca, but there had been something in the woman's voice that had intrigued her. Desperation, maybe. She couldn't put her finger on it, but all would be revealed the next. She returned to her paperwork for the Art School, accompanied with a glass of cool water and an aspirin to dull the mild hangover.

She smiled, as her mind wandered onto thoughts of Julian, the museum and then the fun dinner they'd had at Luigis.

Such a great guy. Funny. Generous and sexy in an unknowing way.

The shrill ring of her phone interrupted her thoughts again. Beth. "Hey girl. How's things? I haven't seen you in forever. How is it going with the new man? What's his name, Julian? Very posh."

"Hi. Sorry. I've been busy. You know beginning of the new term is always a nightmare for me at the Art School. Julian isn't posh as you say. He's a great guy though. You'll have to meet him one of these days. How's Tony? Still working out, and working on you?"

"Yeah. He is great. I'd love to meet Julian."

Emma abandoned her paperwork, grabbed a glass of Chianti and chatted on the phone until her eyes closed, and Beth's voice turned into a distant murmur.

She woke with a start. "Emma, Emma, are you still there? Don't tell me you fell asleep on me. Typical. Go to bed, woman."

"Oh gosh, I did. I'm sorry. Good night. See you soon."

####################

Emma arrived at Cafe Rouge at 11.30 a.m., so she could pick out a good viewing point for the customers entering the busy cafe. She ordered a cappuccino, and found a table near the picture window facing on to The Esplanade. She scooped out the froth, and savoured the hot liquid. A hand on her shoulder made her jump, and turn to see who it belonged to. She recognised the woman as the woman she met at The Spa. "Oh it's you."

"Yes. Hello. I'm Francesca. We met briefly at The Spa but I had to leave suddenly. I'm sorry about that. I was so rude to you, actually. I do hope you forgive me. May I?" Francesca pointed to the chair next to Emma.

"Yes. Of course and of course I forgive you for The Spa. It was a little strange but I'd gone there to be alone, and didn't really need any company, to be honest. It wasn't a problem. Did you order a drink or lunch?" Emma offered the menu.

"No. It's okay. I'm not hungry. I ordered a Latte. They will bring it over."

"You said you wanted to talk to me?"

"Yes. I work for Mr McKenzie in Marketing and PR but sometimes he gets me to do, what he calls, special projects."

Emma's stomach sank. She hoped this was not going to be a confession from a jilted lover. "Special projects?"

Francesca's Latte arrived; she took a sip before continuing. "Yes. One special project was to follow you at The Charity Event. I deliberately bumped into you, and made you spill the contents of your handbag. Do you remember?"

Emma stopped swirling her coffee. "Yes I remember. You helped me collect everything from the floor."

"Well, I added something to the contents. Something like a USB device. I don't know exactly what it was, maybe something to track you or record. Mr McKenzie forced me to do it. I'm sorry."

"Oh. I don't know what to say. I did find something and took it to the guy in that Spy High shop a little further down from here, but he said it was just a USB with movies and music. In fact I still have it somewhere. I thought it belonged to my son but he didn't recognise it or any of the movies on it. That's so strange isn't it?"

Francesca paled. "You know the Spy High store closed down a few weeks ago? They suddenly packed everything up and moved out. Mr McKenzie leased the store to them, and sent me down to find out why they hadn't paid their rent. He wasn't happy at all about that. Have you any idea what is going on, Mrs McKenzie?"

"Oh please call me Emma. No I don't. Tell me, how did my ex-husband force you to plant the device on me?" Emma tapped the side of her coffee cup with the spoon.

"I am from Italy originally and am in the UK on a European working visa. He threatened to speak to the authorities to revoke it and deport me back to Italy. My life would be in danger. My brothers are in the Mafiosa, and they helped me to get here so I would be safe. The people over there are very dangerous. I think Mr McKenzie found this out, and he used this against me when he asked me to do these special projects for him." Francesca twisted her napkin into knots. Her latte shook as she took a sip.

"I can't believe what I'm hearing. How could he do something like that? I'm so sorry." She reached out and held Francesca's hand.

"That isn't everything, Emma. I felt guilty over what I did, and Susie, his secretary—"

"Yes, I know Susie. She is wonderful. What about Susie?" Emma sipped her drink.

"Susie told me that you were always so kind to everyone in the office when you were married to Mr McKenzie. She said you didn't deserve this. She asked me to tell you these things as she couldn't. She said Mr McKenzie hired a private investigator to follow you, and report back on your movements, and who you were seeing. She said the PI told Mr McKenzie you had a boyfriend, Smithfield, I think his name was. He was furious, and arranged for Smithfield to be sent overseas so he would be out of the way, and you couldn't fall in love with him."

Emma's cup clattered to the floor. The waitress rushed over. "Are you okay, Ma'am? Don't worry I'll clean up the mess. Would you like another coffee, a cappuccino wasn't it?"

"Err. No. May I have a glass of water though, please? Thanks for clearing up. I'm sorry." Emma stared at Francesca. "Are you serious? I can't believe what I'm hearing. Andrew hired a private investigator to track me. Oh. My. God. He arranged for John to be sent overseas, so I couldn't fall in love with him." Emma loosened the scarf from around her neck. A chill ran through her veins.

How could he be so callous? What kind of man is he? Who was I married to?

"Was there anything else? Anything to do with Luisa, the woman in the office who was shot."

Francesca's eyes opened wide. "Do you think he had something to do with her death?"

"I don't know. I just don't know what to think anymore. You do know he was having an affair with her, don't you." Francesca showed no sign of surprise or shock.

"Yes, everyone in the office knew that. He was very upset when she died. He gave everyone the day off, and even now he isn't himself. He mopes around, and spends a lot of time by himself in his office. I don't think he had anything to do with it. She kept herself to herself. She didn't realise everyone knew, but it was so obvious." The waitress set down two glasses of iced water, and tidied away the coffee cups.

"Okay. I don't know what to think or do really. I'm shocked that he would stoop so low, and have me followed. I can't get over it. So many strange things happening. I need to go home, and think about this. Thank you for telling me. You did the right thing. Make sure you don't lose your job over me though, please. I would hate for you to go back, and be in danger in your home country."

"I'll be okay. I just do what I am told, and work hard. I keep myself quiet. It's the best way. Luigi is my uncle. He looks after me and said you are one of his favourite customers. I think he is in love with you to be honest." Francesca grinned. "But he is incorrigible. He falls in love with everyone."

"Oh I didn't realise. I love Luigi. He always treats me so well. Please look after yourself, and thanks for telling me. Although I don't know if I feel better or worse." Emma stood, and reached for her handbag. "I'll get this. You get back to work. You don't want to be late."

"Thanks, and sorry if I caused you distress. I felt I had to let you know what was happening. Bye." Francesca disappeared into The Esplanade. Emma sat and finished her water. The cool liquid refreshed her, and cleared her mind. She needed to talk to Julian. As she stood to leave, her phone vibrated in her handbag. An unknown number.

"Hello. Emma McKenzie."

"Do you have the Monet?"

"Hello, who is this?'

"We are coming for it. We want our money back or the Monet."

"Who is this? Who are you?"

"He stole our money for the Monet. We are coming, and do not stand in our way, pretty lady."

"Please. I don't know what you are talking about. Who are you?"

The phone went dead. Emma fell back into her chair. Her heart raced. She held the table to steady her nerves. Beads of cold sweat appeared on her forehead.

What was that phone call about? How did the person have my number and know about the Monet? What now?

She dialled a number in New York. "Can I speak to John Smithfield, please?"

"Who?" The line crackled.

"John Smithfield. He is an architect from the UK, working in your office."

"No. There is no one here of that name. Sorry Ma'am. You are mistaken."

"Are you sure? Please check again."

"Ma'am. I have checked. There is no one here of that name. A few months ago, we received a call informing us that John Smithfield would be coming to work for us, but he didn't show up. We presumed he changed his mind, and stayed in the UK. Sorry Ma'am. Is there anything else I can help you with?"

"Err. No. Thank you for your time." Emma hung up.

What now?

She Googled the UK office of Smithfield, Jones, and Taylor.

"Hello. Can I speak to John Smithfield please?"

"Please hold the line…How may I assist?"

"I'm trying to reach John Smithfield."

"He transferred to our New York office a few months ago. The number is: 555-123-4567. You can reach him there."

"Oh okay thanks for your help." Emma looked at the phone in disbelief.

What had happened to John? I dropped him off at the airport so where did he go? Another mystery.

The walls of the cafe closed in. The lights dimmed. She needed to get out of there. She paid her bill, and relished the fresh air. She leaned against the cafe wall, closed her eyes, and breathed deeply. Thoughts ran around her mind. She didn't know what to think or what to do. Julian would know. He had such a clear way of thinking about him. She would explain everything, and he would make sense of it all.

Chapter Forty

The sun streamed through the window, waking Julian. He sat on the edge of the bed and smiled. They were becoming quite the regular couple at Luigis. Three dinners in as many days. Although he had to admit it had been nice to have an evening to himself the night before. Warmth flooded over him as he picked his way into the bathroom. He relished the white foaming rivets flowing over his body. The day began clean and fresh. A new start for him. He dried off and fastened the towel around himself. He picked up clothes and shoes scattered around the room, putting them away in their place. He straightened the crooked picture frames. He made his bed.

Not bad for a bachelor pad. Now the kitchen.

Buzz, buzz.

He grabbed the phone. Emma's number. His heart leaped. A wave of excitement rolled over him. He sat and composed himself. "Hello."

"Hi, Julian. Thanks so much for bring such wonderful company the other night. I swear my cheeks are still aching from smiling and laughing so much. Do you have plans this afternoon? Would you like to go for lunch somewhere and then come and see The Art Studio?"

He swallowed the frog in his throat. "Yes. I'd love that. What time?"

"Great. Meet me at Luigis at 1 p.m. and we'll go to The Art Studio from there. See you then. Can't wait."

"Okay. See you."

Wow did she say 'Can't wait.' Wow.

His towel dropped as he danced around the room. He grabbed it, and continued with his clean up.

####################

Emma hugged Julian as he entered. Her smile dazzled him. He pinched himself to wake himself up. "Hello. Great to see you, Emma."

"You too. I couldn't wait to see you. Come let's sit down. Luigi insisted on making one of his special lunches for us, so no need for menus. In fact between you and me I think he now expects us to come for either lunch or dinner each day. I would hate to disappoint wouldn't you? I ordered some sparkling water for us. I hope you don't mind." She led him to a table in the back.

"That sounds great. Are you okay? You seem like you are impatient maybe. I'm not sure."

"Well there is something I want to discuss with you, if that's okay?" Emma played with the beer mat.

"Go on."

"Remember I told you about the Monet, that John entrusted to me?"

"Yes. It hasn't been stolen has it?" Julian sat upright.

"Oh, god no. But yesterday I received a strange phone call from an unknown number. I always answer them as they may be art students wanting classes, anyway, the person on the phone said the

Monet was purchased with stolen money and they were coming for the painting. They hung up. It was weird. I couldn't tell if it was kids playing around or something more sinister. I don't know who the person was. No name. Unknown number. And the other thing is, a woman, working for Andrew, met me yesterday, and said he made her plant some kind of listening device on me, something like a USB stick. I found it when I was on the cruise, and when I returned I took it into that Spy High shop for the guy there to analyse. He told me it was a regular USB stick with movies and music. Another strange thing is that the Spy High shop has closed down now, everything moved out. The woman told me that Andrew's company leased the building; the company was late paying the rent so they sent her to investigate, and she found the shop vacated. Isn't that strange?"

Julian shifted in his seat as heat crept up his neck and settled on his face. He scratched his head. "Disappeared, you say. I must admit I went in there once to take a look at what they had. I thought it was all Executive Desk Toys, but it was surveillance equipment. It seemed quite high tech. I hadn't noticed it closed down, but the entrance was inconspicuous, to be honest. A USB listening device. That's interesting. I don't know what to make of the phone call. Where is the Monet now? I hope you have it in a safe place. Did you report the phone call to the police? They can trace unknown numbers, I think, from the cell triangulation at the time of the call."

"Are you okay? You look flushed. It is warm in here isn't it?" Their drinks arrived. "Here take a cool sip of water. No I didn't report it to the police. And yes of course the Monet is safe. It's in the vault at the bank. I didn't know what to think to be honest. There is still more to the story. After the mysterious phone call, I called John's office in New York, but they claim he never showed up to work there. I then called the local office, and they claim he moved to New York. I don't know what to think anymore. Are you any good at unravelling mysteries?" She sipped her water.

"That's interesting. He isn't in New York you say, or in the local office. Okay." John sipped his water. "That's nice. So; we have the USB listening device which wasn't, a painting purchased with stolen money, a spy shop that disappeared overnight it seems, and a missing architect. We need a Cluedo board for this one, I think. I don't know what to make of it all either. Do you think they are all connected or a set of random coincidences?" Luigis specials arrived, along with the largest pepper mill Julian had ever seen. "Wow. That's enormous. I'll have a little please. Not too much though. Thanks." He swirled the pasta round on his fork. "What made you take the USB device into the Spy High store?"

"It had a flashing green light on it that sometimes turned red, so it looked suspicious. The guy that ran the shop was a friend of John's and I met him when we played Laser Tag. I showed him the device, which he took to analyse overnight, but he said it was nothing, and gave it back to me. He even visited my house to do a security check. I must admit he took ages over it, and then said everything was fine. I thought that seemed strange. He gave me his card which had a few numbers on it." Emma searched in her handbag, "look, here it is." She handed him the card. "There's a phone number on it. Should I call it? Maybe he knows where John is? They were good friends as far as I know."

"No. Leave it. I think they're all random coincidences to be honest, and we are reading far too much into them. Let's enjoy our Luigi Special. Clam Linguine is divine." Julian inhaled a large mouthful of linguine.

"Yes. I think you're right. Tell me, what do you do as a job? I never asked."

Julian finished his mouthful of food, and sipped his water. "I'm a consultant on special projects with various different companies. It's a little complicated to explain, and pretty boring to be honest. I'm looking forward to visiting The Art Studio. Tell me about that. It sounds like a real passion."

"Oh yes, it is. I've always loved art, and had a gallery for a while, but that got difficult to manage so I closed it and set up The Art Studio. I teach fine art classes. There are some amazing students. In fact, one of them is friends with John. I just remembered. I wonder if she knows his whereabouts. I'll ask her at the next class. I'll take you there when we've finished here." Emma pushed the remains of her food to one side. "I've finished. Luigi always has such generous portions. Do you want a doggy bag for this?"

"Not this time. I've finished as well. I'm dying to see The Art Studio. Come on. I'll get this one. My treat." Julian signaled for the bill.

"The studio's in walking distance, thankfully. I need to walk off that heavy lunch." She led the way and held his hand as they walked across the park by the river to her studio. "It's locked up at the moment, but the caretakers are around, taking care of things." She laughed.

Julian smiled. "You're quite amusing at times, pretty lady."

Emma stopped. "Oh my god, that's what John used to call me, and that's what the person said on the phone. He called me pretty lady. I wonder if he has anything to do with John's disappearance. That sends shivers down my back. Creepy."

Julian's arm slid around Emma's back pulling her close to him. His lips met hers. "Don't even think about it, Emma. It's all a coincidence. I deal with this kind of stuff all the time. I can call you something else if you prefer. Come on. Show me inside."

She opened the door. "Excuse the mess. We are sorting things out for the new term which starts after the New Year. Actually, I have something I need to discuss with the caretaker if you don't mind?"

"No. Not at all. Can I sit at your desk, and play teacher?"

"Of course." Emma laughed. "When I return you can mark my work, teacher." She closed the door behind her as she left.

Julian scurried over to her desk, and opened the top drawer. Papers, pencils, paintbrushes, tubes of gouache sprung out.

Damn.

He pushed them back into the drawer. He tried the next drawer, but it didn't open. He grabbed a scraper from the pot on the table to pry it open; nothing glue, brushes, and a pot of blue gunky mud.

Nothing.

The last drawer slid open to a few receipts and a lonely calculator. The door creaked; he jumped back into the chair. "Come here. You are late for class. You're such a naughty girl you need to be punished."

"And just how do you intend to do that, teacher?" Emma grinned at him.

He pulled her on to his knees, raised her chin, and kissed her. "Like this. Pretty lady."

She raised her hand. "No please don't call me that actually. It's creepy. Sorry."

Julian pulled away. "No I'm sorry. You are really pretty. No in fact you are beautiful. I'll call you Emma. You're so much more than a silly name. You know that don't you. I, well I, oh it's nothing."

"No. Tell me. What were you going to say?" A quizzical frown crossed her forehead.

He swallowed. "I think I'm falling in love with you, Emma. If you'll let me."

"Oh wow. I don't know what to say. I thought we were going to take things slowly and get to know each other first. I admit that there's a connection that I feel each time I think of you, and each time I see you, it grows, but love and all that entails, scares me. " She pulled away from him towards the long window and caught sight of the birds sitting in a row on the telephone wires, ready to fly away. "Don't get me wrong. I'm glad fate brought us together, I really am, but let's slow down, please."

"Hey it's okay. Don't worry. I understand. I tend to wear my heart on my sleeve, which is unusual for a man I have been told, but it is who I am. I sometimes get carried away with things and say what I feel. I hope I haven't scared you off, Emma?"

Julian held his breath for Emma's response.

"Not at all. I'd just like to get to know you as a good friend before anything else to be honest. I'm so over the whole whirlwind romance thing that; yes was very exciting with John, but it wasn't real. I want this to be real." She moved back to him and held out her hand. He took it in his.

"Emma, I understand. Really I do. I'm sorry for running before I learnt to walk with you. Let's walk together. I have all the time in the world for you. Am I forgiven?"

She squeezed his hand. "Of course you are. It's good to talk isn't it? That's real. Come on let's get out of here and take in some of that fresh winter air. Maybe grab a coffee if you like."

Relief washed over Julian. He exhaled. "Great. Come on. Let's go."

"I need to lock up. See you outside."

"Okay. Don't be long."

Emma grinned. "I'll make it quick. I just need to grab my handbag."

################

Emma found her handbag under the desk. It jumped as her phone rang and vibrated. The screen displayed 'Unknown number'. She hesitated, remembering the last call from an unknown number she received.

"Hello."

"Emma. We need to meet immediately. There is some paperwork we need to go through concerning Anthony."

Andrew. Damn you.

"Today? Can't it wait until tomorrow?"

"No. It needs to be signed today. I'll meet you at the office in twenty minutes. See you there."

"I'm doing something." Emma locked the door, and walked to where Julian waited.

"Emma. This is important. I thought you loved Anthony. It is in his best interest that you meet me."

"Okay. I'll see you there. Goodbye." She hung up, and sighed. "Julian. Something important has come up with Andrew. I need to meet him. I'm going to have to take a rain check on that coffee. I'm sorry but it's something to do with our son."

"Is he okay?" Julian's eyebrows rose.

"As far as I know. It's some paperwork, although I'm not exactly sure what. Don't worry it will be okay."

"I hope so. Let me know if you need me." He squeezed her hand.

"Thanks. That's very sweet of you. I'll be fine. I'll call you." She walked in the direction of the office.

####################

The walk back to Julian's apartment refreshed him. His head cleared and a weight lifted. Sometimes you have to take chances in life and say what you feel when you feel it. Luisa taught him that. Opening his heart to Emma hadn't worked out exactly as he had hoped but maybe that was for the best. She obviously still had things to resolve with Andrew and he certainly didn't want to be involved in that. Andrew was far too smart and ruthless to mess around with. If he knew what was going on then who knows what could happen to either of them.

Chapter Forty-one

Julian pulled out Luisa's phone from its hiding place in his desk drawer. He smiled.

Hiding in plain sight. That drawer is in such a mess. No one would be able to find anything in there.

He entered the security code, and tapped on the photo icon, the camera roll. He knew she had used her phone to photograph important documents and other interesting evidence as she had called it. He scrolled through photos of nature, and wildlife.

Decoys. Where were the other photos?

He found an album called 'Recently Deleted.' He tapped to open it.

A message popped up: '8 Photos will be deleted within the next 7 days.'

He scrolled through the photos, more wildlife, and a bank statement.

That's interesting.

The statement showed a credit and a debit for £1,000,000 within a few days of each other. He restored the 'deleted' photo, messaged it to himself and printed it out. The statement belonged to A M Holdings and the credit account and debit account numbers were clearly visible. He knew exactly who would be interested in this.

"Hello, Ben. Julian here."

"Hello. Do you have anything for me?"

"Yes. What happened to the shop?"

"Things were getting too hot. Too many unwanted visitors snooping around if you know what I mean, so we packed up. We achieved our objective though."

"Okay. I have an interesting bank statement. It's a photo taken on a phone though. I don't know if that is of any use. I have no idea where the original is, probably in McKenzie's office by the looks of the background surroundings. It shows the credit and debit for a considerable sum of money. Are you interested in it?"

"Yes. That sounds perfect, and exactly what we're looking for. I'm going to give you an FTP address. Do you know how to upload to a server and use VPN?"

"Yes I do." Julian fired up his laptop.

"Great. Ftp://spyhigh@ben246.net:Xt24C9!$ put it in the public folder. I'll look out for it. Thanks. Any news on the shipment papers?"

"Not yet. I'm still working on that."

"Okay." The line went dead. Julian set up VPN and entered in the FTP address Ben had given him. There would be no trace on this information, once he cleared the cache on the laptop. VPN ensured the IP address used to send the file could not be traced back to him; just to a large data warehouse with several thousand, if not million IP addresses streaming data out.

His phone buzzed. 'Emma.' He smiled and answered. "Hey you. How did it go with Andrew?"

"Oh that was nothing at all. I think he just wanted to check up on me. There wasn't any paperwork at all. I don't know what the urgency was about. I'm home now so just wanted to let you know and that I really would like to see you again sometime soon. I can imagine it took a lot for you to tell me what you told me especially so soon. I appreciate it, I really do."

"Well I'm kind of actually pleased I got that out into the open and off my chest. One of my weaknesses is that I do wear my heart on my sleeve but that's who I am. Thanks for understanding."

"Not at all. Would you—"

"Actually, Emma. I'm got a lot on over the next couple of days so I'll call you at the end of the week and we can go for dinner. Maybe we can try somewhere different to Luigi's. What do you think?"

"Oh right, yes that's fine. No problem. I've got to get The Art Studio up and running for the beginning of term so yes the end of the week sounds perfect. Take care and thanks again, Julian."

"Emma, I should thank you for not running away from me. Ha ha. Take care, speak soon."

Julian hung up his phone. His heart pounded. Games really didn't come easy to him but he couldn't move too fast with Emma. He knew that.

Slow down. Walk before you can run.

Patience and the long game would pay off in the end. He had waited so long already, what were a few more days or weeks, if that's what it took? In the meantime, he had plenty of time to contemplate the events unfolding around him.

####################

The doors to Emma's Art Studio burst open and Beth rushed in. "Emma, oh my! Emma. I've been trying to call you. Where have you been? Why is your phone switched off?"

Emma laughed. "Beth. You know I switch it off when I'm doing the student accounts ready for the beginning of term. What's wrong now?"

Beth plonked herself down on the old sofa near the window. "You will never believe what Tony just told me. Emma. Oh my."

"What?" Emma grinned, she was used to Beth's melodrama by now.

"Well you know he went to Brighton at the weekend for that strong man contest. Gosh I really should have gone with him, have you seen those guys whoo wheee. Anyway, guess who was competing against him?"

"I have no clue seriously, and you know I'm terrible at guessing games, especially yours." Emma continued with her accounts.

"Only the guy you used to see, that John guy, you know the one Tony knew from the gym, the one that you drove to the airport to get on a plane to New York City for that fancy architect job over there? Well it looks like his plane only went to Brighton."

Emma spun around and Beth caught her pen as it flew across the room. "No way! I'm sure you're mistaken. I dropped him off at the airport, and I know when I called his office in New York they said he wasn't there but you know these huge offices and how the new girl or guy never knows who's who."

Beth shot Emma a look. "Tony was not mistaken. He even sent me a photo. Look."

She offered her phone to Emma. "Apparently he didn't go to New York; he is working in Brighton at the gym as a personal trainer. Tony has a few friends down there in the industry and they confirmed it. I couldn't believe it when I heard either. Men! You can't trust any of them."

Emma shook as she took the phone. John's handsome face looked back at her. Her groin stirred and she swallowed hard as memories rushed back tinged with confusion and hurt.

How was she supposed to deal with this? Forget him, but the Monet? It was rightfully his. Did he want it back?

"Beth. Forget him. It's his loss. He was a time and place and I've moved on now into reality. Julian is real. John was a lovely fantasy. Every girls dream but that was all that was. He rescued me from myself and from Andrew but now, good luck to him. Let him find me if he wants anything."

Beth jumped up and wrapped her arms around Emma in a huge hug. "I'm so happy to hear you say that, Ems. I was so afraid that you'd want to rush down there to find him and pick up things where they left off. You've grown up girl and found yourself. Well done. Well I need to dash. I'm meeting Tony for lunch. Ooh, I can't wait. He says he has something to ask me. I'm so excited."

Emma laughed. "Wow. That's great Beth. He is a real keeper. You know that? Right. He's been so good for you since you guys met. Fingers crossed."

"Fingers crossed. See ya!" Beth picked up her bag and dashed out.

Silence resumed and consumed Emma. She opened the window and refreshed the air in the room. She leaned out and flung her arms wide, throwing away the bad and gathering in the good. She had come a long way. At one point that news would have had her in tears, a trembling wreck, but now she thought 'it is what it is.' Accept and move on. She returned to her student accounts and preparation for the new term.

######################

Julian looked out of his window as the black Mercedes pulled away from outside his apartment building. He opened his notebook. The fourth time he had seen that car in two days. A coincidence? Maybe. He knew all his neighbours and no one had such a car or the means to purchase such a car. Suspicion grew. He knew who drove a car like that. Next time he would get the registration plate to be certain. A sense of foreboding as the watcher became the watched. He secured his documents in the hidden places around his apartment. If someone found one by chance it would be surprising if they found all.

His walk took him along the river opposite the apartments at Riverside Walk, where he had spied on Emma and John. A glint of silver at the window caught his eye. He puzzled.

Wasn't that apartment empty now John had left for New York? What was glinting? A mirror maybe, binoculars?

He continued through the park and down the High Street, where the black Mercedes was parked outside Café Rouge. He mentally made a note of the registration plate and strode past the large windows. A quick glance confirmed who was there and who was stalking him. That would have to wait. His interest lay in that empty apartment. Convinced someone had moved in or had never actually moved out, he rounded the corner by the station and returned to the park. Approaching from the North revealed a clearer view of the apartment and its large windows overlooking the river. The low winter sun glinted off a lens in the window. The curtain moved. A large man with dark hair appeared momentarily and then disappeared into the shadows. Julian headed back to his apartment to pick up his camera and surveillance kit.

The door to Julian's apartment was ajar. Papers scattered everywhere. His sofa ripped open, the contents of his wardrobes and drawers tipped onto the floor. He made sure no one remained and scanned for any bugs then checked his hiding places. All intact. He pulled the video surveillance USB stick out of the unobtrusive socket and inserted it into his iPad.

Andrew. He brought his cronies with him to do the dirty work but he directed the show in plain view. They found nothing of significance only made a mess in their haste.

Julian grabbed his camera that had been left intact and headed out again. He set up surveillance on the apartment in his old spot. He never thought he would be here again so soon and in such different circumstances. He contemplated his next move with Andrew.

Should he leverage his knowledge against him or let this play out. Usually amateurs trip themselves up but with Andrew he wasn't totally sure what he was dealing with.

His movement sensor camera sprung into life. He zoomed in. It was John Smithfield.

Now what was he doing back in town, did Emma know and more to the point how did she feel about him?

Chapter Forty-two

Emma caught her breath as she entered Café Rouge. She always did whenever she saw her son. She smiled as her heart exploded with pride and love. He grinned as he saw her, "Hi Mum, you look great. Is that a new hairstyle or have you lost weight? There's something about you that's glowing." He swept her up in a bear hug.

"Good to see you too and you can put me down now. You may be much taller than me but I'm still your Mum." She laughed as she found a chair at the table. "How are you getting on at Uni? I was surprised you called me to meet I thought it was still term time."

"Oh I'm doing great actually. Got ones and twos in my mid term exams which is good—even the really hard ones which to be honest weren't that hard once I put my mind to it. I just wanted to see my mum and check up on you." Anthony pulled up his chair and grabbed a menu. "I'm starving and," he paused and flashed a smile at Emma, "broke. This is on you. I hope you don't mind."

"Of course not. I'm so pleased to see you. Are you planning on staying over or do you need to get back?" Emma reached over and ruffled her son's messy hair. "I miss you a lot you know. The house seems so quiet these days with only me clattering around in it. I sometimes feel so lost."

Anthony ran his fingers through his hair. "Mum, I know. It must be hard without Dad. I think he misses you too whenever he calls me he ends up talking about you. He still loves you but I understand I guess. Infidelity is the worst and especially after you guys had been together for so long. He tells me he is really sorry and was totally taken in by Luisa's beauty. Ooh, maybe I shouldn't have said that, sorry Mum." His eyebrows raised and eyes opened wide. "Sorry."

"Don't be. It's fine. It's interesting to hear that and good that you talk to your Dad. It's important that you have a good relationship with him. Whatever he did to me, that shouldn't affect it. Whilst I know I'm far from over him, I am coming to terms with it and trying to live my life." Emma played with the edge of the place mat. "In fact I'm glad you brought that up as I've met a lovely man, who thinks the world of me." She raised her eyes from the place mat to meet Anthony's gaze.

"Hi, Welcome to Café Rouge, can I take your drinks order and will you be eating lunch with us today. We have beer-battered fish and chips as our special today. It comes with a green pea puree. We also have a lovely Pinot Grigio on special." The waitress bounced over.

Anthony smiled at her. "Thanks. The Pinot Grigio sounds wonderful. We'll take a bottle and let you know our lunch order shortly. Thanks so much." He turned to his mum, "that's okay isn't it?"

"Oh gosh, absolutely." She glanced around the restaurant with its weekday lunchtime buzz of office workers and ladies who lunch. She wondered how many were in similar situations to her. Probably more than would admit.

"Wow Mum. I don't know how I feel about you meeting someone. It's weird you know. You always think your parents are infallible and it's so unsettling to discover they aren't. But I have been thinking about it and everyone deserves happiness in life. It's something I have to deal with ultimately." Anthony took a swig of the iced water that had arrived on their table.

Emma looked directly at Anthony. "Oh baby, you sound so grown up and thank you for that. It means a lot to me. It's not been easy for either of us and now I've met someone I wanted to tell you before it got any more serious."

Anthony reached across and took her hand. "Mum, I really do appreciate that you know. I want you to be happy more than anything. If the new man is responsible for this glow you have about you then it can only be a good thing. You really do look amazing. You always looked so stressed and worried when you were with Dad but now you look kind of younger even."

Emma stood and hugged her son. "Thank you, sweetie. That's so nice of you to say." She returned to her chair as the waitress reappeared with the Pinot Grigio.

"Did you decide on what you'd like to eat?" She asked as she poured the wine.

"Oh we'll both try the fish and chips special, thanks." Emma handed her the unopened menus.

"Ooh, good choice. You'll love it. I do. It shouldn't be too long." The waitress scurried off to the kitchen.

"His name is Julian and he is a business consultant, although I'm not too sure what that means exactly. He is kind and generous. He makes me laugh and feel good about myself. He is my age or thereabouts. He lives in town, quite close to here actually. I like him a lot but we're taking it slow if that's what you say these days. I met him a couple of months ago now." Emma swirled her wine around in the glass. "Delicious."

Anthony laughed. "Is the wine delicious or is he?"

"Oye, you. I'm not like you young kids. We are taking time to get to know each other before any funny business."

"Eww, Mum. TMI. Seriously. I wasn't even thinking that. I was teasing you as you looked so misty eyed when you were saying all that about him. But I can see you really like him. How did you meet him?"

Emma grinned and savoured the crisp wine. "Oh well, remember the accident I had when I drove into that post. He was on the scene and dragged me out of the car. He made sure I was okay and took me for a coffee. He was so kind then. I felt a real connection to him."

"Oh yes. You didn't mention anyone helping you then though."

"No but it was afterwards to be honest. I invited him for dinner at Luigis as he was so kind and we made a connection then. We have been to the museum. I showed him my art studio, and we've had many, many dinners and lunches at Luigis, who considers us his family now." Her eyes lit up as she spoke and swirled her wine.

Anthony smiled. "Mum. That's great. I can tell you like him a lot. Look how you're talking about him. It looks like young love to me. I'm really happy for you."

"Hi. Here is your order. The fish and chip special for two. Enjoy" The waitress bounced back. "Do you want any sauces, tomato, mayonnaise, mustard?"

"No thank you." Emma picked up her fork and stabbed a chip. "This looks great." She munched away. "This is great actually. Just what I needed."

"Mum. I meant what I said. I am happy for you. When do I get to meet him? Although that will be weird but I guess it's modern life these days isn't it?" Anthony dug into his lunch. "Oh yes this is good. Amazing what they've done to the traditional fish and chips, brought it into the twenty-first century. I guess everything changes doesn't it."

As she ate, Emma considered her son. A rush of love and gratefulness swept over her. She felt lucky. His understanding and maturity had surprised her. His year away at university had helped him grow into a mature, intelligent and balanced young man. A tear pricked the corner of her eye.

"You okay, Mum?" His voice questioned her.

She brushed the tear away. "Yes, sweetheart. I was just thinking how much I love you and miss you when you're not here. And thanks for being you."

"Duh, Mum. I know that. Don't get all sloppy on me now. Please. But I know what you mean. I miss you too. So when do I get to meet this Julian fellow. As I said it will be weird but it's modern life so I'll deal with it." Anthony shuffled his chair around beside Emma. He stretched his arm around her shoulders and nestled into her neck. "Mum."

She stroked his head. "Sweetheart. It's okay, you know. Look you should finish your lunch before it gets cold. And you didn't tell me if you were staying the night or grabbing the late train back."

He repositioned his chair and dug back into his lunch. "This is good. I'm grabbing the late train back as I have classes tomorrow. This is a flying visit, sorry Mum. Hopefully next time I'll get to meet Julian and I'll be around for longer. I'll also bring laundry."

Emma laughed. "Typical." She closed her cutlery over her plate. "Well, I'm done. That was delicious." She refilled their glasses. "Here's to life, love and happiness."

"Yes. Here's to living life, Mum. You only live once you know." Their glasses clinked. "Let's grab the bill and take a walk down by the river. It's a lovely day out and it will be good to walk off the fish and chips and get out of this place. It's a little busy with ladies who lunch isn't it. I never thought it was like that. I used to come here in the evening for drinks and it's a completely different crowd."

"Great idea." Emma paid and they walked out together, arm in arm. Screams and laughter of children playing grew louder as they approached the park. The final few days of the spring holidays, and mothers made the most of the warm weather. A wistful smile crossed Emma's face as she remembered bringing Anthony here when he was young. She hooked her arm in his as they strolled along the path.

"It is lovely here isn't it. So safe for families. I used to bring you here. Do you remember?"

"Yes. I do. I also remember trying to escape from you and giving you the run around in the bushes across the river, but that was before that development was built, at least it's quite stylish." Anthony indicated to Riverside Walk town houses across the river.

Emma inhaled and exhaled in an attempt to remain composed. Vivid memories flooded back of her encounter with John Smithfield in one of those very town houses. As her eyes wandered to the long windows overlooking the park, the flutter of a curtain held her gaze.

Surely that place was unoccupied, as he had left. He hadn't mentioned selling it as it was a present from his father and would be worth a fortune. All his stuff was still here. Was he still there?

She unhooked her arm from Anthony's and picked up her pace.

"Hey Mum are you okay. What's the rush? I thought this was a stroll not a race." He laughed and caught up with her.

"Oh sorry. I, well I. Oh it's nothing. I guess I'm so used to rushing around these days. You're right let's stroll." She threw a glance back at the window but nothing. The curtains hung straight in perfect pleats.

My imagination with Beth mentioning him the other day.

As they exited the park and rounded the road towards the railway station, she noticed a 'For Sale' sign covered with a large 'SOLD' sticker on the entrance to Riverside Walk.

Maybe his place had been sold after all. I don't remember him having those long curtains at all. That explains it.

Relief flooded over her. She turned to her son. "What time is your train? Could you stay for dinner at least?"

Anthony pulled out his phone and checked the train app for times. "Oh there is one in about twenty minutes so that's perfect timing. I'd love to stay for dinner but I have a paper to write due the end of the week. Like I said Mum, this was a flying visit to check on you, but it looks like you're doing really well. I'm pleased."

Emma hugged him. "I understand sweetheart. It's been lovely. Don't leave it so long next time and hopefully next time you'll get to meet Julian. Thanks Anthony for understanding. It was important to me to talk to you about him."

"I know, Mum. I won't. Look, I really need to dash now as I don't want to miss that train. Take care, love you. Bye." He dashed off into the station.

Emma waved until he disappeared up the stairs. She turned and walked to her car at the far end of the High Street. Relief and reassurance encouraged her. She knew what she wanted. Julian. Time to get serious.

Chapter Forty-three

"Would you like to come around for dinner? I picked up a couple of juicy tenderloin steaks on the way home."

"That's sounds wonderful. What time?" Julian's stomach flipped as his groin tightened. He swallowed.

"Anytime you're ready. I'm looking forward to seeing you again it feels like it's been so long." She laughed.

"A week isn't that long you know but great. I have a couple of things to wrap up here and I should be there in about an hour."

"See you soon. Bring a toothbrush." She hung up.

Did she say 'bring a toothbrush?' Oh my. Wow.

A huge grin spread across his face, and a swarm of butterflies invaded his stomach. He closed his laptop and secured it away, packed a small overnight bag, picked up his iPad and jumped in his car. The radio played 'Thinking Out Loud' by Ed Sheeran, about finding love in mysterious ways.

How true.

Each song reflected his feelings.

She stood in the doorway to her house. The fading sun shone through her hair, highlighting the chestnut tinge. His heart leapt. His pulse quickened.

Beautiful.

He pinched himself to chase away any dreams. "Hey you. Come in. It's so good to see you." Her arms wrapped around him in a hug. He didn't want to let go. Heat coursed through his veins. He pulled away. He didn't want to rush.

"It's very good to see you too. I'm starving, and of course I have no food in my fridge so I was very pleased at the dinner invitation. It beats a frozen TV dinner any day."

"You are so funny." She laughed. "Come into the kitchen. You can make the salad. You do know how to do that don't you?" She handed him a lettuce, cucumber and a packet of tomatoes.

"Yes, I think I can manage a salad. Do you have apples, nuts, any seeds?"

"Fancy. Take a look in the tall cupboard over there. See what you can find. This sounds interesting." She turned her back to prepare the steaks. "Would you like potatoes as well or just salad?"

"Yes potatoes sound good." He opened the tall cupboard, and hunted through the jumble of dry ingredients. "Aha. Ooh. This looks good."

"You okay back there?"

"Yes, don't worry about me. Do you have a vegetable knife?" He laid out his salad ingredients on the counter.

"Look in the drawer, in front of you."

"Thanks." He opened the first drawer, and a bundle of paperwork sprung out. As he stuffed it back in, a few words caught his eye: *'Bill of Lading … 2013 Art shipment … Naya Habidin, Rue George V, Paris …'*

That's what I've been looking for. The papers for the art shipment. Now what?

He stuffed the bundle back into the drawer, and turned to find Emma engrossed in peeling potatoes over the sink. He found the knife in the second drawer, and began peeling the cucumber and chopping the tomatoes. His thoughts ran over the papers.

How am I going to take a look at those papers without her knowing?

The knife slipped, and sliced into his forefinger. "Damn"

"What's wrong? Oh gosh are you okay? Here run it under the tap."

He held his finger under the cool running water, his mind still on his discovery.

"You seem far away. Are you sure you're okay?" Emma took his finger, and dried it with kitchen roll. "It isn't a deep cut. Here's a sticking plaster. Waterproof and blue, so we can identify it, if it ends up in the salad."

"Thanks. I'm okay. Sorry about that. It's true it's a while since I chopped and peeled, but that's not to say I can't do it. I used to be a pretty good chef once. In fact, I'll make dessert for you later. I see you have a well-stocked cupboard there. I'm sure I can rustle up something."

"Sounds fantastic. You're on. Help yourself to whatever you need." She returned to her dinner preparations.

He made sure the drawer closed fully, and assembled the salad. "Well the salad is ready. Italian or Julian special dressing?"

"Julian special of course."

"Okay dokey. I hope you like it." He poured olive oil, balsamic vinegar, sugar, and crushed garlic into a jar and shook until the oil emulsified into the vinegar and thickened. "The steaks smell wonderful. I like mine medium rare, please."

"Good to know. I like mine that way as well." Emma turned the steaks onto their plates, and added a scoop of potatoes. "Where would you like to eat? Here in the kitchen or in the conservatory. I'm afraid I'm not one for formalities anymore, so the dining room is out of the question."

"The conservatory sounds good." He had to get her away from the kitchen to execute his plan. "I'll bring the salad. I like to eat mine after the main course."

She rested her plate on the coffee table and pointed a remote control at a corner. Miles Davies filled the room. "I hope you like jazz. Miles is one of my favourites."

"Yes I do. He is pretty cool. The steak is very good. Thanks for dinner. I'm having a great time, despite my injury. I just don't know what happened." Julian munched his way through his steak and sauté potatoes.

"The salad is very crunchy. What did you find in the cupboard? Probably ingredients I had forgotten about, and the dressing is delicious. You'll have to give me the recipe."

"It's a secret. Secret ingredients in both. You'll have to be more persuasive than that to get those secrets out of me." A sly smile crossed Julian's face as he winked at Emma.

"I'm sure I can, what about that dessert you promised. I have a sweet tooth, especially after red meat."

"Sure. No problem. Pass me your plate. You just relax with Miles and your glass of wine." Julian refilled her glass with the

Chianti, and took up the empty plates. The water running into the sink masked the sound of the papers rustling, as he retrieved them from the drawer. He spread them out, and scanned them into his iPad.

Perfect. Now dessert. Chocolate Fondant would be perfect.

Eggs, flour, chocolate. He opened the freezer. Vanilla ice cream. *This is going to be divine.*

"Are you okay? Do you need a hand?"

"No, I'm fine. You just relax. This will take a few minutes. I'll be back with you soon." He assembled the dessert on the plates with a generous scoop of ice cream and a sprinkle of chocolate shavings.

Very impressive.

"Et voilà." He presented the dessert.

"Wow, wow, wow. That looks amazing. Thank you. I love chocolate fondant. How did you know? In fact, how on earth did you make that? I'm very impressed." Emma sat up and patted the seat next to her. "Come, sit. Let's eat this before it all melts."

Julian sat and smiled as she tucked into her dessert. He played around with his on the plate. His appetite had disappeared as waves of anticipation washed over him.

"Don't you like your dessert?"

"I love it, but I'm actually very full from the steak. I don't always have a sweet tooth. It's okay. Would you like it?"

"No, one is enough for me, but come here." Emma's eye glinted with mischief. She took a spoonful of ice cream mixed with the melted chocolate, and offered it to him. As he took the spoon into his mouth, she kissed him. He tasted her warm tongue mixed with the cold ice cream and chocolate. His groin tightened, and he hardened against his pants. He had waited long enough. He replaced the spoon on her plate, and slid his hand around the back of her head. He pulled her towards him, and kissed her. His tongue explored her mouth, danced around her tongue. He sucked, and nibbled her lips. His hand slid under her blouse, and cupped her breast. His thumb searched for her nipple, hard and protruding. She gasped. "Don't stop." She pulled her blouse off and wriggled out of her bra. "Kiss me."

"Like this?" His kisses started on her forehead, brushed over her mouth, and ended on her breast. He sucked and rolled his tongue around the hard nipple. Her back arched.

"Oh, god. Yes." She pulled him on top of her, hitched her skirt up, and wrapped her legs around him. "I want you so much. You drive me wild, Julian."

He reached down, and slid his fingers past her panties into her wet core. She bit her lip, and rolled her head back. He stroked her swollen core, and thrust his tongue deep into her mouth.

She moaned. "That feels so good. Don't stop. Oh, god." She pushed his head down, and his tongue found her wetness. He teased, and swirled until she quivered, and a gush of fluid released. He kissed her.

"Taste yourself."

She sucked his tongue into her mouth, and lapped up her juices. "I want to taste you."

"You will. Don't worry there's plenty of time. No rush. Let me take your clothes." He removed her remaining clothes, and released his bulging pants. He slid his hand up, and down the shaft. She placed her hand on his, and moved with him. "Wow. I want to feel you inside me."

He turned her around, and pushed her face down onto the sofa. Her back arched, and her hips rose towards him. He ran his hands down her spine, and found her soft entrance. He entered, and then withdrew. He teased.

She moaned. "More. Let me feel you."

"Like this." He entered her a little more and pulled out again.

Her hips pushed back into him. "More. I need you."

"How badly do you need me?"

"Oh, god. I need to feel you inside me. I need you to fill me. I need you to fuck me."

"Like this." He thrust into her.

She screamed. "Oh, god yes. Yes. Yes. I love it." With each thrust she pushed her hips back into him. He twisted her hair into a pony tail, and pulled her head back.

"Do you love it?"

"Oh god yes. I love it."

"Tell me how much?"

"I love feeling you inside me. Don't stop. I'm coming. Oh, my. "She quivered, and a gush of warm fluid ran down her leg.

He stroked her back. "I love you, Emma. I love making love to you. I knew I would. Hold my hand." She reached back, and he took her hand in his. "I'm going to come. Can I come inside you? I want you to feel me when I come."

"Yes. Come."

He entwined his fingers in hers, and squeezed her fingers. "Aaargh. I love you." He shuddered. He collapsed on her. Spent.

"Hey. You okay. Sorry but you're pretty heavy. Can you move?" Emma wriggled out from under him.

He shifted his weight to the side. "Sorry. Are you okay?"

"I'm perfect."

He pulled her into his body, and wrapped his arms around her. "Good. I need to close my eyes for a few moments." He nuzzled into her hair. "Beautiful."

She closed her eyes, and the peaceful serenity of sleep washed over them.

Chapter Forty-four

"Julian. It's Emma. Sorry I have to cancel dinner tonight. Something's come up. Call me when you get this message. I had an amazing time yesterday. Love you." Beep. Emma hung up. She hated answer machines. She hated Andrew, but the terms of her divorce dictated that she had an obligation to attend business dinners when requested, and he had requested her presence the following night.

She stretched, and resumed painting. She channelled her emotion from recent events into creating amazing artwork. She had completed one commissioned piece, and had a matching order. Her phone sounded and vibrated. *'Julian'*

"Emma. Wow. You thought last night was amazing, what do you think I thought it was? Sorry to hear about dinner tonight. In fact, I have a last minute appointment as well so I'll call you tomorrow and you can come over for dinner and dessert or we can reserve a table at Luigi's."

"I like your desserts, Julian. I'll come over. Let's speak tomorrow. Enjoy tonight."

"Doubt if I'll enjoy it. It's business but thanks. Take care."

Emma held the phone to her chest, and smiled. A warm glow emanated from her, and she knew she had the confidence to deal with Andrew tonight. She riffled through her wardrobe for her long red dress. She wanted to look fabulous tonight and had a few points to prove to her ex-husband.

The gravel crunched as the chauffeured car arrived. "Just a moment." She slipped into her heels, and grabbed her clutch. Andrew hadn't mentioned who would be at the business dinner, but she suspected the Japanese couple she had met at The Charity Auction.

She admired the facade of The Marriott as they approached. It had been a former stately home, sold by the owners to the hotel chain. The interior had been gutted, and modernised, but the exterior had been renovated and repaired. She felt like Cinderella attending the ball as she climbed the steps with the gargoyle stonework and mullion windows looking down on her. Andrew met her at the top of the steps. "Wow. You look gorgeous, Emma. I always loved that dress on you, and off you." He slid he arm around her waist and her skin crawled.

"Good evening, Andrew. I trust your guests have arrived." She wriggled out of his touch, and stood by his side.

"Yes. I am just waiting for one couple to arrive. The rest of the guests are at the bar. Would you like an aperitif?" He motioned for the waiter. "A gin and tonic?"

"Yes please. That would be nice. I am presuming the guests are the Japanese investors, Mr and Mrs Kaneko?"

"Yes they are. Well done for remembering their name. You always were very good at that kind of thing. Much better than me. There are some other business partners as well I'd like you to meet."

Emma raised her eyebrows. "Why do you want me to meet them? I have nothing to do with the business anymore?"

"You'll see. Here's your drink." He called the waiter over. "I think all my guests have arrived now. Can you show us to our table please? I'm going to meet the last guests outside."

Emma's gaze followed Andrew outside but the entrance columns obscured her view. She turned, and followed the waiter to their table instead. She bowed to the Japanese. She made her introductions, and seated everyone when Andrew walked in with the late arrivals. She gasped, and her glass dropped to the floor.

She sprung up as a waiter appeared to clean up the mess. "Are you okay, Ma'am? You look very pale. Would you like a glass of water or another G 'n T?"

"I, I, I'm okay. Another G 'n T and make it a large one, easy on the T. Thanks." Emma stood as Andrew made introductions.

"Emma, this is Julian. A business colleague, and his partner, Giselle."

Emma heart raced and a sick feeling turned her stomach. She reached out her hand. "Nice to meet you, Julian. Giselle." She turned away. "If you excuse me I need to go to the ladies room." She held her head high as she walked away. In the ladies room, she leaned against the counter.

Oh my god. Why is Julian here and who is that woman. She looks like a whore. Who dresses like that for a business dinner, seriously, does he have no taste. What am I saying? How can he do that to me? Why didn't he tell me he had a woman, partner, wife?

She wiped a tear from the side of her eye.

I need to be strong. Show him I don't care, but I don't understand. How can he say he's falling in love with me but he has another woman? God I'm such a fool.

Her hands covered her face.

God please make him go away. Please make this be a bad dream. Please.

She pinched herself. She refreshed her makeup, and straightened her dress. A few deep breaths and she returned to the table. Julian caught her eye but she couldn't read his look. She didn't know him well enough. She turned away and concentrated on the menu.

"Emma. I'm glad you're back. I was just telling the beautiful Giselle here how long we've been married. Twenty years next week isn't it, sweetheart?" Andrew placed his hand on hers. His ring glinted in the light. "Oh where's your wedding ring? Don't tell me you left it in the bathroom again?"

She glared sideways at Andrew and removing her hand. "I'm not wearing it at the moment. I teach an art class which gets a little messy sometimes so I don't wear the ring. It's in a very safe place though. How long have you been with Julian?"

"Oh I haven't been with him very long. He is lovely though, very attentive, and loving towards me. I am hoping we'll make an announcement one day." Giselle turned to Julian, and deposited a bright red lipstick mark on his cheek. Emma swallowed the bile rising in her throat, took a swig of her drink to untie the knot in her stomach. The strong liquor burned on the way down, and her stomach retched. She held the edge of the table.

"Are you okay, Emma? You don't look well. Here take a drink of water." Andrew filled her water glass.

"I'm fine. I think I ate something earlier that upset me. I'll be fine. Andrew." She drained the glass thankful for the calming liquid diluting the harsh gin in her empty stomach.

"Emma?"

"You have a little something on your cheek." He dabbed his cheek with his napkin.

"Oh that's Revlon Ultrastay. It stains until you wash it off." As Giselle laughed her breasts heaved and threatened to fall out of her low cut top. All the men around the table stopped talking and gazed in her direction. Their wives prodded them to turn back to their business conversations.

Emma pinched Andrew under the table, and whispered. "Stop staring. It's rude. Talk your business with Mr and Mrs Kaneko, please, and I will talk to this whore." A sly smile crossed Andrew's face as he turned to his Japanese investors. Emma set her mouth, and concentrated on the menu. A jumble of thoughts ran around. The menu blurred as tears pricked her eyes. She dabbed the corner of her eye with her napkin and took a deep breath. She looked Julian in the eye. "What kind of business are you in, Julian?"

"Consultancy. I work on special projects." Julian straightened his cutlery, and found interest in his wine glass.

"And how did you meet Giselle?"

"At a business function." He picked up the menu, and studied it again. He kept his eyes away from Emma's gaze. The waiter arrived to take everyone's orders and Julian looked visibly relieved.

Andrew ordered champagne and the hotel's local specialty dish for everyone at the table. The waiter took the main course orders, and returned with the champagne. "I'd like to make a toast. To old friends and new. To international business. To long lasting friendships." Everyone toasted. Emma sipped the champagne but her stomach felt sick. Her vision blurred, and her head spun. She steadied herself against the table, and leaned back in her chair. Her eyes closed.

This must be a nightmare. This cannot be happening to me. I need to pull myself together.

She reached into her handbag to retrieve her headache tablets. She swallowed one and took a sip of water.

"Are you okay, Emma?" A voice asked in the distance. Her mind couldn't make out who asked the question. She grabbed Andrew's arm and whispered. "I have a migraine coming on. Please arrange for a room and make my apologies. I have to lie down."

"Yes, of course my dear. Anything for my wonderful wife." Andrew called the Maitre D' over, who scurried away and returned with a wheelchair. Emma collapsed into it and let herself be taken into one of the rooms. She stumbled onto the bed, closed her eyes, and drifted away into a heavy sleep.

###################

Andrew apologised to the rest of the group. "My wife sends her apologies. She is not feeling well and needs to take a rest. She hopes the rest of the evening goes well. Please enjoy the champagne and the local specialty dish prepared by the hotel chef in honour of our Japanese guests." He bowed and returned to his seat. A smile crossed his face.

Julian turned to him. "Will Mrs McKenzie be okay?"

"Oh, I've no doubt. This happens all the time when she is emotionally stressed. She drank too much as well. Her second drink was a double. Do you know what may be the cause of her stress? I hear that it is quite a common occurrence for an investigator to fall in love with the person he is tailing, especially if she is as beautiful as Emma. You do agree she is beautiful?"

"Stunning." Julian whispered under his breath. "That's an interesting theory, Mr McKenzie. And it is only a theory. I have followed many beautiful women in my time, and never fallen in love with them. It depends on the level of professionalism one brings to the job. You know I pride myself on being a consummate professional."

"I also know you fell in love with my wife and you are seeing her. Stop it before you both get hurt, and I don't mean emotionally. This is dangerous territory you are playing in, Mr Cunningham. I don't care about you, but I do care about my wife."

"She's your ex-wife. Don't forget that. You are divorced. You have no claim over her, and she can see whomever she likes, surely. I will not be scared by your idle threats."

"Idle threats. Look what happened to Luisa. This is beyond my control now. They will stop at nothing to get what they want. You must realise that from your surveillance work."

Julian inhaled sharply at the mention of Luisa. "Did you have something to do with her death?"

"I did not, and I do not know who did, but I suspect they are beyond the reach of the police. She was an unfortunate victim in this story." Andrew placed his glass on the table. "Please take heed of my words Mr Cunningham. Look how easily I found you out, and flushed you out tonight. She is a special lady, and I would never forgive myself if anything happened to her. I need to return to my real business guests now so you and your escort are free to stay and enjoy the meal or you may leave if you wish. I have no further need for your services." Andrew turned his back and engaged Mr Kaneko in conversation.

####################

Julian drained his champagne, followed by his wine, then turned to his companion. "Come on. Let's get out of here."

"Ooh baby, I thought you'd never ask. We can get a room here if you like."

Giselle disgusted him; her tousled bleached hair, thick dark eyeliner and breasts straining the material of her tiny blouse. "No. I'm taking you home to your house and I'm going home to mine. Alone. Is that clear?"

She looked crestfallen, then growled, "Yes. But you can drop me off at Roxies. I'll take my chances there. I didn't get dressed up to the nines for nothing. If you don't appreciate me, then I'm sure there are plenty of men out there who will. Call yourself a man. I bet you can't get it up if you tried."

"Come on. Let's go now." Julian bowed to the party, made his excuses and left. He turned for one last look as he left, and caught a smirk on Andrew's face. All he wanted to do was escape to the sanctity of his home, and plan how on earth he would explain this to Emma, if she would ever speak to him again.

Chapter Forty-five

Julian opened and closed his eyes as the memory of the nights events came flooding back to him. He buried his head in his pillow.

No, no, no. God, what am I going to do? I was set up like a fool and had no idea.

He slouched to the shower and let cool water wash over his body. Maybe the water would wash away the memory of her broken spirit. He couldn't imagine what she thought. He thumped the tiles, and his shampoo jumped out of the shower tray, its contents swirling down the drain. He wished the memory of the night would follow.

He grabbed a towel, and rubbed himself dry. The kettle whistled its tune as it boiled away, but he had no enthusiasm for anything. He studied an ant crawling across the floor carrying a large crumb on its back. He had played a game, and he had lost in the biggest way possible.

What am I going to do? What were those warnings about? Was that just jealousy from an ex-husband or did they mean something? How could he help Emma now if she was in danger?

He tightened the towel around his body, and returned to his bedroom, when he heard the doorbell.

What time was it? Who visited at this hour?

He opened the door, and his heart leaped. "Emma. Come in."

She pushed past him. "What were you doing there and who was that woman? Your lover? God, how could you? After everything we said to each other. You bastard."

"She was an escort, set up by McKenzie. He found out about us, and set a trap."

"Don't take me for a fool. How does he even know you? You told me you didn't know him. You told me you worked on special projects for companies, wasn't that the time to tell me you knew my husband? I fell in love with you. I thought we had something special. God, how could you do this to me?" Emma collapsed into the nearest chair, tears streaming down her face, red with anger.

"We do. I love you, Emma. I am in love with you. Please believe me when I said it was a set up. Surely you know what your husband is like by now. What about the phone call the other night when he said he wanted to meet you. You said it ended up being nothing. Maybe he had followed us then, and wanted to separate us. Come on."

"And, that, that woman. Who was she? She looked like a whore. Is that your taste in women? Maybe I had a lucky escape then. God. You could catch something just looking at her. Where did you pick her up? The street corner outside Roxies. It's disgusting. I feel like such a fool. Don't talk to me again. Ever. I never want to see you again." She stood.

"Emma. No. Please believe me when I say I had no idea who she was until I arrived at the hotel. He set me up with her. He planned the whole evening. It was a set up to bring us out into the open and destroy our relationship. You must know what he is like.

You must. Please. Remember you told me he had someone plant a bug on you. Remember he had Smithfield sent away. He is ruthless. He will stop at nothing."

"This is different. How did he find out about us, and it's none of his business anymore. We're divorced. The bug wasn't a bug at all; it was a music stick, or whatever you call it. That woman, Julian. I, I hope you and she are happy together. You deserve each other. God, to think I slept with you after her. How could you? Just how could you?" Black rivulets ran down Emma's face as her mascara gave way under her tears. She wiped them away and blew her nose. "You hurt me. I hope you are happy. I don't understand what it is with men like you. Do you get some pleasure out of hurting women like me? I loved you Julian. I fell in love with you and you did this to me, and what makes it worse is you couldn't even tell me. I had to find out like that. It was so humiliating." She sat back in the chair, and sobbed. He put his arm around her, but she pushed him off. "Don't touch me. You've done enough."

Julian walked across the room and ran his hand through his wet hair. He smashed his fist into the wall. The mirror jumped. "Please believe me. It was a set up. I can't say it enough. I knew your husband. I have worked for him in the past but I don't work for him any longer. I gave up the work when I met you. He hired me to follow you, and report back to him on your movements and if you were seeing anyone. I did that but as I watched you I fell in love with you. It became a pleasure and joy to watch you. It was hard for me to report back. I gave him the bare minimum and left much out. I was on the cruise with you. I followed you around. I sat next to you on the tour. I retrieved your handbag from the kids in Palma, and gave it to the housekeeper to return to you. I should have told you but I didn't. I'm sorry. Please believe me. Emma. Please." He walked towards her.

She held up her hand. "Stop right there. Do not come near me and I do not want to hear any more of your lies and deceit. Goodbye. Julian. Goodbye." She walked out and the door slammed behind her.

He stood in the centre of the room, not knowing what to do. A wave of desolation and despair hit him. He collapsed on his knees to the floor. Head in his hands, and he wept.

Chapter Forty-six

"Mr McKenzie. I have two gentlemen here to see you. They say they have important business to discuss with you. Should I let them in?"

Andrew pressed the intercom, "I didn't think I had any appointments this morning. Did you ask them who they are?"

"Yes I did. They just said it's very important they see you."

He sighed. "Okay. Let them in. Bring refreshments."

The door opened and two burly men dressed in black suits filled the frame. Andrew walked forward to greet them. "Good morning, what can I do for you?"

"Andrew McKenzie?" The younger of the two questioned.

"Yes, that is I? Who are you?"

"Andrew McKenzie, I am DCI Taylor and that is DCI Jones. We are working with MI6, who have had surveillance on you for several months. Andrew McKenzie, we are arresting you for treason and espionage against the state. You do not have to say anything, but it may harm your defence if you do not mention, when questioned, something which you later rely on in court. Anything you do say may be given in evidence. Do you understand?"

Andrew sat. "Treason and espionage? What? There must be some kind of mistake."

"No there is no mistake. We have evidence to prove that a Picasso painting was shipped from the UK to Paris, to a Naya

Hasidim. Her cousin, Tariq Habidin, accepted the shipment on her behalf. We believe she had nothing to do with what transpired next. A microchip had been painted into the picture by someone you hired to do so. We believe this microchip contained important data, which if in the wrong hands, could jeopardise our National Security. We have evidence to prove that you purchased the painting. We also have evidence to prove that you accepted and transferred on stolen funds of a considerable amount. You will be accompanying us down to the station where we will hand you over to MI6 for their ongoing investigation into these matters."

"Unbelievable. This must be a set up. There is only one person who knows about this, and I know why he wants me out of the way. Damn you, Bryan Smithfield. I know my rights. I need to call my lawyer." Andrew reached for his phone.

"I need to speak to Wilkinson."

"I'm sorry. Who is this?"

"This is Andrew McKenzie. I need to speak to Wilkinson Senior. He knows my business."

"I'm afraid Mr Wilkinson was taken ill this morning. He is in intensive care at the General Hospital. Can anyone else help?"

"Let me speak to his partner."

"Unfortunately his partner has been unavoidably detained overseas. We only have legal clerks here until he returns."

Sweat rolled down Andrew's face. "When will they be back?"

"We really do not know. Is there anything else I can assist you with, Mr McKenzie?"

He hung up. He sat—his head in his hands. "Can I make another phone call, please?"

"You may, but then we need to leave."

"Emma."

"Andrew. I have nothing to say to you. I can't believe you would do something so callous. Julian told me you knew about our relationship. He told me what you did. How could you? I don't want to speak to you. I don't know what to think."

'Emma, listen. You are in danger. You need to leave. Pack up and leave. They have arrested me. Please speak to Kathy and tell her to meet me at the station. I need legal advice."

"Andrew. Is this another one of your games? I don't believe anything you say anymore. I really don't know why I should help you. If you really have been arrested then I am sure one of your business cronies will be able to bail you out. Goodbye, Andrew."

"Emma, Emma …" He looked at the dead phone in disbelief.

How could she abandon me? In my time of great need. What am I going to do now? Who is going to help me?

"Come along. We need to go." DCI Taylor pulled Andrew up from his chair, and handcuffed his hands behind his back.

"Are the handcuffs necessary?"

"Yes they are. I don't want you running from me. Come on." DI Jones led the way out of the door, Andrew in the middle with DI Taylor behind.

"Susie. I have to go to the station to assist the police with their inquiries about something. Try and get hold of Wilkinson for me. His office said something about Wilkinson Senior being taken ill, and Wilkinson Junior being stuck overseas. Try and get to the bottom of it, please." Susie's mouth fell open but no words emerged. She nodded. A silence fell over the office as faces peeked above cubicles to watch the boss being marched out. As the door to the lift closed, a crescendo of words ran rang out from behind doors.

####################

Susie called Emma. "Emma. It's Susie from the office."

"Hello. How lovely to hear from you."

"Andrew has just been arrested. I'm not sure what for but I can't get hold of Wilkinson and Wilkinson. Do you know any other lawyers who he can trust enough to assist him?"

"Oh so it's true. I thought he was playing games with me. He called me just a few minutes ago saying the same thing, but Susie, I don't know what I can do. I can call Kathy but I doubt it's her field. She specialises in family law not corporate or whatever he involves himself in."

"Emma, you realise that if he is not here and arrested then you are in charge of the business, don't you, as the other major shareholder. Have you read the articles of incorporation?"

"No. I had no idea. Susie, I can't run the business. I have no idea what the business is to be honest. Who does what? That's his domain, not mine. Are there any other shareholders?"

"No, but there is a clause that mentions if the main shareholders are no longer fit to run the business then it defaults to the first major stakeholder."

"Who is that?"

"Bryan Smithfield."

"Oh. That dreadful man. I'll talk to Kathy and see what I can do. Can you keep things under control until I can work things out? Isn't there a Chief Operating Officer or someone like that who can run things in Andrew's absence?"

"Yes. Despite everything he does have a good team, and pays everyone well so we can pull together and keep things going for the moment. I'll call you later, okay."

"Great. Thanks, Susie. You're a star. Can you email a copy of the articles to me please so I can read over them? Thanks."

"No problem, Emma. I hope you get everything sorted out with Mr McKenzie."

"So do I."

##################

Emma poured another coffee. She rubbed her eyes and massaged her temple. Her head throbbed from a night filled with strange dreams about love and betrayal.

Is this what living life was about? What happened to the regular life I once knew? The mundane, the routine. At least I'm living, feeling and emoting, even though it all hurts. They say what doesn't kill you makes you stronger.

She sipped the hot drink, and a mixture of thoughts swirled.

What about Julian? Who to believe, Andrew or Julian? I want to give him the benefit of the doubt but he lied to me about knowing Andrew. Are there more lies? I don't know what to believe. Andrew. What has he done, and do I really care? Maybe I should leave him to rot in prison. I'll control the business and maybe make it into something worthwhile rather than just a ruthless money making machine. Can I leave him? Would he leave me? Would he rescue me? I don't know. How could he be so cruel and callous, if he knew about Julian?

A thought struck her. She picked up her phone.

"Susie. Can I ask you a question?"

"Anything, you know that, Emma."

"Do you know a Mr Cunningham?"

"Yes. Andrew hired him as a consultant to work on a variety of special projects for him. He asked him to track you and report back. He swore me to secrecy about the work but as he isn't around I guess it's okay for me to tell you. Do you need to speak to Cunningham? Julian, I think his name is."

"No, but that's useful information. Thanks, Susie." Emma hung up.

Julian was telling the truth after all. Andrew can rot in jail as far as I care.

A weight lifted from her heart as she realised what had happened.

She rang Julian.

"Hi, I'm not here. Please leave a message and I'll get back to you as soon as I can."

"Julian. It's Emma. Can you come over so we can talk? Andrew has been arrested. I don't know what to do and need to talk to you about that as well. Julian, I found out the truth I love you. I really do." She held the phone to her chest, finished her coffee and grabbed her handbag. She didn't want to discuss anything else over the phone. She would visit the office and pick up a copy of the articles. She'd also visit Kathy for a legal discussion about her options, and if she felt generous, Andrew.

Chapter Forty-seven

Julian returned from his run—breathless but invigorated. The fresh air cleared the fog from his mind, and he knew his next move. He would pursue Emma. She had to believe him. He always believed in the truth. He would tell her the truth. She would believe him. The green light flashed on his answerphone. He pressed the button.

Emma. Damn I missed her call.

His heart leapt as he replayed the message over and over. She discovered the truth. He showered and dressed, grabbed his iPad, and jumped into his car. The traffic crawled through the town.

What's the hold up? Come on.

His car crept towards the head of the queue. The traffic lights had been vandalised overnight, and the police had taken over directing traffic. He pulled away but found himself behind a tractor pulling a manure spreader. His nose wrinkled as he closed the windows and put the air-conditioning on recirculate. He maneuvered to the middle of the road, but a blind bend and a slight incline in front made any chances of overtaking impossible. He reached for his phone and dialled Emma's number.

"Emma"

"Julian. So pleased to hear from you. Did you get my message?"

"Yes I'm a few minutes away from you. I came as soon as I could."

"Oh that's great. I had a few errands to run so I'll be back soon. You know where the key is don't you? Under the flowerpot on the right of the door. Just make yourself at home. I'm looking forward to seeing you."

"Me too. And Emma?"

"Yes."

"I love you."

"I love you too."

The tractor pulled into the field on the right, and Julian sped up. He passed a black Mercedes parked on the lane and pulled into the drive. He found the key where Emma left it, and turned it in the lock, the bolt slid and locked instead of unlocking. He frowned.

Maybe she forgot to lock the house. Strange.

He pushed the door and entered. A hand grabbed him from behind the door, and a cold hard barrel poked him in his back.

"Don't move. Are you armed?"

"No. Who are you?"

"Walk into the kitchen, and sit on the chair." A rough voice commanded.

Julian's stomach lurched and tied in knots. Sparks flew through his body as his nerves jumped. He walked into the kitchen. The cold hard barrel grew bigger by the second. His world moved in slow motion. He turned, and sat on the chair. He recognised his assailant.

"Smithfield. Aren't you John Smithfield?"

John grinned. "Well done. Yes I am, indeed. The one and only."

"Aren't you supposed to be in New York? Emma said she wanted to talk to you, but she couldn't get hold of you." Julian employed distraction tactics. He tried to create a relationship with his assailant and increase his chances of staying alive.

"I didn't go. Women are such fools. Give them what they want. A bit of love and affection and they do anything for you. She loved it as well. She begged me for it. She was wild. I drove her wild, and she couldn't get enough of me. We did it everywhere we could. Her pussy was wet just at the thought of me. Are you with her now?"

Bile rose in Julian's throat as he listened. He whispered. "Yes. I'm with her now. Don't talk about her like that. She deserves more. You should know that."

"She doesn't deserve anything. She supported her husband for all those years. Do you think she deserves anything? She has everything. Well she thinks she has everything but not for long." John placed his gun on the counter. "What are you doing here? I was expecting her."

"I'm meeting her here. What do you mean, but not for long?" Julian estimated the distance between himself, the gun and John. Too far.

"Oh, come on. Don't pretend you don't know what's going on. Mr Private Investigator." he snickered. "You know more than anyone. I'm sure you've got everything worked out, and you did us a huge favour by working with Ben and feeding him all that evidence on the shipment and the money laundering stuff. That was classic. Even we didn't know about that, and that really sealed the deal on McKenzie's demise. Those judges don't like money laundering or selling secrets. It will be a long time before he sees daylight. Especially since we dealt with his lawyers and made sure no one else will touch him within a fifty-mile radius of this town, and forget the law in London. We have that sewn up as well."

"But, Ben worked for MI6 didn't he?" Julian inched to the edge of the chair.

"Yeah, sure he did, if that's what you want to believe. Shame MI6 has no record of his activities or employment with them. Come on. He was a set-up from day one. Do you really think there was a market for a spy store in a quiet town like this, MI6 or not? Even MI6 wouldn't do anything like that. It would be far too suspicious. She fell right into his hands. We suspected McKenzie had planted a bug on her and we needed to get our hands on it, especially after she and I became lovers. It was my father who gave him the idea about the bug, and employing you to follow her. We needed some evidence on him, and knew she could provide it." John placed his hand over the gun.

Julian perched on the edge of the chair. "But it still doesn't make sense, why do you need him out of the way? What difference does that make, and how is Emma involved in all this?" His knuckles turned white as he grabbed the arms of the chair.

"Really. You don't know. Let me explain." John folded his arms across his chest. "Andrew and Emma are the only shareholders in McKenzie Associates. Everyone else is an associate, or a stakeholder, so with both of them out of the way, then the articles state that the company will pass down to the major stakeholders. There are two major stakeholders in McKenzie Associates. Bryan Smithfield and John Smithfield. Father and son."

Julian's face paled. His grip tightened. "But McKenzie has only just been arrested. I'm sure he has enough connections to raise bail, and will be back at the helm before the week is through."

"As I said, no one will be foolish enough to post bail for him or represent him. In a case like that, without adequate representation, he doesn't stand a chance. The articles state that sole ownership passes to the next major shareholder, if one shareholder is arrested and charged with illegal activities."

Julian swallowed the vomit rising in his throat, and whispered, "And Emma?" An air of dread filled the room as he waited for the response.

"Yes, the wonderful Emma. It will be such a shame, but it has to be done. I tried a few weeks ago but ended up shooting that Iraqi whore instead. Silly cow disguised herself to look like Emma. Good disguise. It fooled me. So here I am. I was hoping for one last reunion with her, but I guess that's out of the question now. She had such a sweet pussy, and loved to suck my cock. You should have heard her scream for more when I fucked her."

Without warning, Julian launched himself at John. He swung, and aimed for his face. John ducked, and punched Julian in the stomach, winding him. Doubled over, gasping for air, Julian reached for the gun, but it slipped to the floor under the kitchen counter. John pushed him backwards over the stove. He felt the sharp edge of the burners digging into his back. Julian's hands grabbed the edge of the stove; he leveraged his weight, and kicked John off him. John flew back, hitting his head with a loud thump against the kitchen cupboard. The contents rattled to the ground.

He shook his head, and gave a half-groan, he threw himself at Julian. Julian's knee rose looking for his groin, but missed, and John grabbed him by his hair. He pulled his head down and dragged him across the kitchen into the hallway. He slammed him against the long mirror. It shattered, sending shards of mirrored glass everywhere. An excruciating pain shot through Julian's head. His hand found the spot where his skull stung, and his fingers slipped on the warm liquid matting his hair. Dark red blood covered his hand. He slumped, leaving a trail down the wall.

"Is that all you have? Emma must be disappointed if you finish so soon. I kept her up all night. She loved it." John goaded as he moved in with a long spike retrieved from the floor. "I'm not going to kill you now. No you can watch when I fuck her one last time. At least she will die happy."

Julian hung his head. Blood ran over his face, and blurred his vision. He closed his eyes. Adrenaline coursed through his body. He needed to compose himself. A few deep breaths held for a couple of seconds, calmed his racing heart. He waited.

"Defeated already. You make me laugh. Call yourself a PI. Private dick, pathetic dick, if you ask me." John moved closer. "She is mine. God, I am going to enjoy this. I'm hard already just thinking about her."

Julian positioned his hands behind his back for leverage, and kicked John in the chest. He sprung up and grabbed him as he fell backwards. He slid the spike of glass into his stomach, pulled it out and slid it in again. "Do not underestimate me. Do not talk about Emma like that. Do you understand? You will never ever, ever go near her again." He slammed his head into the broken mirror, over and over again.

John bent over, and held his stomach. Two large red circles spread across his shirt.

"Do you know how long it takes to bleed to death once you've been stabbed in the liver and the kidneys? I am very precise you know." Julian dragged him back into the kitchen, but stopped when he saw a figure standing at the open door.

"Stop. Both of you stop. What are you doing?" Emma's hand shook as she pointed the gun. "Stop."

"Emma. How long have you been here?"

"Long enough. I heard everything. I thought I would surprise you when I saw your car in the drive, so I crept around the back. I saw, and heard, everything through the kitchen window."

"Oh god, Emma. I'm so sorry you had to see this." Julian pushed John down into the centre of the kitchen. He lay on his side, groaning as a pool of thick red liquid spread beneath his body. "He is fatally wounded. I stabbed him in his liver, and nicked an abdominal artery. Let him bleed out. Emma, put the gun down. Please."

Emma paled. "We need to call the ambulance and the police. I don't know what happens in these situations. We need to help him. We can't let him die." She placed the gun on the counter, and half bent down to look at John. She hesitated then moved away.

"We can, but he will be dead by the time they get here." Julian kept his foot on John, to hold him down. He wanted no sudden revivals. He dialled 999, and requested an ambulance and police to the address. He gave a code used for retired members of the police. "I used to be in the police force. I'm not sure I told you. I retired a few years ago due to ill health. I had a cancer scare but I'm fine now. In fact I'm fitter than I've ever been, but I decided I no longer wanted to be at the frontline. Pass me some kitchen towels." He pressed the towels against the wounds. "I'm only doing this for you. If it was up to me, I'd let him bleed out. He is a nasty piece of work. The towels will stem the flow of blood but I suspect it may be too late already."

"Thank you."

"I presume you heard what he intended to do to you." John twitched under Julian's foot. The towels turned red.

"Yes. It's disgusting. Heartbreaking. I feel so violated, to think he was using me to get the business from Andrew. I heard everything. I can't believe it. I just came from the lawyers, and know it's true what he said about the articles and the business. With Andrew and myself out of the way the business would fall into the hands of the major stakeholders."

Julian reached out, and held Emma's hand. "We'll have to make sure that doesn't happen now then won't we. Although I'm not sure what to do about his father."

Emma smiled. "I don't think he will be a problem. I heard that the police have arrested him, as the money Andrew laundered was traced back to an offshore account in his name. There is a paper trail as long as your arm. Someone is going to have a huge amount of work unravelling that."

John groaned, and whispered something. Julian bent close to his face.

"He says he is sorry. He says he loves you. He is asking for your forgiveness." Julian looked at Emma.

Emma turned away. "Tell him I forgive him, but I will never forget what he tried to do. I only forgive because I need to move on."

Julian relayed the message to John, who gave a weak smile, gasped and closed his eyes. Julian searched for his pulse. "He's gone."

They turned as the gravel crunched under a flurry of activity as the police and ambulance arrived. Julian stepped back to let the medics work on John. One turned to him, "What about you? You are covered in blood. Sit down, and let me take a look at you. That looks like a nasty cut on your head."

"I think it looks worse than it is. You know how head wounds bleed a lot even if they are minor. But please take a look."

Emma took a damp kitchen towel and cleaned Julian's face. "That's better." She reached in and kissed him. "I don't know what to say. Thanks don't seem to be enough but thanks. I don't know what I would have done if you hadn't been here. It doesn't bear thinking about."

He waved the medic away, grabbed her waist and pulled her on to his knees. He held her in his arms. "Don't think about it, pretty Emma. Just don't. I'll protect you always. You do know that don't you. I loved you from the first time I saw you. From the first time your ex-husband asked me to follow you. You filled my dreams. I felt like I was sent to watch over you, and protect you." He lifted her chin towards his, and kissed her. "For always, Emma."

"For always, Julian."

BIOGRAPHY

From West Yorkshire in the UK originally, Karen moved to Grenada in 2003 with her family. She discovered her love of island living—wide open spaces, the beautiful sea, warm sun, cooling breezes, forgotten times, and people with no cares and no reason to hurry. This sparked her creativity and her passion for writing was born. Unexpected Monet is her first novel and an unexpected achievement. Karen lets her imagination run wild and lead her down unexpected paths as she writes from experience with a whole lot of fiction thrown in.

For more of Karen's work, or any of the JaCol authors, please visit: www.jacolpublishing.com

She also runs www.simplycarriacouwebdesign.com